ON THE WINGS OF A WORD

BY
C. M. SINNER

BOOK ONE OF LOKI'S MONSTERS TRILOGY

·ASGARD·
BIFRÖST
JOTUNHEIM
MUSPELHEIM
VANAHEIM
LFHEIM
IFELHEIM
NIDHOGG
MIDGARD
JÖRMUNGANDR
SVARTALHEIM
THE NINE REALMS
OF THE
YGGDRASIL TREE
HELHEIM

This book is dedicated to my family. For the hours you dealt with me clacking away on the keyboard, the nights you suffered through cheap frozen pizzas because I was "in the zone", and the countless times you had to hear me reading my book aloud. For you three, I am forever grateful!

AUTHOR'S NOTE

While I attempted to stay as true to Norse mythology as possible, I took a few creative liberties in order to fit the lore into the storyline of my book. If you are interested in learning more about Norse mythology, I highly recommend Anthony Faulkes's translation of The Prose Edda by Snorri Sturluson and Carolyne Larrington's second edition translation of The Poetic Edda. If you are interested in learning more about Old Norse pronunciation and/or prefer audible learning, I highly recommend visiting Dr. Jackson Crawford's YouTube channel: www.youtube.com/@JacksonCrawford.

Possible triggers: foster care, violent scenes with blood and gore, emotional/verbal abuse, bullying, character death (including parental), substance abuse, and fire/arson.

NORSE PRONUNCIATION GUIDE

AUTHOR'S NOTE: SOME PRONUNCIATION HAS BEEN
SIMPLIFIED FOR EASE OF READING

- Aesir (eye-sir)
- Aksel (ax-el)
- Alfheim (alf-hame)
- Algiz (all-gyeez)
- Angrboda (ung-er-bow-da)
- Arnar (ar-nar)
- Astrid (ah-strid)
- Baldr (bald-er)
- Bifröst (bee-frost)
- Bragi (brahg-ee)
- Eihwaz (ay-whaz)
- Ek ann per (eck-awn-pare)
- Fjalar (fya-lar)
- Fenrir (fen-rear)
- Fensalir (fen-sah-leer)
- Fimbulvinter (fim-bowl-vin-ter)
- Folkvangr (folk-vong-er)
- Freya (Froy-uh)
- Freyr (Froy-er)
- Frigg (freeg)
- Galar (guh-lar)
- Ganga (gang-uh)
- Garm (gharm)
- Gulltoppr (gool-top-er)
- Gunnlöd (gunn-luth)
- Hati (haht-ee)
- Heimdall (hime-dahl)
- Hel (hell)
- Helene (huh-leen)
- Helheim (hell-hame)
- Himinbjörg (hee-min-byur-g)
- Höd (hode)
- Hoenir (who-neer)
- Hrym (her-rim)
- Huginn (hoog-in)
- Idun (you-duhn)
- Isa (ee-sah)
- Jarnvidr (yarn-vinth-er)
- Jörmungandr/Jorm (yorm-un-gone-der)
- Jotunheim (yo-tun-hame)
- Kvasir (qwa-see-er)
- Laguz (la-gooz)
- Leif (lay-if)
- Lítilvölva (leet-uhl-val-vah)
- Loki (low-key)
- Mani (mah-nee)
- Megingjord (mayg-in-yord)
- Midgard (mid-gaurd)
- Mimir (me-meer)
- Mjolnir (myol-neer)
- Moa (mo-uh)
- Muninn (moon-in)
- Muspelheim (moo-spell-hame)
- Naglfar (nah-gill-far)
- Naudhiz (nowd-ease)
- Nidhogg (nid-hog)
- Niflheim (niv-uhl-hame)
- Njord (knee-ord)
- Odin (oh-din)
- Opna (op-nah)
- Þorbjörg (poor-be-yorg)
- Ragnarök (rag-na-roke)
- Seiðr (say-der)
- Senja (sen-ya)
- Sif (siff)
- Sigel (see-gul)
- Skadi (ska-dee)
- Skidbladnir (skeed-blad-neer)
- Skor (score)
- Skuld (skoold)
- Sleipnir (slipe-neer)
- Skoll (skal)
- Sol (soul)
- Suttungr (sut-tung-er)
- Svartalfheim (svart-alf-hame)
- Teiwaz (tee-whaz)
- Thor (thore)
- Unnasta (oo-na-sta)
- Urd (ourd)
- Uruz (oo-rooz)
- Vala (vah-lah)
- Valaskjalf (vah-lesk-galf)
- Valhalla (val-hal-uh)
- Valkyrie (val-cue-ree)
- Vanaheim (van-a-hame)
- Vanir (vah-neer)
- Verdandi (ver-don-dee)
- Völuspá (vol-us-puh)
- Völva (val-vah)
- Yggdrasil (eeg-drass-il)

CONTENTS

PROLOGUE

December 21, 2006. First day of Yule.

A hazy mist clouded the moonlight on a silent and eerily gray winter evening, blanketing the world in an orangish hue. Moa stared at the starless sky, an excited energy pulsing through her. Her breathing, even and deep, fogged the glass of the icy window before her. She turned toward the living room to admire the crackling fire and realized how much she loved the house she and her husband, Leif, had turned into a home. They were especially fond of it during the holidays.

A juniper wreath graced the inside of the front door. The deep green spindly foliage spread across the wood paneling like elven fingers and frosted blue juniper berries complemented a shimmering golden ribbon that weaved gently around the branches. The home smelled of aromatic berries and dozens of delicately placed cinnamon pinecones her husband loved.

"It smells incredible in here," Leif said, sneaking up behind her and resting a hand on her belly. "What are you thinking, my love?"

"Mm," she hummed, looking his way. Moa's handsome husband easily distracted her from her thoughts of the impending snow. His luxurious blonde hair was styled in a man bun; some of the silken strands had fallen loose to frame his chiseled jaw and high cheekbones. Horn-rimmed, black glasses framed and emphasized his ice blue eyes, and his tattooed, muscular arms peeked out from beneath the slightly rolled-up sleeves of his navy button-down. As he loosened his beige paisley tie, Moa knew she'd never get tired of gawking at his appealing professorial style.

"Look at the sky, babe. It's going to snow tonight."

Nearing the middle of her second trimester, Moa thrived on the comfort Leif gave her as his face nuzzled into her untethered blonde hair. His breath tickled her ear as he whispered, "My most beautiful Moa. I am unsure how you always know, but I trust you are right. You predict the first snow every year."

"It is a gift."

His arm snaked around her body, and he interlaced their fingers to spin her around gently. He kissed her lips and dropped to his knees, placing both hands on either side of her slightly distended belly button. She giggled in delight as he whispered against the loose black flannel nightgown, "Little one, you hear that? Your momma is gifted."

She laid her hands over his, and her whole body tingled when his mouth gently kissed her bump. A loud knock on the front door interrupted their sweet moment, and both their eyes filled with questions.

"Who could that be?"

"I'm not sure. I'm not expecting anyone." Leif rose to his feet and opened the door to reveal a towering man with a mane of long, tousled gray hair and a thick beard. He wore a cloak lined with plush, white fur, heavy brown leather boots, and a sleek leather eyepatch.

"Odin!" Leif exclaimed. The two men wrapped opposing arms around the other, leaning forward to touch foreheads together—a warrior's welcome.

"Hello, Odin! What a pleasant surprise," Moa greeted. The giant man wrapped her in a gentle hug, taking considerable care not to jostle her too much.

"Moa. Leif." Odin removed his cloak, hanging it on the posts behind the door. "It has been too long, and I had to see for myself." His eyes drifted to Moa's midsection.

Her eyes glittered with pride as he rested a giant palm over where the tiny baby grew. "I have seen, Odin. She will be here in May, and she will be exquisite. Everything we hoped for and more."

As Moa prepared hot water for tea in the kitchen, the men chatted quietly in the dining room. Words like "prophecy" and "destiny" were exchanged, filled with excitement and joy. But a hint of despair also lingered in the air, a general foreboding cutting through the warmth like the chill breeze that snuck through the door upon Odin's entrance.

A female voice joined the conversation, and Moa ran to throw herself into the newcomer's waiting arms. The woman wore a long-sleeved, floor-length gold filigree gown that contrasted beautifully with her dark chocolate hair and emphasized her beaming smile that lit up the entire room.

She held Moa in a maternal embrace, rubbing her lower back in soft, gentle strokes. A pastel pink glow surrounded them, and Moa sighed in relief as a deep pain seeped from her.

"Nana Frigg! I've missed you so much. Whatever you just did, please teach my husband! My back has been aching for weeks."

"My sweet girl, the babe growing within you is taking her toll," Nana Frigg said sweetly. "I merely gave you a small reprieve."

"Even if it only lasts a little while, I am grateful. Leif gives a good foot rub, but healing magic isn't in his wheelhouse." Moa motioned toward the kitchen. "Would you mind helping me with the tea?"

As the women chatted about the unborn child and the wonders of pregnancy, Odin's joy slowly diminished. "Leif, we have come to visit you on this first day of Yule, but we do not bring the gladdest of tidings." Pity creased his face, sinking deeply into the man's wrinkles and aging him even more.

"What is it, Odin?"

The women rejoined the room, placing the tea kettle and steaming mugs on the table with a tray of holiday cookies. Knowing Odin wouldn't touch the tea, Moa set an empty mug in front of him. He reached into his pocket, removing a leather flask filled with a deep crimson liquid that he poured into the mug. As Moa pulled her chair close to Leif's, Frigg shot a solemn look at Odin across the table, and they nodded at each other in unspoken agreement.

"I have seen…" Frigg started with an air of seriousness.

Leif reached under the table and grasped Moa's hand. His voice shook when he asked, "Nana Frigg, what… what have you seen?"

"A sacrifice."

The pair inhaled audibly, their dread painting a shadow over the room.

"We knew that he would find out," Odin stated. "Do you remember when we talked of all the risks?"

"Yes," Moa murmured. Recognition painted her features as she shakily squeezed her husband's hand. "I, too, have seen."

"Moa, what?!" Leif's stared at his wife with a slack jaw. He gathered his wits and asked, "Why didn't you tell me?"

"I didn't want to believe it. I saw nothing we haven't already mentally prepared for, but a part of me still hoped it wasn't to be."

"What did you see?"

"Flames."

"And your daughter, rising from the ashes," added Frigg. Moa nodded, a tear sliding down her cheek.

"He will come. One way or another. The best we can do is prepare the child for the fight of her life in the meantime," Odin said.

"Vala," Moa whispered so softly that it was nearly incoherent.

"What was that?" Frigg asked.

"Our daughter's name will be Vala. She will have wisdom and foresight. She is the chosen one." Her free hand rested on her belly, prone and ready to protect her unborn child. Tears openly streaked down her cheeks, but her voice exuded strength. "Her name is Vala Boddason."

CHAPTER ONE

I lived in a foster home that smelled of stale cigarettes and rancid beer. The kitchen's sticky dining table was strewn with empty beer cans, and the coffee table held a stained ashtray brimming with half-smoked butts.

I had to leave.

My phone buzzed, and I checked the time: ten on the dot. The new text was from my best friend, Helene, telling me she was waiting outside. I could always count on escaping my seething hatred for a few hours with her.

I hated that house. I hated the drab, yellow-stained walls and the jumble of flagrant scents. I hated the slow drawl that my foster dad, Steve, took up after he'd been drinking. I hated my foster mom, Brenda. She constantly bitched about his inebriation but did nothing to change it. Like I said, I had to leave. I texted Helene:

Be right out.

Sneaking out of the house was never that hard because my room was on the ground floor. The last place I lived in had iron bars on the windows, which was inconvenient. It may have seemed a bit harsh, but most foster kids my age were known for attempting to run away. I learned a saying during my years as a foster kid: better out than in. It became the motto for most of us who were doomed to the system.

I threw on my favorite tattered black hoodie, the one with the Luke's Diner logo—Gilmore Girls may have been an older show, but I loved watching it every year with my mom before she died—and headed for the window.

The "FPs"—as I called all foster parents—wouldn't even realize I left. For them to notice that I slipped out, Brenda needed to take her attention off her drunk husband, and Steve had to take his attention off his bottle. Both were highly unlikely.

Bye-bye, psychos.

I snuck out in a flash. The darkness granted me grace and helped shield me from prying eyes. Not that anyone seemed to care about me or my whereabouts besides Helene. She cared. I crept quickly toward her beat-up, used-to-be-white Honda Civic and hopped in the passenger seat. The vehicle was ancient! The poor car even smelled old. Her *"solution"* was to spray so much perfume it hurt my nose, but it didn't cover the scent of sweaty gym clothes and old McDonald's cheeseburgers.

Helene was a quintessential blonde bombshell. She was tall and muscular, having played years of volleyball throughout middle and high school, and she often kept her hair down with small, earth-colored beads braided into her long, wavy locks. The shades of brownish-green beads drew out the hue of her eyes, making them glimmer the color of honey. Her sun-kissed skin always made me a bit envious, but never enough to mess with our unbreakable bond.

She wore her favorite worn-out daisy dukes with a cream-colored crop top and dangerously tall fire engine red wedges. I always thought Helene was crazy for dressing like it was summer year-round, but she claimed that she ran hot. Apparently, her Scandinavian roots made Oregon weather feel like living on the equator all the time.

"Hi, cow!" Helene squealed and giggled as she raised her hand.

"Hi, jerk face." I gave her our token fist-bump, followed by cheek kisses. Left, right, left.

"You got out easy-peasy tonight, huh? Let's Shania Twain this bitch and go, girl." My friend gave a ridiculously loud "Yeehaw!" as she took her foot off the brake and slammed on the gas pedal. *Oh lordy, my best friend is such a dork.* I rolled my eyes at the fleeting thought.

The road I lived on wasn't too busy, so Helene's speeding never caused any real destruction other than the painful sound of the brakes whining when she slowed at the four-way stop. We listened to music as we drove around aimlessly with the windows rolled down to feel the air on our faces despite the chill in the air.

Helene came from a seemingly pleasant family, but her parents argued a lot. She heard them; despite their efforts to hide their issues from her, and that's what started our nightly adventures. She escaped. I escaped. We escaped together.

We became best friends in kindergarten. And considering that we were seniors in high school, we had a lot going for us. All our other friendships hit dramatic, youthful snags, but she and I remained close. I loved her because she knew everything about me and still tolerated my quirks. Hell, she seemed to enjoy being around me. That was more than I could say for most people. *You'd have been lost without her, don't kid yourself. Poor girl has taken on an enormous load of baggage.*

I was considered strange, not that I was funny-looking or anything; some people even called me pretty. "Too bad you are so weird," was the typical follow-up statement to any comments about my looks. I never tried to be odd, but I guess it came naturally. I bore a scary pale complexion, long, harshly blonde hair, and piercing, ice-blue eyes. Despite my short stature and lean frame, my body curved in places that drew male attention—even if they'd never admit it.

My greatest downfall was that I was supremely awkward. I tended to be noticeably quiet unless I was around Helene. Years of being talked down to, ridiculed, and essentially ver-bally abused in a revolving door of foster homes had a way of doing that to a girl. I heard people giggle and call me "that awkward albino Wednesday Addams" or Elsa's long-lost sister, destined to live alone in an ice castle or something. It didn't help that I never found a boyfriend. Kids could be dumb... and hurtful.

The last day of elementary school was when I stopped caring about what people thought of me. It seemed like an ordinary day, but that changed quickly. When I got home from school on that bright, sunny day, I was excited that it was finally summer. I couldn't wait to hang out with all my friends and discuss middle school. We finally made it to sixth grade. We were finally the *big kids*.

As I entered my house, the scent of lemony sweetness bombarded my senses. Instant feelings of comfort mixed with unease always accompanied the smell of Mom's homemade lemon bars. *Oh no. What's wrong?* When she felt guilty about something, she would make them because they were my favorite. The homemade graham cracker crust was always perfectly crisp and magical when combined with creamy lemon custard and a fine dusting of powdered sugar.

My parents were murmuring in the dining room.

Dad should not have been home yet; he was a professor of Scandinavian Studies at the local community college and was typically in class until at least an hour after I got home. Setting aside my worries, I followed their voices to say hello and brag about my middle school status.

They both stopped talking when I walked in.

"Hey, kiddo. Mom and I have something to tell you." Dad's statement felt foreboding, and the rest of what he said fell on me like a ton of bricks. Between the pounding in my head and my heartbeat, I made out fragments of his speech. "Moving." "New teaching job." "Fresh Start."

No, no, no, no. I loved my small group of friends. Life was good! They couldn't take it all away. My parents told me we were moving to an entirely different state and didn't seem to care about my opinion! How could they do this to me?

Anger roared as I ran to my room, sobbing uncontrollably, and grabbed my most prized possession: my poetry journal. Tears spilled from my eyes, the droplets smudging the words that bled onto the page. The passion in my writing felt different—unparalleled—compared to any other time I wrote. In those moments, my eleven-year-old self was the most hurt and broken I had ever been in my life, and I could tangibly feel my rage emptying onto the page. *I hate them. They are ruining my life!*

That night, my parents died. I woke up coughing. My lungs stung from strangling smoke, and it took everything in me to move toward the front door and push my way outside. After several deep inhales of fresh air and sickening hacking coughs, I started yelling, "Mom! Dad!"

No response.

Neighbors ran out of their houses as I stood on the front lawn screaming. Mrs. Miller—the kind lady from next door who had given me cherry popsicles on scorching summer days—ran to me and dropped to her knees, checking my body for burns. My other neighbor, Mr. Johnson, was frantic as he spoke into his cell phone. "Drive as fast as you can! The Boddason house is on fire! There are two adults still inside…"
This can't be happening…

His voice seemed to trail off as the pressure in my head built, blocking my ears from all sound. I stood planted where I was, wrapped in the arms of Mrs. Miller, as an emergency crew arrived. Firefighters ran by. Water hoses erupted. The muffled sound of sirens blaring got louder, and police officers arrived. I stared at our home as it burned and silently sobbed. *I don't hate you. I was wrong!* I waited for someone to come out with my mom in their strong arms or help my dad walk toward me. But my parents never emerged from that house.

I stopped writing poetry that night, allowing the numbness of my parents' loss to cut off my creativity. Instead, I burrowed into my anxiety, allowing awkwardness to clothe me in a new, odd skin. I became comfortable in my grief, wearing my agony like a cloak.

Helene nudged me. "You good, Vala?"

Nope, far from. I am anything but good right now, but nothing can change the past. So I will do what I always do: pretend. I can pull an Elsa and "conceal, don't feel."

CHAPTER TWO

I only nodded in response and turned the radio up. Helene could always tell when I was thinking about my parents but never pushed me about how I was feeling. I hated it when people did that. With my friend, I could be sad. We were together, commiserating silently. She smiled limply, reaching over to quickly squeeze my hand before moving forward when the light turned green.

The town, which I never ended up leaving, featured many awesome spots for teens to hang out at night. Bend, Oregon, was just rural enough that most parents still allowed their teenagers to roam without fear of kidnapping or murder, regardless of the overwhelming number of homeless folks that moved into the area. *"Just a small town girl, livin' in a lonely world..."* The Journey song played in my mind.

The favored city park was sprawling and open, but as we exited the car and headed down the dark and winding path of the walking trail illuminated only by the full moon, the underbrush gradually got taller and fuller. Once we found the rock pile we created in middle school to mark our path, we pushed through a thick bush. There it was—our favorite spot, tucked away from prying eyes.

The area wasn't much bigger than the space in Helene's Honda, but a big, flat rock sat right above the river like a natural dock. It was low enough to the water that we could take our shoes off and dip our toes in. In our spot, we were just two best friends enjoying the still of the night, the chill on our toes, and the warm breeze on our skin. Over the years, we laughed, skipped rocks, talked about boys, and let the troubles of the world melt away.

"I love it out here," said Helene.

"Me, too… Thank you for the silence in the car."

"Girl, I know you. No need to say thank you." She removed her heels and winced a little as she dipped her bare feet into the water. "God knows I don't always want to talk about my parents."

I dipped my toes in and quickly pulled them out with a tiny shriek. "Holy crap, dude! The water is cold today."

"Don't be a boob, Vala," Helene chuckled as she scooped up a handful of water to throw my way.

"Do it and die," I warned in mock terror.

Helene giggled, reached into the shallow water and pulled out a smooth, spectacularly flat stone. She had a knack for always finding the perfect skipping rocks.

"Here."

"Why, thank you, my love." I grabbed it with faked en-thusiasm; my mouth hung cartoonishly open as if it were a diamond ring or something equally spectacular.

"Don't forget to make a wish!"

I held it like my father taught me, with the flat weight resting on my middle finger while my index finger and thumb hooked around the stone gently. I pulled my arm back and lined my shot up with the water, inhaling a slow, steady breath. As my arm shot forward, I flicked my wrist gently, releasing the rock. *This one's for you, Dad.*

One skip. Two. Three. Four. Five. It skittered and skipped at least ten times before the stone finally submerged in the deepest part of the river.

"That was perfection! What did you wish for?"

"Girl. You know I can't tell you." I was still awestruck by one of my best throws. "It won't come true." *Who cares if it's a childish notion. I will put my hope in wishes if it means getting the hell away from the FPs and figuring out what to do with my life without my family. Come on, mom and dad. Please be listening.*

I wished for a purpose but didn't want to tell Helene that. I searched for something, anything, since my parents passed. What was the meaning of their deaths? Why did I survive?

"I bet you wished Emo Nathan would ask you to prom," she joked, eyebrows waggling.

"Eww, no!" I punched her arm. "I have standards, Helly! If anyone was to ask me to prom, it better be Jock McGlock!"

Ethan McGlock was the star football player at school, and I would *never* want him to ask me out. He was the cockiest misogynist, and at the mention of his name, both our faces scrunched in disgust. We erupted in laughter simultaneously.

"Standards, my ass!"

As we basked in the moonlight, we talked crap about our biology teacher, Mr. Smass—Mr. Ass as he was referred to behind his back. A frog dissection lesson was coming up, and we planned to skip that day.

Eventually, we left our little zen place and lay on the grass in the middle of the park. It was well after eleven, and stars glittered across the night sky. They were prettier and more visible in the sprawling field. *Mom, are you up there? Dad, can you guys hear me?*

I could feel sleep taking over as we gazed at the constellations. We would usually head home, but the plushness of the blanket beneath my body and the soothing chirp of crickets made my eyelids heavy, and I sunk into the comfort of the night.

"He's dating that girl—Ella. You remember? The cheerleader who moved to town last fall." I could hear Helene talking about Tyson—the boy she had been "in love" with since freshman year—and the cadence of her voice lulled me to sleep.

I breathed deeply, smelling the tart sweetness of my mom's infamous lemon bars baking in the oven. My eyes snapped open. What the hell? I was in my old bedroom, in my childhood house. I could hear my dad and mom talking in the other room. I looked at my bed, and... sitting there was eleven-year-old me, sobbing over my poetry journal. How was that possible?

Damn, I looked like a hot mess.

When the younger version of myself saw the actual me, she snapped to attention, almost zombie-like, and whispered, "Remember," with her palm flat on our poetry journal. I froze in place, and my pulse quickened, nausea churning my stomach. But I could not move.

The scene shifted suddenly, and I was in the small dining room, where my entire world changed. I had thought my life was ending. *If only I had known then what was to come.* My eyes darted to a tiny flicker that was barely noticeable. The flame came out of nowhere and spread so quickly I had to step back to avoid it. The fire engulfed the room almost instantly and licked at my heels, but I felt nothing. I reached out to touch it. No heat. How was that possible?

"Remember," the fire seemed to sing to me as it wrapped around my outstretched hand and grew into an even larger blaze. *What am I supposed to remember?* I ran to my parents' room. They were still asleep, and I started to scream at them. "Wake up! It's coming! Get up! I don't hate you guys, I never did. I *miss* you!" It was no use. They couldn't hear me, and the fire spread. The younger version of myself was outside screaming for them, too. "Mom! Dad!" *Okay, self, if you're trying to remind me of how useless I was—am—I freaking get it!*

In that dreamlike state, I was nothing more than a ghost. I leaned down and kissed their foreheads one at a time. "I love you always, and I love you more," I whispered as they finally started to rise and cough. They jumped up from the bed, eyes wide, but too close to escape the flames. The foundation crumbled with a heavy thud and blocked their door. I couldn't stay for what I knew was to come. I could not witness my parents' deaths.

Tears stung my eyes as I left their room to walk around my childhood home once more. The house was ablaze, but it couldn't hurt me, so I wandered, soaking in every memory I could. I remembered cozy fires in the hearth during the holidays. The overwhelming smell of cinnamon. All the stupid pinecones Mom loved to place throughout the house seemed to be ablaze, choking the memory with their scent. I remembered my dad's office, littered with history and mythology books.

Walking past the dining room reminded me of the family dinners where my dad would hide his brussels sprouts in his napkin each time my mom got carried away in a story, her eyes closed to recall each detail. He always winked at me as if he thought he would get away with it. I smiled at the memory. I could still smell his aspen cologne mixed with the stench of the veggies he'd thrown in his pocket. Needless to say, mom always caught him.

The living room brought me back to those rainy-day Gilmore Girl binges I'd have with mom. She'd get all the junk food that Rory and Lorelei had, and we would laugh at the pure wit of the show while stuffing our faces and cuddling together under blankets. She paused the show throughout to ask me about my life. It annoyed me then, but I wish she could ask me now.

Each room held a plethora of memories. Joy, love, broken hearts, and family moments. *Gosh, I miss you guys.*

I walked past countless family photos in the hallway: all the family trips, school photos, and snippets of our fleeting time together. I watched the memories burn physically as they seared into the recesses of my heart. I could feel the hot tears running down my face, but the vicious fire still didn't affect me.

I returned to my bedroom and walked through the burnt doorway. Amongst the flames on the bed was my poetry journal. It was open and—impossibly—not on fire. *What the hell?* I walked over to get a closer look.

What. The. Hell.

I woke up sobbing and dripping in sweat. My breath caught in my lungs as I replayed the dream over and over again. My mind clung to that final poem like a bloodied murder weapon. What had I done? My heart was ripped out, sliced through, and replaced with a shriveled version of what it once was. Endless tears streaked down my cheeks, and my head ached. *What did I do? What had I done?*

Helene startled awake and gawked at the state I was in.

"What is wrong, Vala?"

"I... I... think... I think I killed my parents."

CHAPTER THREE

*H*elene's eyes were wide as saucers. "What on earth would make you think that?"

Oh, you know, I wrote a stupid poem that somehow caused the fire my parents died in. Because there is no logical explanation other than that...

I was gasping so hard I thought I'd throw up. I couldn't catch my breath. Splaying my hands out in the grass, I attempted to calm my breathing—as if touching the earth would ground me. It helped. Feeling calmer, I opened my mouth to speak.

"Do not tell her," an unknown female whispered behind me. The rich Scandinavian voice was calming and smooth, maternal and commanding. *Um, excuse me?!*

My mouth almost involuntarily snapped shut, and tears stung in my eyes. I turned my head, looking around to see who had spoken. Was I losing my mind? I stared at Helene helplessly, and she wrapped her arms around me. I started sobbing against her shoulder, extremely grateful for our voiceless bond. *I'm going insane. Steve always calls me a "crazy bitch". Maybe he's right?*

My friend allowed me to stay in her embrace as long as I needed, and I enjoyed the comfort of being close to someone, but what did I say to her? The voice did not speak again, and I was dealing with an internal argument about whether I even heard it in the first place. As I finally pulled away, I whispered, "Thank you."

She nodded understandingly, and we started getting our stuff together.

"I think we may have broken our record tonight." Helene casually checked her watch—as if she was trying to sweep what happened under the proverbial rug. She knew me so well; I hated dwelling on my emotions. "Three in the morning is the latest we've ever been out. We better not get caught on the way back in."

Dear universe, thank you for sending Helene to me. I would surely float away without her here to ground me. Sincerely, a crashout queen.

By four in the morning, I was lying in my twin bed at the FP's. Sneaking back inside the house was simple. Steve always passed out before the early morning hours. Nothing short of a wrecking ball crashing into his room would wake him up. Brenda was also likely passed out, exhausted from dealing with her husband all night. I never understood how they could afford the house because she was the only one who worked, and the measly checks sent by the state for fostering me weren't much to gawk at. *No wonder you kept getting passed around. You probably aren't worth the hassle.*

Instead of going to bed, I searched for my poetry journal in the box that held my few remaining belongings. There was a photo of Mom, Dad, and me at our favorite local hiking spot in Oregon called Blue Pool, my father's ash-covered copy of *The Poetic Edda* from his Norse collection, and my mom's nearly empty bottle of Angel perfume—my favorite scent. Subtle hints of praline and patchouli always reminded me of her. Finally, I pulled out my drawn-on poetry journal.

I cuddled under my thin comforter and flipped through the journal's messy pages. Each page was covered in silly, childish nonsense. I started creating poems immediately after I learned to write, and my parents always encouraged my creativity.

There was no way my poem could have... what? Come to life? Even just thinking it sounded stupid. It was impossible. As I read, though, memories flooded my mind.

My kindergarten teacher assigned a creative project to our class, and whatever we chose had to involve our favorite animal. I decided to write a poem about my imaginary friend, a friendly spider:

About five minutes after giving my poem to Ms. Spalding, the room erupted in squeals and giggles. She was having a full-blown meltdown, standing on a chair and shrieking like a little girl. I went over to see what the commotion was about, and on top of one of the classroom's little plastic horse figurines sat a black spider. Helene laughed about it for years, but little did I know that Ms. Spalding was a severe arachnophobe.

Flash forward to third grade. A new boy had joined our school, and I thought he was so cute. His name was Jack, and his hair was the perfect Ron Weasley-red. When he smiled, his cheeks would indent with the cutest dimples.

Helene and I would pass notes about him during class and giggle. She liked him a lot, but I didn't tell her how much I liked him, too. One day, I passed a note to her with the following poem:

That day during lunch, Jack asked us if he could sit at our table. He talked and flirted with Helene as much as a third-grade boy knows how and placed a folded-up note on the lunch table when he left. I nearly spit out my chocolate milk when she opened it.

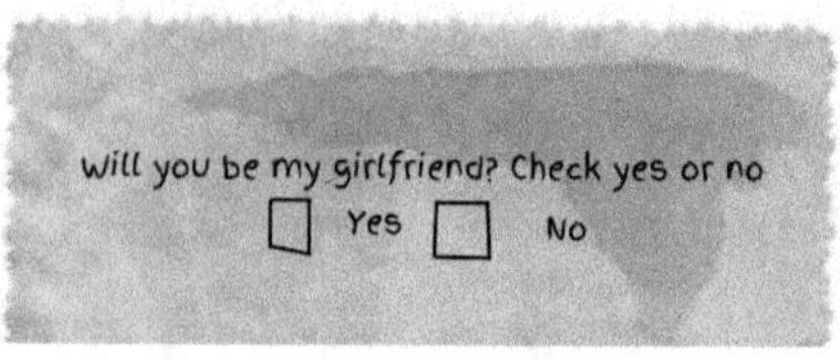

I bet his parents were big fans of George Strait. They dated for two weeks—an eternity in grade school.

My mind spun as I read my poetry. Bits and pieces of my words had come to life throughout my past. How had I not noticed? Instances that once seemed inconsequential were becoming stark, burning points in my memory. *Okay, time to do some experimentation*

I had to test whatever was happening. I stumbled out of my bed and crawled my way to my closet. I rummaged through the front pocket of my backpack until I found a pen and made my way back.

I sprawled the journal out, flipping to the empty half of the book. I tapped the pen against my lips as I formulated what to write. An idea hit me, and I began. The words started hesitantly but then flowed as though they'd always been there.

"*You are Völva,*" whispered that ethereal, accented female voice.

My whole body jerked from surprise. "What the hell?! Who are you?"

"*I have many names, but you may call me 'Wisdom.'*" Her voice was symphonious, a lulling melody that held a hint of humor. *As if that makes everything make sense? Sheesh. Whatever. Let's see what the voices in my head have to say.*

"*Where* are you?" There was no one else in the room and nothing to attach the voice to. "And what the hell did you just call me?"

"*I am here. I am there. I am everywhere.*" The richest and deepest laughter I ever heard burst forth, and I could not help but smile despite my fear. Was I going insane?

"*You, Vala Boddason, are unaware of who and what you are. You have been chosen. You have a purpose, my dear girl. You are part of a plan.*"

Excuse me? Chosen... "Wait, what?! But... why me?" *And by whom?!*

"*You* were chosen many generations ago. It will end with you. Do not fret. You will learn all in time. For now, sleep.*" Warmth spread over my entire body as a low, lullingly hum filled the room. The voice comforted my weary mind and gently tucked me in. Despite my attempts to stay awake, I fell asleep as soon as my eyes closed.

I dreamt of a terrible, ominous darkness. A dense, chilly fog sprawled across my vision, forming a spiraling passageway. I heard the reverberation of wails floating upward. The cries were melancholic. *Don't do it. Don't go down there. You have no idea what the hell is causing those cries.* Despite common sense urging me to stay, I followed the pathway into the dark depths.

The deeper I descended, the muskier the air became. On the last step, my foot fell heavily into something that squished beneath my weight, releasing a vulgar scent. I gazed down and realized I had planted my foot within the decomposing body of a huge rodent-like creature.

Ew, ew, ew!

The rotting body audibly whooshed as I pulled my leg away, leaving my converse covered in innards and wriggling maggots. I screamed as I shook the insects off.

I fell back into a stone wall behind me, instantly feeling something tickling my skin. My head swiveled to the right to come face-to-face with a black spider as big as my hand.

Oh, hell no!

I launched myself from the wall, brushing the cobwebs from my skin. The wailing echoed off the walls, becoming louder and beckoning me forward. I continued on, despite my utter disgust. As I walked, broad gnarls of rotten roots jutted out along the path.

The decayed undergrowth led to a giant, majestic, macabre throne of twisted twigs and human bones. Sitting upon it was a beautiful woman who had an elaborate crown made of giant, craggy antlers atop her head. Her long blonde hair was so light that it was almost white, and despite the softest blush on her cheeks, her pale skin was nearly translucent. She had an unusual eye color. It was a hypnotic shade of violet rimmed in lilac. Something about her demeanor radiated sadness.

A low, menacing growl rumbled from the shadows behind her. And from their depths emerged a large wolf held in place by a thick iron collar chained to the throne. The beast's eyes beamed at me in the darkness, stalking my every move. The sound of the metal raking against the rusted iron as the creature fought for freedom was akin to nails on a chalkboard. Utterly unbearable.

Come on, Vala, turn back. This whole situation feels like a big nope, But... I need to know why she is so sad. Maybe I can help?

The woman stared off into the distance forlornly and seemed to be crying. The sight was nearly painful. The sound of wailing all around us was brutal. But as I stepped forward to ask what was wrong, she turned her face to me, and I drew back in horror. The other half of her face was ruinous decay, an utter juxtaposition to the beauty I originally saw. Bits of sinewy flesh had been torn away, leaving oozing gashes that leaked sticky, silver blood. The remaining skin looked rotten and putrid, framed by stringy, black hair that fell from her partially exposed skull, glowing glassy gray in the darkness. Her left eye socket was devoid of anything but bits of gelatinous vitreous tissue.

She stood, and I could do nothing but stare and wonder how she could stand when the entire left side of her body was decomposing.

Shit, she's coming. She's making her way, and I can't move. Useless as usual.

As she moved towards me, I could hear the crack of exposed bones. Her mouth opened and soft lips parted on one side, while the jawbone disconnected with a garish click on the other. "Welcome to Hel, Vala." Her rasping voice made a chill slither down my spine. Her bony left hand extended toward me, and I jolted awake just as her bare phalanges brushed the skin on my shoulder. *Shit, shit, shit!*

Fear was replaced with... nothing. I was somewhere, but nowhere. And I was alone.

"This could be your future," the rasping voice slithered through my mind.

Everything around me changed. Fire erupted and within the burning bubbles I saw the form of a man. The scene changed, and I was plunged into deep, dark water. Amid the roiling waves I spotted a ship sailing through the abyss. Again, the world around me shifted, and I was surrounded by a green field dotted with purple flowers. The Sun was setting just as the Moon made its debut, stars freckling the perfectly black sky above. Howling infiltrated my eardrums.

"What is this? What do you mean?"

"You'll see."

My eyes flew open, and the light that flooded into my room blinded me momentarily. I sucked in a harsh gasp as my lungs burned; I must have been holding my breath. I *remembered* my dream. I *never* remembered my dreams. As if on cue—and to freak me out further—the disembodied voice of Wisdom said almost nonchalantly, "*Vala, I trust you slept well despite your dream of Hel. Don't allow her to frighten you.*"

Instinctively, I drew away from where I heard the voice. "What the… Hel?!"

"*Do not be afraid, child.*"

"'Do not be afraid?' How can you expect me not to fear that I am either: A. Losing my mind. Or B. Hearing a bodiless voice?"

Her gentle laughter sent a cool breeze across my skin, and I wrapped my arms around myself, glaring at the nothingness before me. *That's just rude. I'm having an existential crisis, and she laughs. I despise when people laugh at me.*

"*I realize this may seem… how shall I call it… abnormal? But I promise I am not here to harm you. And neither is Hel.*"

"Was Hel that woman? What happened to her face?" It was odd that Wisdom's words comforted me. I was talking with someone I couldn't physically see, and it felt normal. *Yup, you're freaking nuts.*

"Hel is both the woman and the domain she rules over. She is both dead and alive. Hel, the place, is not the same 'hell' that most humans know about. It is where those who did not die in battle go to rest. The Valkyries retrieve those who fall as warriors and take them to Valhalla. The others spend eternity with Hel, fated to her kingdom of death."

"Oh my gosh! The overload of information! Let me start with something I can wrap my head around. How did she know my name?"

"You are known throughout the nine realms, including the Earth and Below. As I've told you, Vala, you were called for a great purpose. You are Völva."

"What does that—"

"All will be revealed to you in time. But I shall leave you with a gift. A guide. You will find him at the place where the rowan trees grow, and he will bear a mark which you will know once your eyes behold it. Peace be with you, Vala."

And just like that, Wisdom's voice was gone. *Could she be telling the truth?*

I rubbed my temples and contemplated my sanity. Bits and pieces of my father's academic discipline flooded my mind. The nine realms referred to Norse mythology. But that was all they were. Myths… Maybe I had finally snapped and gone looney from the survivor's guilt that haunted me daily? *Dad. I wish you were here to talk to about this.* The thought was painful enough that I continued to muddle through the delusion, feeling closer to him than I had in years.

I had to ask Wisdom if anyone could hear her or if it was just me the next time we spoke. Her voice was as clear as someone sitting next to me, but I was the only one who caught her voice the night before. Helene had not. Sometimes, my friend could be clueless, but she would have never ignored a woman talking to me right next to her. She was too nosy for that.

Another thought occurred to me. When were the guide and I supposed to meet? Was it an actual person or another disembodied voice? If it wasn't a person, how could they bear a mark? I was beginning to feel overwhelmed when my phone buzzed.

Hey, are you ok?

Yes. I'm sorry for being an emotional mess last night.

Girl, don't apologize for that. I got you, boo!

:D I got you 2!

Plans today?

Wisdom made it clear that this was *my* journey. If she wanted Helene to know, she would have made her voice heard or allowed me to tell my friend last night, right? *I'm sorry, Helly.*

> The FPs want me to clean the house. I will let you know when I'm done.

> Damn. Well, hit me up when you are free, jailbird.

> You got it. TTYL!

Guilt about lying ate at me, but I didn't yet understand what was happening or know what to say. So, I rolled off the bed and walked to my closet. What do you wear to… what? A divine meeting? A destined meet-cute? That last thought left me giggling as I changed into denim cargo jeans with a black long-sleeved crop top. It was the middle of April, but unlike Helene, I was always cold, and the weather was only hitting the mid-fifties for the past few weeks.

The silence in the rest of the house indicated that Steve's bender was one of the worst he had yet. I was okay with that. *Screw Steve and his wandering eyes when he asks what my plans are. None of your business, perv.* If the FPs were asleep, I had no questions to answer before leaving the house for the day. So, I tiptoed to the front door and gently shut it behind me, barely making a noise.

CHAPTER FOUR

My destination was Rowan Grove Park—the only place where you could find rowan trees in our town. It was less than a mile from my foster home, and it was a sparkling day in Central Oregon, so it was a perfect opportunity for a walk.

I loved walking. I enjoyed the sun on my skin, the wind gently sliding across my cheek like a mother's caress, and the solid ground beneath my feet. I often walked to clear my head and ease my overwhelming anxiety, allowing a sense of peace to wash over me when I was one with nature.

As I strolled, a memory of walking toward Rowan Grove Park with my father popped into my mind. It must have been the scent of the previous night's spring rain or the sweet, heady scent of the rowan flowers in bloom that released it from my subconscious.

"Have I ever told you the story of Skoll and Hati, Vala?" my dad asked me quizzically. I was riding atop his shoulders and let out a delighted squeal, kicking my feet to avoid his tickles.

"Daddy, are those the woofs?" My dad chuckled at my inability to pronounce certain words, reveling in my childish vernacular. I

giggled at the skip in his step, my body weaving from side to side in a scary yet faithfully secure way.

"You remember! Yes, they are wolves. They are the chasers of light, remember?"

"Yup, I renember. Why do they chase the light, Daddy?"

"They want the entire world covered in darkness forever, my sweet Vala. Skoll has been hunting the Sun from the east to the west each passing day for generations. Meanwhile, Hati chases the Moon from the west to the east, trying to take a bite out of it. But don't you worry. Nana Frigg won't let those mean and icky wolves cover you up in darkness." He grabbed my leg and gave it a reassuring squeeze.

That snapped me back to the present like a slap to the face. *Nana Frigg.* I hadn't heard that name in over a decade. Fragmented and blurry recollections attempted to resurface. I tried to focus on one, but the memory was like the images in those old, bright red View-Master toys my mom kept from childhood. Each flashback was a still I could click through, but it was worn and hazy around the edges.

I couldn't hold onto a memory of any conversations with Nana Frigg's name, but I could envision the shape of a woman. I could feel her name ignite recognition but could not figure out how or why.

Who was Nana Frigg, and where was she now?

A low, snarling growl hummed from the shaded area to my left, pulling me out of my puzzling thoughts.

"Get down!" a deep, male voice boomed. A sudden blast rammed into me, knocking all the air from my body. As everything turned black, I caught a glimpse of messy chestnut hair surrounded by a glowing, emerald aura.

I woke up in the shade of a rowan tree just outside the entrance to the park. *What just happened? And…* I groaned in pain as I attempted to sit up.

"You must be more careful, Vala."

"How do you know my name?" I whipped my head toward the voice, only to wince from the sudden movement and closed my eyes tightly, trying to stop the world from spinning. Behind my lids, white spots mixed with black swirls.

Come on, girl! Now is not the time to be defenseless.

When I could finally open my eyes again, I peered dazedly down at my torn, wet black crop top. I touched the slickness, and red dripped from my fingertip. Blood.

"He got you pretty good, eh?" What kind of accent was that? I couldn't quite place it. Scandinavian? Icelandic? The man sounded like a freaking Viking warrior from those shows Helene loved.

"He…? What… what got me?" I stuttered in bewilderment, still staring at the blood.

Who was *this guy?*

The answering hearty guffaw stunned me. "Oh, that was Skoll. Stupid wolf didn't see me coming." How could he be laughing? Was he unaware that I was bleeding? As if the man could hear my thoughts, he said, "Here, give me your hand."

Uh, no thank you.

A large palm swung down toward me in my peripheral, and I turned, ready to face the man who knocked me off my feet.

Whoa. There went the wind again.

Holy hotness! Tamp it down, girl. You don't know this guy from Adam.

My towering savior looked to be about nineteen years old. Thick, chestnut hair cascaded past his shoulders, and chunky braids framed his head, keeping the long locks out of his face. Sideburns emphasized his sharp jawline, forming a picture-perfect beard with hints of red and gold. The rich colors contrasted with his stark white shirt, which I couldn't help but notice was so thin that I could see his tanned, chiseled chest covered in black tattooed symbols. And his eyes were pools of emerald, radiating energy.

Damn! He had muscles for days! He was strong all the way down to the deep brown linen pantaloons covering his thick legs. Pantaloons? Who the Hel was this guy?

Ignoring his still outstretched hand, I repeated, "I asked you how you know my name! And what are you talking about? Wolves don't come this close to town, like, ever!"

He only gazed at me with those steady, piercing, viridian eyes. I shivered a little at his ability to hold my gaze without a single movement, but I held his stare right back out of contempt. He wiggled his arm a little and hummed as if to say, "*Here, take it already.*"

"I am Heim. I was sent to find you." It was an offering, so I would finally allow him to help me.

Fine. Time to show no fear.

Warily, I accepted his assistance, and the moment our hands touched, a shock shuddered through the point of contact. The emerald aura came back, surrounding Heim as the skin of the arm I grasped started to crack open.

At first, I was horrified, unable to look away. But the transformation wasn't gruesome; beautiful gold filigree worked its way up from where our skin touched, and a thick, black tattoo formed at the base of Heim's wrist. I watched in awe as the etching formed a straight line upward, bisecting a slowly emerging V. The symbol reminded me of a man lifting his arms to the sky in praise.

A single word slammed into my subconscious. "Protector."

Heim pulled my body from the ground. The ease with which he maneuvered me was stunning. I had never met him before, nor had I ever laid eyes on anyone so attractive, but I suddenly felt a complete sense of peace. As soon as I was upright, he put his other hand on my waist, allowing me a moment to gain my bearings until I was steady. Heim bent his head toward mine—which was a feat because he must have been at least six feet tall while I was a mere five feet and three inches—and murmured in his thick, tantalizing accent, "Völva."

His breath brushed against my ear, and he lingered for a second, which gave me a moment to calm my racing mind despite the aroma of freshly cut juniper invading my senses. Gradually, my comfort bled into unease. Why on earth would he whisper female anatomy into my ear? What a creep!

He started to pull away, and I yanked my arm back before throwing it in the general direction of his face with all my strength. I let out a loud yelp when my fist connected with the bone around his eye socket.

"What the Hel?!" Heim's expression was a mixture of confusion, humor, and shock as he stood his ground.

"You're a pervert! A stalker! Somehow, you know my name. Then, you say something inappropriate. You have a lot of nerve, sir!" I stomped away, cradling my throbbing fist. Damn, that was more painful than I expected.

"Listen to me, Vala! *Vahl*-vah." Heim drew the syllables out slowly, exaggerating his lip movements for emphasis. The distinction was incredibly obvious. "Did Wisdom tell you anything, girl?" Despite his obvious frustration, he wore an annoyingly smug grin. "Völva is what you are. I was *not* referring to anything else."

Well screw you, sir. How the hell was I supposed to know? Do you think I'm just going to allow you to stand there and make me feel stupid?

"Oh," I said, sounding sheepish.

I guess so.

"Your accent is so much thicker than Wisdom's." He raised his hands in surrender and took a step closer. I rolled my eyes, allowing him to tend to my still-bleeding wound.

The man was proficient as he bandaged me up with items from a medicine bag that looked like it was from biblical times. With each step, he described the ingredients of the salve he rubbed gently on my skin, which burned under his touch. He used yarrow for wound healing, plantain for its antibacterial properties, and honey-infused bandages for quick recovery.

I pointed at the fresh tattoo. "What is that symbol on your arm?"

"It is the algiz rune. It stands for protection, among other things."

As he tenderly cared for my injury, I allowed my mind to wander.

What was a Völva and how did that fit into whatever Wisdom had meant I was chosen for? Heim seemed to know more about me than I knew of myself. I had a lot of questions, but the only words that left my lips next were, "I'm sorry about your face."

His eyes met mine, and he smiled; there was only a small blemish from my weak punch.

"I forgive you. But you only get the one punch, okay?"

"Got it."

CHAPTER FIVE

Heim reached into the ancient bag, pulled out an antique-looking leather bottle, uncorked the top, and took a swig of its contents before passing it to me. My nose squished in disgust before I realized what I was doing. "Eww. I have no idea where that has been." When I noticed his look of offense, I gently added, "But thank you for offering."

"Suit yourself," Heim muttered. He turned away and started walking toward the park gates. "Follow me. We need to find the Norns. Help me look for anything that resembles three women holding spools of thread."

"I have no clue what you are talking about," I stated pointedly, and my "guide" stopped but didn't turn around.

Yep, you are about to get a piece of my mind. Who do all these people think they are, barging in and bossing me around?

"You asked what Wisdom told me; honestly, she didn't say much. Then, you literally come out of nowhere, talking to me about a wolf with a strange name and saying words I don't understand. I feel like an idiot because I have no clue what you are talking about! I mean, what the Hel is a Norn anyway?"

"Vala… I'm sorry. I easily forget that you don't know what I speak of; every soul that inhabits the nine realms knows of your calling. The Norns are the sisters of fate and destiny, the first step on our journey. They possess the power to bless—or curse—your quest." He turned to look me in the eye, and seeing my clear confusion, he added, "I suppose if you have any further questions, you may ask them now, and I'll answer what I can."

Wow… how generous of him! I rolled my eyes, but he ignored my clear annoyance and started walking again.

Mainly out of pure curiosity, I followed him and asked one of my original questions—one of many that swirled in my mind. "What did you mean when you said a wolf did this to me?" When Heim glanced back, I gestured to the bloody mess of my shirt.

"Ah, Skoll. I heard his growl before he pounced. Sorry for knocking you down. I did not want him to hurt you any more than he already did," Heim said as if it were the most normal thing in the world. "That beast is fast. He must be if he thinks he will ever catch the Sun. The stupid animal has not, and probably will never, take the sweet bite he desires. Gods bless him for trying, though. I do not think he meant to harm you."

"How on earth did he not mean to harm me? How does this happen by accident?"

"You… uhm… I don't know how to tell you without frightening you, Vala." Heim's voice had lost the surety it held prior.

"What the Hel are you talking about?"

"Vala, you are Völva. When a Seeress becomes aware of her gifting, the Seiðr magic immediately manifests physically. You, specifically, radiate a much brighter light than any other Seeress I've ever witnessed throughout time. It is golden like the Sun. Skoll was more than likely confused and thought you *were* the Sun. As I said before, he is not the smartest creature on Midgard—I mean, Earth."

"Oh my gosh, Heim! Stop adding *more* confusing words to this already confusing heap of confusion!" He shrugged with a sly smirk. The asshole seemed to be getting off on my bewilderment.

Big, white, tufted blooms of rowan flowers and tiny green buds sprinkled the trees above us on our walk through the park. The clusters of blossoms always reminded me of the softness of a blown dandelion: fuzzy and fluffy white. As I surveyed my surroundings, I tried to focus on asking more questions from my growing mental list but couldn't help but get sidetracked by Heim's backside. *Pay attention, Vala. Nice assets do not equal trustworthy.*

"Can everyone see me glow?"

"No. Humans cannot. Only members of the nine realms can see it. I am sure you are curious about Midgard, so let me answer that eventual question, too. Humans know of Earth,

Heaven, and the Below. In our world, there are more than just those three. Are you familiar with the Yggdrasil?" my guide asked, genuinely curious.

As I started to shake my head no, a distant memory buzzed in my mind; something my dad used to whisper to me before bed:

"My Vala, I love you more than all the Aesir in Asgard. More than all the light elves in Alfheim and the dark elves in Svartalfheim. More than all the humans in Midgard. More than all the giants in Jotunheim. More than all the fire and ice in Muspelheim and Niflheim. More than all the darkness in Helheim, and more than all the Vanir in Vanaheim. That means I love you more than all the inhabitants of the Yggdrasil, and that, my dear, is an awful lot!"

I recited my father's words in my head like a prayer. "I know a little bit."

"Midgard is the land of humans, where we are currently. 'Earth' is the physical planet, whereas 'Midgard' is the realm. Midgardians can see your glow, but those who do not inhabit the realms cannot see your light—as with all Seiðr magic. Humans cannot see Skoll, either, nor would he harm them in any way." The anxiousness that riddled my body eased slightly.

"Thank you," I whispered, almost too quietly for him to hear. His head bowed ever so slightly as he pushed aside a branch for me. We continued to search for something I knew nothing of when a new thought came to mind. "Who are *you,* Heim? Why were *you* sent to find me?"

"I am Heimdall, son of Odin. I am the guardian of the Aesir and watchman of the Bifröst." His tone was commanding as he recited his title, taking a small bow. I stifled a laugh. At his massively offended expression, I quickly contained my giggle and curtsied back. "I am the only one who can guide you across the realms."

The soft whooshing of the breeze was replaced by a gentle thrumming.

"Do you hear that, too?"

"Yes. Follow me." Heim gently grabbed my arm, and we followed the sound around the maze of Mountain Ash trunks. Like a gentleman, he lifted drooping branches out of my way. Left. Right. Forward.

As we rounded a corner, the thrumming abruptly stopped.

Before us stood a statue of three women. The one on the left sat, the middle one stood tall, and the one on the right kneeled. Each figure held a spool of thin stone thread that crisscrossed between the women, connecting them. I had never seen anything like it before—I certainly had no recollection of it from the numerous times my father and I had visited the grove—and wondered distantly how the stone thread held up over the years.

In front of the statue was a pool of clear water that glittered in the sunlight. Heim looked at me, mouthed the word "Midgard" with a single lifted brow, and opened his ancient bag to retrieve a wooden cup. He dipped it into the pool and poured a little of the liquid on each spool. The stone flaked away to uncover a shimmering thread of silver. As the transformation rose to the statue's layer of stone, it slowly turned to ash and blew away on the light breeze, revealing three beautiful, living women.

"Hello, Urd. Verdandi. Skuld. It has been an extraordinarily long time," Heim greeted, turning to each woman as he spoke their name.

"Heimdall. To what do we owe this pleasure?" the three figures hoarsely whispered in unison.

"I bring Vala to you, sisters of fate and destiny, to bless her journey."

"Bring her here," they crooned. The creepy trio of voices left me uneasy. "Don't be frightened, child."

Easy for them to say.

Heim motioned me forward, and I grabbed his outstretched palm for balance as I joined the women on their platform. Each woman silently reached for my hand and tied the end of their silver string around my wrist. Despite my raging curiosity, I didn't ask what they were doing; it felt too sacred and important to disrupt with my endless questions.

"Vala Boddason, we are past, present, and future. With this twine, we thread your fate together." As the low and harmonious words were spoken, the thread on my wrist weaved into a silver-knotted bracelet with a small, flat disk. Thin scratches began to mar the smooth surface of shining silver, creating an etching of the same rune that appeared on Heim's forearm when we touched.

Algiz. Protector. Heimdall.

Dear girl… Algiz also means Awakening. *You come from an extensive line of Völva and Skald. You are a seeress, a holder of the Seiðr magic, and a wordsmith, a master of verse. This is your awakening, Vala. This is the time to hold your destiny in the palm of your hand. It is your chance to choose which path you would like to take. The power lies within you. Only you can decide how to wield it. Choose wisely…*

Those words were for me alone, but they sent a shiver down my spine. In response, I nodded silently to each woman and turned to Heim. The experience had changed me. I stood taller and straighter, allowing the Norns' words to build my confidence from the inside out.

"Okay, Protector. Now what?"

"Now, we go to Asgard."

CHAPTER SIX

Asgard. Scraps of knowledge I learned from my father flooded my memory. The home of Aesir. The home of the Norse gods.

"Why are we going to Asgard?" Everything seemed so surreal, and I vaguely felt like I was losing my mind. *Was this my life now?* Heim looked amused, no doubt seeing my mind racing toward a possible mental break. "How is this real?"

"I am quite impressed with your adaptability. You *go with the flow.* Humans say that, right?" A hint of sarcasm laced his deep voice. *Is he goading me, or is this genuine?* His ability to go from teasing to serious was incredibly annoying. "Your destiny calls you to Asgard, Vala, as it has to all nine realms. We go there first because Odin has been waiting to meet you."

We began walking again, and I followed blindly until Heim stopped so abruptly that I ran into him, falling back flat on my bum.

He gave a rich and hearty laugh. "Here, let me help you up." I glared up at him, grabbed his outstretched hand, and let him pull me up… again. I was sick of needing his help, and I promised myself I would not let it happen a third time.

Hanging from the nearest rowan tree was a ropelike branch that twisted and grew into what eerily looked like a hanging noose. I reached up, allowing my fingertips to graze the bundle of twigs. Heim grasped the loop tightly and pulled down.

"Odin's Gallows."

When I looked up at Heim quizzically, he blinked one eye at me awkwardly, and the other eye twitched oddly. Was that an attempt at a wink? It was the worst excuse for a wink I'd ever seen. I howled in laughter and bent over, clutching my aching abs until the earth started to shake, and I had to grab his arm to steady myself. Then, it was Heim's turn to belly laugh, and the ground seemed to rumble harder as if in response. All around, roots started to rise from the dirt. They were twisted and gnarled like the roots in Hel, but these were alive, healthy, and thriving.

They twisted into an ever-growing trunk, sprouting branches and green foliage. What was once nothing morphed into a monumental rowan tree—certainly the biggest one in existence. It was so large I couldn't see the entirety of its width or height. *Well, there is one way to put your puny life into perspective.*

"Welcome to the Yggdrasil, Vala," Heim said proudly with a wave of his giant arm.

"It's huge!"

"The size should come as no surprise. It *does* house all the realms." If I weren't worried about the inevitable pain, I would have punched him.

"Now what? Are we supposed to climb it?" I immediately wanted to hide in shame for even asking, and my cheeks grew warm. Not knowing about everything around me was new territory. Living in foster homes had taught me to crave control in any way I could grasp it. I may not have been able to control Steve's drunk ass or Brenda's weak character, but I could damn well control how I reacted to it by always observing and understanding my surroundings.

"Not exactly. Do you remember why Wisdom sent me?" *Right. He told me he'd take me across realms.* Before I could answer, Heim placed his outstretched hand on the trunk and whispered, "Opna. Open."

Bright light spilled from beneath his touch. It was so intense I had to shield my eyes until it dimmed slightly.

"Behold, Bifröst." Heim nodded at the medley of colors that burst from beneath his palm.

A rainbow formed before us. The reds, oranges, and yellows were ablaze, like the fire that licked my heels in that horrible dream. The greens were like the lushest meadow, and I swore I could smell fresh-cut grass. The blues and violets—together yet separate, like a starless mid-evening sky—finalized the perfect blend of colors.

The elements should not have been able to coexist so close together, but they combined seamlessly to create a sturdy bridge connected to stairs that formed right in front of my feet. Heim held out his hand to me, offering stability as I took the first step onto the magical stairway.

Tingles flitted along my wrist as my silver bracelet thrummed with the colors of the rainbow. The scent of praline and patchouli wafted through the air, tickling my nose.

Are you here?

I could feel my mom and dad; their presence surrounded me, and I instinctively knew my journey across the Bifröst was safe.

Vala, Algiz has many meanings. Spiritual connection is one. We are *with you.*

My father's voice was a comfort in my mind. As I closed my eyes to say a silent thank you, the world fell beneath my feet, and I plummeted into endless darkness.

I was back in Hel. Metal scraped against iron, and I knew that I would see the giant wolf when I turned around. Was it Skoll? I thought he belonged in the sky, chasing the Sun.

"Don't mind Garm," stated a familiar, raspy female voice.

"Garm?"

"He is my Hel Hound, but he is harmless to you, Vala." Hel's words were reassuring, but they still sent a chill down my spine. "Do not be afraid. We intend you no harm."

"Why am I here? What do you want from me?"

"You have a purpose in each realm. Here in Hel, if you choose to help me, your purpose is to correct the wrongs done to me and my siblings by my father. In exchange, I will owe you a sizable favor."

"How can I help you?" Dread filled me.

I have a feeling I'm not going to like the answer to this.

"Hel, who exactly *is* your father?"

"My father, Loki, has sealed the fate of my two siblings and me. It is a fate no one would choose, and I would greatly appreciate a chance for redemption." I remembered little of Loki and his legends but knew he was a relentless prankster. Could I even trust his daughter?

"What has he done to you and your siblings?"

"His poor actions have damned us, banished us, and restrained us. His children, the monsters, have paid the price for his wrongdoings." Venom and an overwhelming melancholy laced her words, and I was starting to understand the intense sadness I saw in her the first time we met.

"I am so sorry, Hel. But how do you expect me to help you?"

"You will learn soon enough if Wisdom has anything to do with it."

My brows creased in frustrating confusion.

Why is everyone so cryptic? How do they expect a girl with trust issues to be so nonchalant about all this... craziness? But maybe I can get something out of it.

"You said you would owe me a favor, right?" I kept my tone hesitant and polite, given I was bargaining with a goddess. "What will you give me in return?"

"Hel is home to those not lost in battle. I alone can save a soul from my realm, but I can offer the release of two souls if you choose to undertake such a task," she divulged as if it were a secret. "Take it or leave it, Vala."

My parents did not die in battle; they had ultimately surrendered to smoke inhalation. Did that mean they dwelled in Hel? If that was the case, saving them was worth any risk.

"I will take it." Her fleshy hand was cold as we shook in agreement.

When my eyes opened once more, I was back on the Bifröst, in the same exact place as before. Heim stood right behind me, incognizant of my disappearance. I decided not to tell him about my conversation with Hel; I needed to sort through the information on my own first. I stepped onto the bridge path that seemed to go on forever and was pleasantly surprised when the whole thing moved beneath my feet.

"I suppose we were a bit ahead of the times with this feature. I once visited an airport to see the flying metal birds and was impressed that someone stole my idea and modernized it."

It took me a moment to realize that Heim was referring to moving sidewalks like the ones at Portland International Airport. He reminded me of a giddy boy, but I had no idea how old he actually was. So, I chuckled along with him and gave him a thumbs-up for being so innovative all those years ago—however long ago that was.

The multicolored travelator moved upward at a steady rate. When we could see the city of Asgard floating above us in the distance, I noticed a towering building not far off to the left of the Bifröst. "What is that, Heim?"

"Himinbjörg. It is my home." He looked up at the tower with an emotion I couldn't place. Disdain? Loathing? Longing?

"It is... huge." Wow, that seemed to be the only adjective in my mental dictionary.

What do you expect when the most beautiful man you've ever met is standing right next to you. Brain cells are dying in the heat of his stare.

"Yes. It is massive. Living there can be quite lonely." My companion's eyes were unreadable, and a darkness cloaked his joyful spirit. The teasing ceased, and only dead air remained. We rode the rest of the way in awkward silence despite the multitude of questions that still buzzed about in my brain.

Could Heim tell me what it meant to be both Völva and Skald? I still wasn't entirely sure what a Skald was, only that it had something to do with my gifting with words.

And what did I need to know about Loki? Was he good or evil?

What was my purpose in each of the realms?

Most importantly, why did everything feel so normal to me? Less than twenty-four hours prior, I was an ordinary girl living a typical life in a regular small town.

CHAPTER SEVEN

The Bifröst ended abruptly, joining with the earth before us seamlessly. I almost tripped as the ground suddenly stopped moving beneath my feet, and I had to wobble for a second.

Heim finally broke the silence between us. "We have made it to Asgard."

Asgard was more magnificent than anything on TV about the lost city of Atlantis or the Greek's Mount Olympus. It sat atop the Yggdrasil, and when I looked down, I could see the earth spanning far below while the other realms diverged from the enormous branches of the World Tree.

Holy fear of heights! It's okay, I'm okay.

I peered up at the towering palace in front of me with its jutting towers, gleaming windows, and silver roof in silent awe. The reassuring pressure of Heim's hand on my lower back steadied me when I started to lose my balance from craning my neck so far back. I turned to him and gave a silent nod of thanks. He smiled and attempted to wink again, sending me into another fit of giggles.

"Heimdall, you have a way with the ladies, don't you, son?" said an older man from the palace's central doorway. "Hello, Vala. I've been waiting an exceptionally long time to meet you."

The newcomer had a shock of long, wavy gray hair pulled back from his face by an intricately woven leather headdress adorned with the skull of some small beast. He wore a long, charcoal tunic cinched tight with a hefty leather belt and a giant iron buckle carved into the shape of an eagle. A fur cloak the color of freshly fallen snow was draped over his shoulders, and fur-lined boots engulfed his feet. His pants—traditional kirtles—were black leather and laced up the sides of each leg with thin leather straps.

Enlightenment was etched into the lines and wrinkles of the man's face. His bright smile told a million stories, and a worn, black leather patch covered his left eye. Odin.

"Hello, Father." When Heim knelt on one knee and bowed his head, I tried to follow suit so as not to be disrespectful. I had no idea how to act in front of a king or a god. *Goodbye, control. Hello, anxiety.*

I was filled with so much uncertainty that I wanted to crawl into a hole and die. "Uh, hello."

Odin laughed. The sound was so joyous and rich that I smiled and lifted my head to look at Heim, who returned my smile and offered his hand to help me to my feet. I silently refused, pushing myself up from the ground gracefully. *Atta girl.*

"Vala, welcome to Asgard. We are so pleased that you have finally arrived after all this time," Odin stated as if I should understand what he was talking about. He made me nervous despite his jovial welcome. "This is my home, Valaskjalf. Please come in and make yourself comfortable."

"Do not be afraid, Vala. No harm shall come to you by the hands of Odin."

Wisdom! Her voice surrounded me like a gentle caress, and I was instantly at ease. Of all the unbelievable things I learned and experienced, she was my first taste of the realms, and her presence instilled peace. *Yup, I'm crazy. Comforted by the voices in my head while I'm guided through a freaking* kingdom! I nodded to Odin and followed him up the steps and into the building.

The king of the Norse gods talked boisterously with his hands as he guided Heim and me through the palace hallways. We passed pictures of Aesir and other creatures of the realms. There was a hauntingly beautiful picture of Hel kneeling before her helhound and another of a forlorn Heim gazing at the Bifröst from his lonely tower.

Odin's voice cut into my musings. "Here is your room, Vala. I hope it is to your liking. Now, rest. You can clean up for dinner later. We shall introduce you to the rest of the family tonight."

I silently observed Odin and Heim as they walked away from my accommodations, and panic struck, nausea rising and stealing my breath. I was about to be alone in the vast palace. I hadn't paid attention to how we got to my room. I pleaded wordlessly with Heim when he turned his head back toward me.

I don't even know if I trust you, but you brought me here. Give me a sign that I'm safe here.

He gave me a lopsided grin and one of his stupid one-and-a-half-eyed winks. I inhaled deeply, mouthed the words "thank you," and turned to enter my room.

Rooms, to be more precise. The walls were painted gold. The floor tiles were white marble dusted with shimmering golden flakes. The art decorating the walls rested in aged gold frames. The chaise lounge, which was creamy white, had gold trim, and a long golden side table was piled with shiny golden apples and rich, golden grapes.

The decadence reminded me of a sexy guy in a loincloth who'd feed me the fruit at my whim. I chuckled at my random imagination until I caught myself picturing Heim as the more-than-half-naked guy. Heat rushed to my cheeks, and I shook my head to clear the alluring image.

A large doorway led to the bedroom on the left. It was mostly black and accented in—you guessed it—gold.

The king-size bed had a thick comforter embroidered with longships sailing on amber waves. And cushy black and gold throw pillows nearly covered the oak headboard that was ornately carved with a kraken overtaking a longship. It was stunning.

Exhaustion crashed over me like a tidal wave, and I eagerly jumped onto the bed. As I sunk into the plush bedding, I examined the stunning painted mural on the ceiling. It depicted a story from Norse mythology that I vaguely remembered my father telling me about as a child. *What a coincidence that my father chose to specialize in Scandinavian Studies.*

The scene showed Odin sacrificing his left eye for divine wisdom. As I stared, the artwork blurred into a jumble of colors, reforming into a fresh image of Odin hanging from the branches of the Yggdrasil. He had hung there for nine days and nights to gain knowledge and to give his people a language, the Norse runes. The art continued to blur, change, and form image after image of the Allfather's adventures.

Only Odin. *Vain much?* Eventually, my tiredness overtook me, and I allowed myself to drift into a deep sleep.

Slowly, I roused from unconsciousness as something grazed the skin of my arm. My eyes remained closed, but every nerve in my body seemed electrified from that goosebump-raising touch. The light sensation became more substantial as masculine hands splayed over my collarbones, running across my shoulders and down my arms in a slow caress. The bed sank under the weight of another body as muscular legs straddled me. Strong arms moved to bracket either side of my head as hot breath blew across my neck. "Vala," a deep, delicious voice growled.

Heim.

My body overturned every rational thought my mind tried to grasp onto as he gently cupped my chin, and his other hand tangled in my loose hair. With my eyes still closed, I envisioned his gorgeous chestnut tresses cascading down to frame his face, shielding us from the outside world as he towered above me.

He placed two fingers on my brow and, with a downward motion, rounded and splayed his palm on my cheek, his thumb grazing my lower lip softly. His body lowered slightly, his face mere inches from mine.

Oh my.

I wanted him to close the distance. I wanted to feel his lips on mine. *What is wrong with me?*

"Do you want me to kiss you, Vala?" His lips were so close that I could feel his breath tickling my mouth as he spoke.

Yes. No.... Yes.

I dug my hands into his hair, trying to pull him closer in answer to his lingering question.

As our lips nearly touched, I opened my eyes to witness his beauty before my first kiss.

My mouth opened on a silent scream, and high-pitched, maniacal laughter erupted from the man above me. "Got you!"

"Who the Hel are you?" I thrashed my legs, pushing the man away with both arms. Without so much as a word, the unknown male jumped back and disappeared in a cloud of shimmery, red smoke. *Who was that, and what the Hel just happened?*

I stared around in absolute shock, trying to find something I could use as a weapon, when a knock sounded. "I'm coming!" After falling out of bed, I grabbed a gold candelabra and placed it behind my back before heaving the door open, breathless and probably a bit wild-eyed.

A meek young woman with long, flowing, gorgeous red hair and bright green eyes that drew out the pretty freckles dotting her pale cheeks stood on the other side. "Hello, Miss Vala. I am here to assist you in dressing for dinner. Are you quite alright?"

No, I'm not! But I'm not going to tell you that.

"Oh, uh, I'm fine. Come in," I said, still hiding the candelabra as best I could. I wasn't sure who I could trust anymore. She quietly moved past me into the room and walked straight to a set of double doors. I set my makeshift weapon on one of the tables before following her.

We stepped into a huge closet, and I felt completely… underwhelmed. The large space was empty. Just as I was about to ask the girl why we were in an empty closet, she turned to me, her green eyes shining in an otherworldly way.

"Alright, dear. You need an outfit to wear to dinner. We must make haste so that we aren't late. Odin does not enjoy waiting."

"But there is nothing in here," I retorted.

"You do not need to see with your eyes to truly see. Envision what you want and write it, please, Vala."

"Write *what?*"

"Harness your Skaldic power, and you shall see."

Come on lady, do you not see the look on my face?

I honestly hoped she could see how lost I was. "How?"

"You are Skaldic. Own that. Think of what you want. Form an image in your mind and use your words to write it. Then, it shall be," the woman declared, sounding almost bored.

Our ancestors were skalds. Poets.

My father's voice drifted in and out of my memory like a dream.

"Uh, ok. I need something to wear to dinner, right? Is there a dress code? Also, what am I supposed to wri—?" Before I could finish asking what I was supposed to use to complete this task, a writing desk, parchment, and the most gorgeous quill and ink set appeared before me. *That's handy.*

"The gods enjoy the finer things in life while staying true to our Nordic roots." I nodded in slight understanding and leaned over the desk, imagining an old Norse-style dress I saw in one of my father's books.

Well, here goes nothing. Please let this not backfire.

I dipped the quill in the ink and let the words flow from my fingertips.

Intricate and soft.
The deepest shade of crimson.
Clothe me to belong.

I looked up at the girl and handed her the paper. She read it and looked at me quizzically.

I shrugged. "Haiku."

After reciting the poem, I felt ridiculous and was about to start laughing at the absurdity of it all when my cargo pants and torn shirt disappeared. *Holy crap! What is happening?* My hands flew up to cover my semi-nakedness, and my cheeks flushed bright red before warm air enveloped my entire body.

The magic felt warm and tingly as the most exquisite material I'd ever touched caressed my skin. The deep crimson dress that formed from nothing was cool and creamy like silk but also soft like cashmere. The neckline dipped slightly, elongating my throat. A deep emerald smokkr—an apron— draped over the bodice and skirt and was fastened over my shoulders with intricately carved bone brooches. Glass beads adorning the top lip of the apron caught the light, reflecting rainbows throughout the room. And a leather belt cinched tight around my waist, accentuating my chest and torso.

As I moved, the bottom of the dress billowed around my feet. I turned to the girl, and she handed me a pair of leather slippers that magically appeared in her hands. I placed the shoes on my bare feet and felt the soft brush of a snow-white, full-length fur cloak skim my arms as it magically buckled around my neck.

"Did I do this?" I asked breathlessly as I walked to the mirror in the still-empty closet.

"Yes, Vala."

The girl was so kind. Immediate shame slammed into me when I realized I didn't know her name, but she had called me by mine numerous times. My parents had raised me better than that before their untimely demise. It had been rude of me not to ask.

"What is your name?"

"I am Idun, goddess of immortality." Her aura erupted into a bright halo, the same otherworldly green that her eyes were earlier.

CHAPTER EIGHT

Idun's entire appearance changed into that of a blonde, fair-skinned woman. Her cheeks had the same whispered freckles, but her once long, loose red hair was swept into a beautiful, long braid that brushed the floor. Her face looked wiser but not older, and on top of her head sat a dainty crown of delicate, white flowers. She also held a basket of the most amazing golden apples I'd ever seen.

"Much better." The goddess smoothed the wrinkles from her simple, floor-length white dress. "Would you care for an apple, my dear?"

"I… uh, no, thank you," I stuttered.

I don't need a Snow White moment, even though she's given me no reason to doubt her.

She smiled, reaching out to grab my hand. I stared at her outstretched offering before my gaze flicked back to her ethereal eyes. "I thought you worked for Odin. Before you… changed. Like a servant or something?" Her head tilted back as she gave the softest little giggle, but her kind eyes looked at me almost pitifully.

"Sweet Vala, I work for no one, but I can understand your confusion. I sometimes change forms to discreetly move about the realm or, in this case, to meet the infamous Vala Boddason," she replied after she regained her composure. "I live here in Asgard and keep the gods eternally young by feeding them my apples. Truth be told, I could get any of them to work for *me* if I wanted to. We can blame that on their selfish vanity. To live forever is one thing, darling, but to remain forever young is an entirely different story."

I pondered that for a few moments. "Idun, what would happen if *I* were to eat one of those apples?"

"My apples have a different effect on Midgardians than on the gods. As you are from that realm, the fruit would do nothing for you in the long term. They would, however, have several effects on your human form for a short time. You would gain increased strength and speed. They may also provide calmness and clarity in stressful situations."

"So, kind of like a caffeinated apple?" The goddess stared at me slack-jawed, and I had to hold in a chuckle.

Lady, you are making this difficult since humor is my shield.

"How did you know I could do that with my haiku?"

"I suppose I could have started with that. Despite how incredible I look for my age, I am quite old." An air of superiority laced her youthful voice. She set down her basket of apples and started to pace. "My husband is Bragi. He is the god of poetry, the son of Odin and Frigg. He is the rea—"

"Did you say *Frigg*?" I interrupted as all the fragmented memories of Mom and Dad talking about Nana Frigg danced around in my mind. Idun's glare was instantly humbling, and I shut my mouth. *Don't interrupt this goddess. Got it.*

"As I was about to say, he is the reason your bloodline became Skald. He had a soft spot for your ancestor, Bragi Boddason, so he sent me to help ease you into our realm." I had so many more questions, but I could tell that the goddess was becoming exasperated, so I kept them to myself. "If that is all, I think we should head to dinner. I am sure everyone is waiting for us by now."

As I followed Idun, the eyes in the artwork seemed to follow me as if I were doing a walk of shame. I internally giggled as I thought of the images talking to me like the art at Hogwarts. *"Hello, Vala. Why do you look so sad? Is it because Idun is such a sourpuss?"* the Fat Lady inquired in my head. I chuckled aloud this time, and Idun turned around to scowl at me—her age certainly showed in her hasty annoyance. Properly chastised, I walked silently, following obediently until we arrived at the dining hall.

"Idun. Vala. I'm glad to see you both have finally made it," Odin's voice bellowed through the dining hall. I glanced around the large table that dominated the space, feeling entirely unwell—Heim was not in the room with us. Odin wore a long, royal blue tunic, brown trousers, and the same handsome fur-lined leather boots. His unruly gray hair was swept away from his face, tucked beneath an iron crown that boasted two horns etched with runes. "Come, come, child. Have a seat by me."

The feeling of a familiar hand across my lower back made me jump. The situation with the unknown male from my room left me questioning not only who I trusted but also myself. Why had I allowed the situation to progress, even if I *had* thought it was Heim?

"You look beautiful, Vala," Heim murmured against my ear, his warm breath sending heat waves over my skin. *That's why.* My heart picked up its already quickened pace.

"Don't worry, Lítilvölva. I'm over here," mocked the nameless male's voice from the other side of the room. I froze at the sight of him. He was tall, thin, and very toned. His face was long and slender, and his head was covered in a shock of red hair that seemed to float around his nearly incorporeal body as if he were underwater.

Everything about him was angular and sharp but not un-attractive. His unlaced red tunic and black trousers hugged his muscular body in all the right places. The smile plastered across his face instantly made me think of the Joker in The Dark Knight. I had always thought Heath Ledger was the creepiest Joker of them all—and the most attractive.

"Are you alright?" An involuntary shudder ran through my body in response to Heim's words. I wasn't sure if it was be-cause of his proximity and warm breath on my skin or the fact the ghostly redhead was getting to me, even from across the room. Couldn't Heim see the eerily handsome specter across from us? As though the man could hear my thoughts, he stared at me pointedly and winked! The wink—unlike Heim's awkward attempts—was a successful promise of trickery and douchebaggery to follow. Suddenly, his body disappeared in front of my eyes in a cloud of red smoke.

"Vala, did you hear me?" Heim's voice was laced with concern as he guided me to my seat.

"No, I'm not alright. Who was that guy?" I pointed to where the man evaporated in thin air.

Great, now on top of feeling *crazy, I am going to* look *crazy since no one is there.*

"Who are you talking about?" He followed my gaze to the other side of the room. "There is no one over there."

"He was just there. He was in…" I could not articulate to Heim—or anyone for that matter—what happened in my bedroom earlier out of fear of embarrassment. What would my guide think if he knew I thought it was him and had been okay with what was happening?

"Never mind. I'm fine," I stated curtly as I sat in the chair beside Odin, who sat at the head of the table. I couldn't help the annoyance dripping from my tone. Heim was infuriatingly confusing, Idun wasn't exactly a spoonful of sugar, and the unidentified male had successfully debilitated every one of my nerves.

"Vala, I apologize for my family and any incongruous behavior," Odin interjected as if he could read my thoughts. I sent him a questioning glance, and he lifted one side of his lips in a smirk and gave me a slight nod of understanding. Oh. My. Gosh. My eyes widened in horror. He *did* know what I was thinking!

"I can't read minds if that's what you are wondering, but I must say that your expressions are effortless to read." *Thank the gods!*

Everyone else at the table silently watched our exchange, including Heim, who sat in the seat to my right. How had I not noticed how handsome he looked? Dressed in a black tunic that brought out the green of his eyes, tan trousers, and gray fur-lined boots, my guide was hard to look away from. His sleeves were rolled up to his elbows, showing off the fresh tattoo on his tanned, muscular right forearm. Unconsciously, I breathed him in without realizing what I was doing.

Sitting beside Heim was Idun, and next to her was a man who looked like he could be her grandfather. He was gray personified—curly gray hair that grazed his shoulders, a long gray beard, and a charcoal cloak. It wasn't until Idun leaned over to kiss his lips that I realized he must be her husband, Bragi. *What an odd couple.*

On the other side of the table was the largest man I had ever seen. He had classic red hair, a flawlessly fluffy Viking beard, and a uniquely muscular, chubby build. His outfit, which was less clothing and more armor-plating, was heavy-looking and covered much of his upper body. On the table next to him was a giant Viking hammer.

When the man's eyes met mine, he grinned. "Nice to meet you, Vala. This right here is Mjolnir." He lifted the large mallet and kissed the flat head. "And I'm Thor."

My eyebrows scrunched together in instant confusion, and Odin guffawed. "Oh… please don't say, *'But you don't look like Thor.'*" Thor said that last part in a poor impression of a little girl.

"I… I'm… well…" I stuttered. I vaguely remembered watching Marvel movies with one of my foster brothers, Andrew. The memory of the character clashed distinctly with the man before me.

"I'm only joking. I swear you humans take things way too seriously."

I regained my bearings and smiled back at the ornery hulk of a man. His teasing put me at ease, although I was still shocked by his appearance. "I am sorry, but in my defense, you are not what I was expecting."

"Yeah, I know. I'm way more handsome!" His laughter was so contagious that the whole table erupted in a giant fit of giggles.

Finally, someone with my kind of humor.

"*That* was hilarious. Thank you, Vala. It has been a long while since I've enjoyed a decent belly laugh like that." Odin held his sides, still trying to catch his breath. "Human eyes have greatly altered my son's depiction. You envision—oh, what is his name again? Christopher Hem-something. That Stan fellow was incredibly talented, but he did take a lot of creative freedom with Thor's appearance for his picture books."

Thor was banished to Earth by Odin. Don't you know anything, you stupid bitch.

The memory of Andrew's cruelty slammed into me. I thought I remembered that Thor lived among the gods based on my father's teachings and was telling him so when he screamed the words at me. That type of berating behavior only got worse when I moved in with Brenda and Steve. He was agonizingly adept at calling out my inaccuracies, even if I was not, in fact, wrong. No one is smarter than a drunk dude.

The only thing worse than feeling out of control in my life was being made to feel stupid or less than. I began to contain my thoughts to guard myself from unwanted accusations against my intellect. *The only person that can make me feel dumb is me. Got it?* Self-consciousness washed over me like acid rain before Odin gripped my shoulder in comfort. "I apologize if our laughter felt like it was at your expense, child."

His smile and the kindness it radiated reached his one good eye and crinkled the crow's feet on his weather-worn face. Immediately, I relaxed into my chair, feeling more like myself than I had in many years.

Screw you, Andrew. Looks like I was right all along.

Thor placed a huge arm around the woman at his side. "This is my wife, Sif. She is my better half and way better looking… obviously." The god had a gift for replacing awkward discomfort with humor.

"Hello, Vala," Sif greeted. A light blush spread across her pale cheeks.

The goddess' hair was magnificent; it spilled from the top of her head to the floor and glittered gold everywhere the light touched. If I had thought my rooms were awe-inspiring, they were nothing compared to her glorious strands of glimmering honey and lustrous flax. Her gown was a mixture of cream and gold, cinched with a thin, glass-beaded belt that sparkled. When her bright blue eyes met mine—she obviously saw me ogling—her smile instantly put me at ease, and I found myself smiling back.

"You have now met most of my family; I have two more for you to meet. Then, we may begin our meal," Odin stated. He tilted his head skyward and released a low whistle between his teeth.

A cool breeze grazed my skin as the sound of wings sliced through the air. Appearing out of nowhere, two massive, black ravens circled the table above us, gradually gliding lower until they came to rest on Odin's shoulders.

"Huginn. Muninn. Welcome home, my boys. Give a warm welcome to Vala." Each raven turned toward me and let out a small coo as if to say hello. "What news have you brought me?"

One of the ravens opened its beak and started... speaking.

CHAPTER NINE

"Allfather, we traveled near and far within the realms and come home with news. There have been encounters."

"Where at, Huginn?" Odin's tone was urgent

"Midgard was his last known location, Father. But there have been other sightings."

"The red smoke," the king god mused to himself as he stroked his beard.

"Excuse me, did you just say, 'red smoke?'" I interjected. Everyone stopped what they were doing and stared at me.

Uh oh.

"What do you know of the red smoke, Vala?" Heim asked, sensing everyone's unease.

"Did you not see it earlier? Just there." I pointed to where the unknown man disappeared earlier. I glanced around the table and saw concerned faces. Everyone started talking at once, the buzzing of their voices becoming a cacophony.

"Enough!" shouted Odin as he banged both fists loudly on the table. Silence fell over the room. "Vala, did you see anything other than the red smoke?"

I rubbed one thumb over the other in a nervous habit. Heim must have noticed because his hand dropped to my thigh. I was positive he meant it to be a reassuring touch, but it made everything much more difficult to proceed.

Well, this should be interesting.

"Yes," I finally admitted in a hushed tone.

"Tell me what you saw. Now." Odin's order was commanding yet gentle.

"There was a man in this room earlier, but he disappeared in a cloud of red smoke." I didn't want to say the rest, but I could tell that the god was analyzing my face and would pick up on any omissions, no matter how minor. "He was also in my room before Idun came to me."

Heim shifted in his chair, and I could feel his penetrating stare. A rush of heat blossomed from his palm, and I swore I could hear his heartbeat quicken. I kept my eyes on Odin, fearing I would lose my nerve if I turned to look at my sworn protector.

"Why are you just now telling us, Vala? What happened?" Despite the calm in Odin's voice, I could feel the tension in the room. It had grown steadily since the ravens arrived, and Odin's question was the eye of the storm.

Here goes nothing.

I breathed deeply, counted to three, and admitted, "I thought it was Heim in my room." Heim's hand left my thigh, and I winced, my cheeks flushing an even deeper pink. It was best that I was wholly honest—for the most part—since

I had revealed so much already. "I was relaxing on my bed, still basically asleep, when Heim's voice woke me up. When I opened my eyes, a man with bright red hair and an angular face was standing over me. Before I could find out who he was, he vanished! When I came into the dining room earlier, he was here mocking me until he disappeared again in a cloud of red smoke. Who is he, anyway?"

"He is my brother." A shudder of fear ran from the base of my neck down my spine. The next words out of Odin's mouth seemed almost inevitable: "His name is Loki."

An awkward silence cloaked the dining hall. Palpable tension settled in the room like a heavy fog. Despite the mood, I was constantly amazed by new and unusual happenings. For instance, once Odin went silent, the empty table suddenly filled with food.

Full loaves of bread, seared vegetables, huge slabs of spit-roasted meats, and large goblets full of a deep burgundy liquid materialized on the table. A lone goblet full of the burgundy beverage sat before the Allfather. But Thor's empty plate filled magically—there was enough to feed at least four men. He grinned slyly at me and lifted a giant turkey leg to his mouth, devouring it in almost a single bite.

I smiled at his antics but quickly became lost in thought about Heim's reaction to what I told Odin. *Could he see through my half-truth?* I tried not to let the blush touch my cheeks, but he was sitting close to me, making it difficult to hide. I was suddenly incredibly parched. Was it the memory making me so thirsty? I couldn't recollect the last time I drank anything. I reached for my full goblet to quench my thirst, but Heim's hand caught my wrist before I could touch the glass.

"Excuse me?" The words hissed between my teeth on an exhale.

"You cannot have any of the mead, Vala."

"Why the Hel not?"

He looked taken aback but amused. "First of all, you are underage. Secondly, the liquid in your glass is the mead of Suttungr."

"As if I understand what that means…"

"It is the poetic mead. For Odin, it is all he needs to survive. For the other gods, it brings about eloquence and understanding. For a human, it could cause…" He paused briefly, trying to find the words. "…undue distress. The magic within the alcohol flows through the Boddason line. Bragi, the god of poetry, gifted your ancestor a taste of the fermented beverage. A mixture of honey and the blood of Kvasir, the original god of poetry, combined to make a libation worthy of scrimmage. We keep it under strict protection after the many theft attempts made throughout the years. For a Midgardian, it is too easy to become addicted to the magic, the taste of the honeyed drink, and the power it gives."

"So then, why do I have a goblet?" I countered.

"You must forgive the help, but look around the room, Vala." Idun didn't look like she could be any older than me. Thor looked about twenty years old, and Heim was—well—Heim. "You are in a room full of gods. Our servants are not accustomed to checking ages, so they are unlikely to withhold a goblet from anyone. Also, while no one here is worried about you stealing the mead, I highly warn against it. I have witnessed the downward spiral of an addict, and it is not something I wish to see you struggle with."

Suddenly, a giant hand reached over my head and snatched the goblet from my place setting.

"I'll take that." Thor swallowed the contents in one gulp and lumbered back to his seat. I liked him. He had big brother-like tendencies and an entertaining attitude. I smiled, and he returned it with a goofy, lop-sided grin.

"Fair point, and fine," I whispered, returning my attention to Heim. "But I *am* thirsty." At that, he lifted his hand, and a crystal-clear glass of water appeared in his grasp.

"This is an enchanted dining hall. Everything here will magically appear again tomorrow, the day after, and so on. If there is something you desire, think of it, wish for it, and it shall appear. Go ahead, try it."

Seriously? Get ready, Asgard. I'm bringing you a special treat.

I closed my eyes and thought of one of my favorite foods. Expectations running high, I peeked one eye open but was met with only an empty plate.

"Why didn't it work for me?"

"Hmm. It would depend on what you were thinking of. There is a limit to the hall's magic, as in all things. It only works for items readily available in Asgard. Sometimes, I forget that."

"Damn. I was *really* looking forward to my mom's lemon bars."

"I am not sure what those are, but I apologize that they aren't available," Heim said seriously.

"You've never tasted a lemon bar?!" I exclaimed louder than I intended, and everyone gave me a weird look. "Sorry, but lemon bars are superior to all other desserts."

"We do not have lemons in Asgard, only my golden apples, plantains, and a few other local fruits," Idun explained. Instead of feeling chastised, I felt sorry for them. The comfort I found in speaking my opinion so freely reminded me of who I was before foster care.

"Well, we are going to have to fix that someday, and when we do, I will bake homemade lemon bars using my mom's recipe," I announced proudly, forgetting the sour mood that coated the room since before dinner. Everyone stared at me briefly as if I were an oddity but then returned to their conversations and meals.

"I'd like that," whispered Heim, his breath tickling my neck. Yet again, my body betrayed me, and I shuddered at his closeness.

After dinner, my protector offered to walk me back to my room. The sprawling hallways intimidated me, so I graciously accepted his offer. It seemed surreal that just the night before, I was with Helene…

Oh my gosh, Helene!

"Do cell phones work here?" I asked before realizing I didn't even have my cell phone. "Ugh, never mind."

"Do not worry about your friend, Vala. Time works much differently here in the realms than in the earthly world." That was a relief, but there were still a lot of questions on my mind.

Yeah, like how you feel so comfortable here despite all the weird shit going on?

"Loki is known for his tricks." Heim interrupted my internal tornado of thoughts with the one topic I wanted to avoid like the plague. "He is not pure evil, but he is far from good. That is why there was a layer of unease at our meal this evening. Odin trapped Loki far beneath the ground, lower than even Hel. If he has escaped, that could mean terrible things for us. It also makes this entire situation make sense."

"What do you mean?"

Heim looked like he was choosing his words before he said them; it frustrated me to no end because I didn't know what to do with his long pauses.

"You are Völva. Settled within the marrow of your bones and throughout your being is Seiðr magic, the power of your people. It shouldn't have flourished. Not until you come of age. There must have been a special circumstance that awoke your powers early. Loki escaping is one Hel of a circumstance.

There were rumors before, but this solidifies his return to Asgard."

"What do you mean by 'come of age?'" I asked, hoping to put off the inevitable awkward conversation a little further.

"Eighteen. In our culture, men and women come of age when they turn eighteen."

My birthday was only in a few short weeks.

Thanks, universe. This is an interesting choice for an early birthday present.

"What would have happened if there had been no circumstances?"

"Nothing," Heim stated. "You would be in the earthly realm and know nothing of our kind yet. Blissfully unaware." My breath caught in my throat. I imagined what it would be like to be in Bend—in my bed at the FP's house—"blissfully unaware." *Blissful, my ass.* Even though I didn't know Heim well, I would have missed him even if I never met him. Our bond filled a hole I hadn't known was there.

"So, Loki escaped. What should I do now? I don't know anything about being Völva, and I don't know how to harness my magic. I know nothing about what being a Skald entails. I don't even know how he found me. I am just a human!" My emotions were quickly overwhelming me.

Heim was in my space within a second. His hands gently clutched my face, and he bent slightly to touch his forehead to mine. "Vala Boddason, you are far from just a human. Within you lies the power of an entire clan of powerful women. With one poem, you could tear down an army. With one thought, you could rewrite the stars. With one word, you could lead a man to Valhalla or have him follow you straight to Hel." His breath hitched on the last sentence, and I burned at his confidence in me.

Slow down, heartbeat. They are just pretty words.

"How do you know, Heim?"

"Because Loki came for you," he said with clenched teeth. That was not what I wanted to hear. Despite that, I knew Heim was right. "I'm not sure how he found you, but we will find out. I promise you."

And powerful promises.

"Thank you." I stepped back, his fingers lightly grazing my skin before fully leaving my cheeks. Instant cold replaced the warmth of his hands. "For making me feel better."

"You never have to thank me. I am your protector." The proof of that statement glowed from the rune on his right arm. "Out of curiosity, what happened with Loki in your bed chamber?"

Well, shit.

CHAPTER TEN

What happened with Loki in your bed chamber?

I did not want to answer. How could I begin to explain? The situation was inappropriate, and I hardly knew the man who had become my protector. In the short amount of time since we had met, I realized Heim had a knack for infuriating and enraging me while simultaneously stirring emotions I had never felt before.

He was also an incredibly old god, which made me feel weird because he looked only a year or two older than me. My brain went straight to age-gap romances and how gross I always thought they were unless the male was an immortal Fae or something. Did an immortal Norse god count?

Heim was gorgeous, and I swore I could feel the chemistry in our connection. When he touched me, I could feel every atom sizzle from the heat that exploded between us. My bracelet warmed when he was near—his empowering words were a power source, and the thing was casting gorgeous rainbow rays all over the hallway, like a diamond catching the light of the sun. Remembering how Loki touched me while mimicking Heim's deep voice quickened my pulse as a blush stained my cheeks.

"I…um…" Wow, I sounded like a blubbering idiot. *Well done, Ms. You-can-rewrite-the-stars-with-one-word.* I mustered up all the courage Heim's monologue gave me and spoke as evenly as possible. "I think it's safe to say that you know I find you attractive."

Heim tripped over his feet, stumbling before quickly righting himself. I stifled a laugh. He kept walking as if nothing happened while I attempted to tamp the fire blazing under my skin. *Did I just make* him *nervous?*

"With that being said, I think the rest is just going to have to remain a mystery, and you, sir, are just going to have to respect that," I declared sassily.

My companion gave a heavy sigh like he had been holding all his breath in for an eternity. When he collected his thoughts, he finally broke the heavy silence that had fallen over us. "I vow to respect you always, Vala. Respect and protect you. There *will* come a point where we will have to discuss this more… for safety reasons."

We had reached my chambers, and he opened the door for me. As I passed him, one of his big, sturdy hands wrapped around my wrist and pulled me back to face him. I kept my gaze on the floor, but he cupped my chin and raised my face.

He looked at me with a hunger I hadn't seen before. He grazed the fabric on my shoulders before trailing his touch softly down my arms. "I think this shade of crimson is my new favorite color."

Oh... good... lordy.

Heat rushed to my cheeks again, and he traced the blush with his fingertips. He gracefully bowed his head, stepped back, and left. I couldn't breathe. I couldn't move. How on earth could I relax after that?

I woke up the next morning to a knock on my door. The comfy bed was difficult to climb out of, but a deep need for coffee won out. I dragged myself from the plush bedding and tossed on a gorgeous cream bathrobe over my gold silk pajamas. The night before, I was too exhausted to be shocked that someone had laid out clothing that fit me perfectly. Instead, I had graciously put them on, crawled into bed, and fell instantly asleep.

The intruder knocked harder as I stumbled to the door. "Patience! I'm on my way!" I was grumpy in the morning without coffee. *Whoever it is better have a steaming cup of black coffee, or I'm going right back to sleep for a hundred years.* The knock reverberated again, and I flung the door open with as much force as I could muster. "What the Hel?!"

"Good morning, Vala," Heim greeted with amusement. In his hands, he carried two large wooden mugs. Thick rivulets of steam rose from them, teasing my sapped senses. *Thank the gods!* I stood on my tiptoes to see their contents, but I was too short and breathed an exasperated huff. Heim chuckled and passed me a mug. I grabbed it a little too excitedly. It smelled like… apples.

My nose scrunched. "What is this?" I was too tired to care about the disappointment that laced my voice.

"This is Idun's cider." Heim drank deeply from his mug.

Just as I was about to take a sip, too, I caught myself. "Idun told me that eating her apples could have a strange effect on me."

"Not a strange effect per se, but it *will* heighten your senses. That is one of the reasons I brought it to you this morning." He paused, and as if he could sense my annoyance at the unnecessary silence, he added teasingly, "You also seem like the kind of person who needs a warm beverage in the morning."

"Why cider instead of coffee?" I asked blankly, ignoring his relentless ribbing. Heim seemed smart, but if he decided to come between me and caffeine, he was in for a rude awakening.

"I tasted coffee while visiting Midgard, but it was introduced to civilization well after our beginning here in Asgard. Remember, if something didn't originate from here, then it doesn't exist in this realm," he explained with a hint of empathy.

"That may be the saddest thing I have ever heard."

"I hate to say it, Vala, but I must agree."

I allowed Heim to enter my room, and we both relaxed in the main sitting area, drinking our cider in silence. It was as if he knew not to talk to me too much until the coffee-shaped hole in my heart was filled, even if it was satisfied with a fraudulent alternative.

Oddly enough, the cider was the most incredible warm beverage I had ever tasted. The amber liquid was the perfect blend of tart, sweet, and aromatic, with notes of cinnamon and nutmeg.

As the spicy-sweet drink hit my tongue, I could feel it spreading throughout my system. The heat traveled down my throat, entered every blood vessel, and pulsed through my enlivened veins. Each beat of my heart pulsed out a new sensation.

Beat. Peace.

Beat. Energy.

Beat. Power.

I was invincible and limitless while reveling in deep tranquility, unlike anything I'd ever felt before.

"Heim, not that I am complaining… at all… but why do my senses need to be heightened this morning?" I inquired in a daze.

"The time has come," he said with a certain je ne sais quoi, "for you to meet Frigg."

"Nana Frigg?" Maybe I could finally learn more about myself and my parents. Perhaps I could finally ask all the questions that had been swirling around in my head.

"Yes. I believe your parents originally introduced her to you as Nana Frigg." I was unsure if it was the cider or the adrenaline-fueled excitement at potential answers, but I jumped up immediately and was dressed and ready to go within five minutes. "Okay, Vala, off to Fensalir."

"Fensalir?"

"Yes, each deity of Asgard has a home, and each home has a distinct name."

"That makes sense. Odin called this place, uh…"

"Valaskjalf. I figured that would be simple since it starts with your name."

"Hey, Heim?"

"Yes, Vala?"

"Shut up."

His eyes widened in feigned offense, but his mouth was lifted in a wicked smirk. "Make me."

I walked over to him, clad in nontraditional trousers and a blouse, and lifted my hand to strike his arm. Before I could make contact, he grabbed my wrist in his large, strong hand and pulled it above my head, rendering it useless. "That's what I thought, you stubborn little thing."

What the Hel did he just call me?

As he stared down at me with an expression of success, I glared back in defiance. Once his eyes broke contact, I lifted my foot and slammed it hard onto his.

"Ouch!" he laughed.

"That's what you get for calling me stubborn."

Asgard was speckled with many palaces besides Valaskjalf. Some were constructed of glass, while others were adorned with jewels. And the land was made up of rolling hills with flourishing green foliage and tall amethyst flowers that released an odd scent.

"Wolfsbane. Odin planted it everywhere surrounding Asgard to keep Fenrir imprisoned," Hein explained when I asked about them.

"Who is Fenrir?"

"Fenrir is one of Loki's monstrous children."

That reminded me of Hel's request. Why had Loki's children been punished for *his* misbehavior? That hardly seemed fair. I decided to hold onto that question, trusting that I would find the answer when the time was right.

As we walked, Heim told me about the different homes and landmarks along the way. He was quite the tour guide, describing the inhabitants of Asgard and explaining how their homes complimented their godly gifts. Idun and Bragi lived in a palace filled with musical instruments and writing tables. The land surrounding their home was a thriving orchard brimming with Idun's golden apples. Thor had the Norse equivalent of a multi-level home gym, and Sif had thousands of brushes everywhere.

We arrived at a fence of flowers, and my protector guided me toward a small outbuilding on the outskirts of a dense field. He opened the large wooden doors, and within stood a stunning horse. The beast was a creamy tan with a mane that matched my own locks. The horse reared back and whinnied until Heim stepped in close to stroke the animal's snout lovingly. "Hello, Gulltoppr."

Heim motioned me forward and grabbed my hand, guiding it toward the horse's nose; the whiskers on its chin tickled. Gulltoppr nudged me for more attention, so I ran my hand down its long neck and felt the creature rest its giant head on my shoulder.

"He's beautiful."

"He is mine, but today he will be ours."

After saddling Gulltoppr, Heim hoisted me onto the horse's back and mounted gracefully behind me, wrapping his arms around my waist to grab the reins. We rode across the field of poisoned plants, weaving through the flowers gracefully and leaving each purple petal untouched.

Above us, Huginn and Muninn followed our path in leisurely flight. Odin sent them to watch us from above. They were to report sightings of red smoke. Thinking of Loki sent a shiver down my spine, but I tried my best to ignore it and appreciate the beauty and history of Asgard as told by Heim. The deep timbre of his voice could make just about anything interesting.

He pulled back on the reins just as Gulltoppr's breath became ragged from the hard gallop. In front of us stood two towering willow trees that stooped and bowed together to create an arch draped in drooping branches. We dismounted, and Heim pulled the branches back like a curtain, waving me through.

On the other side, the environment shifted abruptly from hills and forests to marshland covered in the greenest grass. Channels of azure water spread out like billowing veins, creating little islands of solid ground. High above in the sky and dotting the terrain were mighty blue herons. They were majestic in flight and peacefully present on the land.

"Beautiful, isn't it?" The serene scene had struck me dumb, so I merely nodded. "Let me prepare the boat."

Heim pulled a little wooden canoe free of some overgrown grass, and after helping me sit on the back bench, he carefully got into the vessel. I was incredibly relieved when he started rowing. It allowed me the opportunity to enjoy the beauty and stillness that was only disrupted by the oars brushing through the water and the gentle breeze swishing through the marsh grass. Even the herons were silent.

"What happened to Huginn and Muninn?"

"Frigg is powerful and erected a blockade around her territory. The tears of a grieving mother created this marshland. Thousands of years of despair since the loss of her son and my brother, Baldr, have formed the canals you see. There is much to her story that is not for me to tell," Heim stated with reverence.

Interesting. He can be trusted with secrets.

"Your brother? Is Frigg your mother?"

"No, but Odin is our father. I have profound respect for Frigg, and she has never treated me as less than any of her children, even and especially after the loss of Baldr."

"I am so sorry for your loss." I reached out to lay a hand on his thigh.

"It was a long time ago, Vala, but thank you." My protector looked out at the marshland again, clearly lost in thought. "We are almost there."

The narrow canal we rowed down opened into a sprawling, clear lake. A light fog danced over the glassy surface, creating a haunting, rising veil. Thousands of delicate violet orchids mottled the marsh grass, daintily dangling toward the ethereal water. And spanning far in the distance was a raging cerulean ocean with white-capped waves that crashed against the shore. "Whoa."

"Welcome to Fensalir, Vala." That was Wisdom's voice, and it wasn't in my head.

Behind me, standing on stairs made of dense fog, was a beautiful young woman with knowing, compassionate hazel eyes. She wore a flowing white gown lined with gold, and her long, chocolate-brown hair was braided into a powerful and regal updo. When she spoke, her words dripped like sweet nectar. "Nice to finally meet you in person, Vala. I am pleased that you are here."

When I just stared at her in shock, Heim cleared his throat, and I shook myself out of my stupor. "Hello, Frigg," he greeted, solidifying my suspicion that Wisdom was Frigg—also known as Nana Frigg.

"Wisdom."

"Vala, do not be afraid. Do you remember when I told you time would reveal all? That time has arrived, and we must prepare you for what is to come," Frigg declared.

My brows bunched in confusion. "Time for what?" I asked.

"Vala, it is time to prepare for Ragnarök."

CHAPTER ELEVEN

Was Frigg for real? Ragnarök. Wasn't that the end of the world or something? Both deities must have sensed my general unease because, within seconds, they were by my side.

Frigg wrapped her arm around my shoulder. "Vala, I did not mean to frighten you. I apologize for my directness."

"In her defense, Frigg has been alone for quite some time. Her way of conducting herself around others is clearly out of practice." Were Heim's words meant to instill faith in me? At least I felt less nuts since I could finally put a face to the voice that spoke in my mind.

"Regardless, frankness is necessary. We need to begin her training. The sightings alone are cause for preparation."

"I assure you, Frigg, Vala can handle anything," Heim declared between clenched teeth. It was really annoying that they were talking about me while I stood there, all but ignored.

"I know you think that, but until she is trained in Seiðr and accepts her true Völva and Skaldic powers, she is defenseless."

"Okay! I am standing right here!" I yelled. "I will do whatever I must to learn, but I want a few questions answered."

Frigg's eyebrows lifted quizzically, and she looked almost impressed. "What would you like to know, Vala?"

"First of all, what are we preparing for? Second, how is training going to help with Ragnarök? Is that not the end of the world, and, oh, I don't know... inevitable?"

"Vala, there are prophecies foretold that must come to fruition before Ragnarök can occur. One of those prophecies tells of Loki escaping after centuries from his binding prison. Your recent sightings prove that Loki has indeed escaped the chains that bound him."

My next question seemed rather inconsequential. There was no time for silly questions when apocalyptic words flew around me like candy at a kids' party, but I couldn't help but ask, "Why did my parents call you Nana Frigg?"

"Your parents were both from lengthy lines of Völva. For a woman of these lines, harnessing Seiðr magic is not unusual. For a man, it is almost unheard of. Your father was set apart because he was one of the few men with the gift of sight throughout history, albeit his ability was not as strong as the women's. I am the goddess of motherhood, Vala. All Völva report to me after their training. Many view me as a maternal figure, and 'Nana Frigg' is a common nickname. I loved your parents as my own, just as I love all the realm's creatures, big and small."

Whoa. My parents were like me. Why didn't they ever say anything? An aching urge to talk to them hit me—I needed to yell at them and hug them simultaneously.

We are with you, sweet Vala.

I inhaled deeply and closed my eyes. *I know.* My head buzzed with a never-ending trail of questions, but I latched on to the only one I could sanely wrap my mind around.

"Can I ask you one more question?"

"Of course, Vala."

"What do you want *me* to call you?"

"Darling girl, you can call me whatever you like," Frigg replied gently, kindness radiating off her like a diamond shimmering in the sunlight.

I reluctantly followed the deities up the stairs. Upon first glance, they appeared to lead to nothing, but once Frigg stepped onto the solid ground, an entire palace formed within the dense fog. Thick pillars, doorways, and windows formed from the water vapor. Curious, I reached out to touch a handrail. It felt cool and solid beneath my fingers.

The building that materialized in front of me reached completion, and it was gorgeous and... alive. Each surface rippled at the slightest touch and sent small waves across each facet of the structure, creating an endlessly undulating plane. The languid movements—liquid, yet solid enough—captured within the confines of each floorboard and wall panel were mesmerizing. Fensalir was an aquatic anomaly.

"Vala, do you remember the stories that your father used to tell you?" Frigg inquired.

"Bits and pieces... It is like I can't fully remember all of it. It is almost like there is a wall separating me from my memories. Some are clear, and others are hazy. They come back to me in broken segments sometimes. Does that sound crazy?"

"Not at all. Someone put a magical block on your memories to protect you. I will investigate and see if we can figure out how to lift the spell. Is that okay with you?"

"Of course. Do you think there's a way to get my memories back?" I was feeling hopeful despite the confusion surrounding said memories.

"I do." My stomach flipped. "There will be time for more questions as we progress. For now, I will have Heim take you to your room so you can change. Once you are ready, you will come back down here to train."

Heim guided me down an ethereal hallway. No art hung on the walls. Instead, etched silvery, metallic runes rippled on the eddying, yet solid, fog. The place was certainly mystical, and the runes only added to the witchy vibe. I vaguely remembered that witches were the most well-known approximation for Völva in the human world.

We are not witches, Vala. We are prophetesses, seeresses, healers, spirit speakers, and leaders. Frigg's voice penetrated my wandering thoughts. She was everywhere. Perhaps that was why she adopted her original moniker of Wisdom.

My protector opened a door. "There are clothes in the closet for you, Vala," he stated politely before stepping back to leave.

"Wait. Heim, what do I wear for training?"

"You will know. Don't worry. This is not a test." He gave me one of his half-assed winks, which got me giggling.

Once I entered the closet, my eyes were instantly drawn to what I was supposed to wear to train—a multicolored dress with a simple bodice and a honey-colored leather corset. But it was the skirt that made the dress extraordinary—the strips of fabric were a kaleidoscope of every color and shade one could imagine.

I exited the room to find Heim standing guard in the hallway, waiting for my return. Giddy, I twirled just like a fairy princess and was delighted when all the light, dainty pieces of fabric lifted like multicolored streamers. The dress was perfect. When I looked up at Heim, his slightly parted lips spread into a wide smile, revealing dimples beneath his sculpted beard.

"What is that dopey smile for?" I asked jokingly.

"What does 'dopey' mean?"

"Dopey means goofy or silly, and that is just how you look, sir." I poked him gently on his large chest.

"Well, I suppose seeing you look so cheerful could make anyone dopey," he mused. The compliment left me shy, timid, and quiet.

I'm beginning to wonder if these aren't just pretty words.

The awkward silence made me flustered, so I retreated toward the stairway. "Did I say the wrong thing?" My heart broke a little at his question.

"Absolutely not! You said the exact right thing. Sometimes, that is more difficult for me to understand than the wrong thing. Does that even make sense?"

"Surprisingly, yes." Vulnerability laced his tone as he continued, "I grew up with brothers who were perfect or strong or graceful. They have storybooks written about them, each called for amazing purposes. Their names will come from your lips more times than mine because *they* are those who history chose. They are who Odin chose. I am but an afterthought. Called only to be a guide and a protector.

"The Bifröst doesn't *need* a guide. I feel stuck despite the straightforwardness of the task. I will remain rooted at the bridge between realms. It is part of the storyline within the book of my life, which I had no say in writing. Frigg showed me kindness and called me for more. She bade me to guide you. I will be eternally grateful for her trust, but it's hard to accept someone's praise or acknowledgment when I've been alone for so long and do not feel worthy of taking on such a task."

Now I've seen kindness, protectiveness, and vulnerability. Now I know I was too quick to mistrust this one.

I wrapped my arms around his big body. He stiffened at first, but after a couple of seconds, he melted and wrapped his arms around me, leaning his chin on my head.

"You are worthy, Heim. I have only known you for a little while, but I know I can trust you with my life. Look." I lifted my wrist, showing off the bracelet as it rested next to the inked rune on his forearm.

"We are in this together. I have no idea why—and I am slightly afraid—but I have you by my side. I will say your name as many times as possible until you know you are the only man I want to guide me. I will say your name repeatedly if it means I can rewrite the stories. You are no less than any other. In our story, you are my main character. I can't do this, whatever *this* is, without you."

I leaned back to look up at him just as a tear streaked down his cheek, but he looked stronger and even more powerful than before. He touched his forehead to mine and whispered so quietly I could barely make out the words, "Thank you."

Heim pulled away and kissed my forehead gently. The touch was fire on my skin, temporarily freezing me in place before I could shake off the shock.

I grabbed his hands and pulled him toward the staircase. "Let's go, *Heim*." I enunciated his name slowly as I winked at him, making him laugh.

Downstairs had transformed in our absence into a magical oasis. White pillar candles were strewn everywhere, bathing the area in an ethereal glow where before there was only a vacant room. A large table hosting both familiar and unfamiliar items sat in the middle of the once-empty space. Herbs, wooden bowls, animal bones and a long, craggy staff were among them. Light from the glowing candles bounced off the walls, creating moody shadows all around us.

Frigg stood in the middle of the room, wearing a dress almost identical to mine, her hands lifted skyward. "Vala, welcome to my training room. Völva have gifts that manifest differently in each person. The main ones are healer, seer, prophetess, and spirit speaker. You have been double blessed, Vala. Your mother is a purebred Völva, while your father was a gifted seer and Skald. Do you know what that means?"

"It means my father was a poet and could see into the future, right?"

"Yes, but it's more than that. A Skald that is also a seer can take a word and give it life. The gifting has long roots in our history, spanning back to the ending of the Aesir-Vanir war. The truce was sealed when the gods spit into a vat, thus creating Kvasir. Then the greedy dwarves Fjalar and Galar murdered the poet, combining his blood with honey to create the mead of poetry. One would hope the violence would end there, but no creature of the realms can withstand the call of the mead.

"Those nasty dwarves lost their ownership of the mead after murdering Suttungr's parents. It was either they relinquish their rights to it, or Suttungr would allow them to drown in the sea where they had killed his parents. From there, the mead was hidden deep inside a mountain, guarded by his daughter Gunnlöd. Her father should have known the loneliness would affect her. Odin surely did when he found out where it was hidden. He infiltrated the mountain, playing at the young woman's weakness and tricked his way into obtaining the mead. He retreated from the mountain in his eagle form, chased by Suttungr all the way to Asgard.

"Odin held the poetic mead in his mouth, returning that power to his people so that mead would run through your father's veins and now in yours. With that power, he could harness his poetry and will it into existence which is why the mead is so heavily guarded in the kingdom of the gods. From what I have witnessed and heard, you can do that, too, to a certain extent. Part of your training will focus on harnessing your power. With control, you can use it as both a blessing and a curse." Excitement glittered in the goddess' eyes.

"Did my dad know that he could do that?" I couldn't recall him ever telling me about it, writing poetry, or much else for that matter. He was a professor of Scandinavian Studies at the local community college and knew many stories about Norse mythology, but I could not remember him doing any form of writing.

"Yes, but that is all I can say about your parents. More will come with time, Vala. I know that is not what you wanted to hear."

"It's not, but I suppose I've waited this long, so I can be patient," I sighed.

We spent the next several hours going over the Völva history and origins. I felt like I was back in high school.

All that was missing was Helene. My mind wandered as I wondered what time it was at home.

Home? I had only been in Asgard for twenty-four hours, and it felt more like home than anywhere else since my parents died.

"Did you hear me, Vala?" The sternness in Frigg's tone snapped me out of my downward spiral.

"Yes… uh… you were talking about Freya, who taught the Seiðr magic to the Aesir."

"Yes. And why, pray tell, is that important knowledge?" I stared at her pitifully, knowing I got caught in the act of not being attentive. "Just as I thought. Pay attention, please. We don't have much time. Freya taught us magic to try and save my son, Baldr. A prophecy told us his life was in danger, but she granted him invulnerability to magic. As we know, magic has its limits. Loki figured out Baldr's one small weakness; he learned the loophole in the spell. He used that to trick the blind Höd into accidentally killing his brother—my son—with a mistletoe-dipped arrow. That act resulted in the trickster god's banishment to the deep below."

"Where is Freya now?"

"Freya is the Queen of the Valkyries and resides in Folkvangr. She is fond of the men and women who died as warriors, so she visits the hall of Valhalla frequently. Those ripped from this earth with their lifeblood soaking the ground surrounding them are her reason for being. She visits them to vanquish her regrets."

"Because of Baldr?"

"Yes, because of Baldr." A deep sadness resonated in Frigg's voice as she continued, "He rests below. He has found favor with Hel but cannot escape the domain because he did not pass in battle."

Perhaps liberating Hel could create a new loophole for Baldr to return to his grieving mother. I placed that idea in the back of my mind and paid closer attention to every word the goddess spoke with a newfound understanding of the importance of each.

By dinnertime, I had not written anything or learned how to harness power like I thought I would. Frigg saw my frustration and reminded me that foundational training was key, and the rest would come with time. I didn't argue. I had only witnessed a small amount of what Loki could do, but that alone made me realize I needed to be fully prepared before going head-to-head with him.

Dinner at Fensalir was different than Odin's, but in some ways, even better. Frigg's enchanted dining room boasted a variety of savory seafood, matching the aquatic theme of her home.

Huge clam-shaped plates piled high with bright pink shrimp, lobster tails as big as my arm, and little rolls formed into the shape of conch shells appeared on the table. Creamy, melted butter rested in small wooden bowls beside each plate, and pretty purple drinks served in ice-filled, clear goblets sweated enticingly, trailing droplets onto the table.

"What is this?" I asked Heim.

"It is orchid iced tea. Frigg brews it for its immunity bene-
fits."

"It's delicious."

We spent the rest of the evening eating without awkward
silence or looming unease, laughing and joking about the
happier parts of the lessons. Frigg even asked me questions
about the past several years of my life. I enjoyed every minute
and left the table full and happy.

I drifted into a deep and peaceful sleep on the big waterbed
in my room, lulled by the sound of waves.

I knew it was a dream—I could still breathe even though I
was undeniably underwater. My hair fanned out around me,
floating and flowing like mermaid locks. The depths were
dark and murky, but a dim light ahead seemed to beckon
me forward. The closer I got to it, the brighter it became,
illuminating something iridescent...

The thick wall of scales moved, and I realized I was looking
at some kind of creature. Its giant body shifted in odd, serpentine undulations, spanning as far as my eyes could see in both
directions. Gradually, a snake head with two huge, yellow
eyes came into view. Its mouth was firmly biting down on its
tail, creating a never-ending ring around the sea floor.

"Hello, Vala," the snake hissed in my mind. I would have been more startled if I hadn't gotten used to such dark dreams, voices in my head, and the unending strangeness that had become my life. Everything was real but felt so surreal. I swore I would wake up one day to the sound of the FPs arguing and pray to fall back into the dream I was living.

"Hello," I said, trying to sound unphased while bubbles erupted from my open mouth. "What is your name?"

"Oh, you can hear *me?"*

"Of course, I can hear you," I replied, wondering why he would ask such an odd question when he called me by name.

"I am Jörmungandr, but you may call me Jorm. I am the son of Loki, the endless ouroboros."

"Uh, it's a pleasure to meet you, Jorm. How did you get so large?"

"My banishment began many years ago," he hissed. *"Odin threw me into the sea, and I have grown and grown. The oceans are endless, and so is my size."*

"Why did Odin banish you?"

"He heard from a prophetess that my siblings and I would cause chaos, so he banished us when we were quite young."

"Oh. I'm sorry. I bet it has been lonely down here." The snake's gaze became mournful, and I wanted to lift his spirits. "Why is your tail in your mouth?"

"I bite my tail to contain myself. My father wants to free me to bring about Ragnarök, but I would not choose to end all things. I long for freedom, but not in this form. I wish to be small again."

I brushed a hand against Jorm's scales. They were smooth and cold to the touch. "I will help you. I'm not sure how, but I vow to try." His eyes glimmered with hope and kindness. This poor beast was no monster. He was a misunderstood, lonely child cast out because of a misunderstanding.

"Thank you, Vala."

In the space of a blink, I was awake, curled up in the big waterbed. I sat up and smoothed down my bedhead only to find damp, dripping hair. Interesting.

CHAPTER TWELVE

I showered immediately; I hadn't felt wet while speaking to Jorm in the dream but waking up damp seemed wrong and uncomfortable.

When I opened my door to head down for breakfast, Heim was already waiting for me, leaning against the wall opposite my door. He looked serene, eyes closed, arms folded above his head, and legs crossed. Had he slept there?

"Vala." I jumped, and his chest shook with laughter. "Sorry, I didn't mean to frighten you. Let's join Frigg for breakfast and figure out the game plan for the day."

"Do you think *Frigg* has coffee?" I asked, already knowing the answer but remaining obstinately hopeful.

"Nope." I gave an exaggerated sigh, and he chuckled again at my obvious disappointment as we walked downstairs.

What an ass.

"I had a strange dream—" Sitting on a plate in front of my place at the table was a perfectly browned pastry. "Oh my gosh! Is that an Ocean Roll?!"

Delight sparkled in Frigg's eyes upon seeing my excitement. "I heard it was one of your favorites and thought you may be getting a little homesick." How did she know? Ocean rolls were only available from a little bakery in my hometown. They were crispy, flaky croissants, finished with an egg wash to ensure their golden perfection during baking and a light dusting of sugar, cardamom, and vanilla. Helene and I would go to the bakery early every Saturday morning and pick a few up before the bakery sold out.

"Thought you might like this, too," said a familiar female voice behind me.

"HELENE!" I jumped up and threw my arms around her.

"Dude, Vala… coffee," my bestie scolded. Creamy brown liquid bubbled up from the lips of two to-go lids. She deposited the tray of coffee cups onto the table and embraced me tightly.

"Wow. Are women always this loud?" Heim's question broke through our excited giggles. Helene and I both turned in unison and stuck our tongues out in his general direction. Goodness, I missed her more than I realized.

"Wait. Helly, what are you doing here?"

"Well, I suppose it's time I told you. But I need you to promise you won't be mad, ok?"

"Be mad? Why…" I glanced from her to Frigg and then to Heim, and they all looked like they knew something I did not. "…would I be mad?"

"Vala, I know Frigg. I knew your parents long before I met you." Helene's voice was gentle despite the bomb she had dropped on my lap.

"Excuse me?"

"I am one of Frigg's attendants. I am also the goddess of compassion. Your mother and Frigg knew the path your life would take. They knew it would be difficult for you. So, they made me young again and sent me to be your companion. I want you to know that I am still the Helene you know and that, until about a week ago, I didn't remember who I was except for my fierce protectiveness of you. Please don't be angry—"

I threw my arms around her again. "I could never be upset at you for that, Helene. You are my best friend. So what if you are a goddess? I just found out I'm a magical poet, so there's that." I honestly wasn't mad; I was just so exhilarated that she was there. "I love you, jerk face. Plus, you brought me coffee!"

"I love you always, cow." We both laughed at Heim and Frigg's audible intake of breath. "Now, drink your coffee, put on your big girl pants, and let's take Loki down."

"Yes, ma'am!" I agreed, grabbing a cup of delicious, life-giving coffee.

The lessons for the day focused on the prophecies of Ragnarök. Helene and Heim joined me as Frigg educated us about the impending events. I learned that, among the many prophecies, three main things needed to happen for the end to begin:

1. Skoll and Hati needed to catch their prey. Fimbulvinter would be a consequence of the lack of Sun and Moon. That

would lead to the Yggdrasil withering and set another ice age into motion on Midgard.

2. The Midgard snake—Jörmungandr—must rise from the ocean floor. His giant body would disrupt the seas, creating a terrible path of destruction. Jorm's destiny included killing Thor, the god of Thunder, with his venom.

3. Fenrir's liberation from his prison in Asgard; he would wreak havoc among the realms and—in the end—swallow Odin whole.

"Odin and Thor will die?!"

"The prophecy does say that. Vala, you are their only hope. You are the only hope for the nine realms and their inhabitants. Your parent's purpose was to create an heir that could save us all," Frigg explained gently.

"Whoa, that is… a lot." Helene had been away from Asgard for so long that she related more to Earth than to the realms.

You're tellin' me.

"Heim told me that the wolves were too stupid to catch their prey," I said to no one in particular.

"I may have been saying that to calm down a young woman that I just met who was also bleeding from the gut."

I shot him a glare. "I am no weakling."

"I know that… now." He winked, and my hand flew to my mouth to hold in a laugh. Helene's brows flew to her hairline as she jabbed me under the table.

"Later," I mouthed.

"The written word cannot naturally change," Frigg lectured. "That is where you come in, Vala. When your Völva magic and Skaldic gift combine, ultimate power is the result: the ability to see and change the future through your words."

"Do you think I can actually do that? I mean, why couldn't my dad have been the one if he harnessed the same magic?"

"I think you can do anything you endeavor to try, Vala. Your father was a gifted Skald, but his Seiðr magic could never be as strong as your mother's or your own. It is an old magic that manifests more robustly in females. Today, we will continue working on Völva training. Tomorrow, I have someone I'd like you to work with."

We spent the rest of the day learning important tools like scrying, hexing and blessing, divination, fortune telling, and healing. Healing was difficult for me because I had to practice on Heim. Each time he cut into his palm with the ceremonial antler-bone knife, I heard his pained intake of breath and wanted to yell for it to stop. At least I was able to use that passion to clot the bleeding and bind his wound with a shamanic spell. *Uruz. Heal.*

At the end of the training session, Frigg bowed her forehead to mine. "You have done well, my child."

"Thank you, Nana Frigg." Enjoying the closeness of her maternal aura, I radiated a golden luminescence while her magic enveloped her in the softest rose-pink glow. She was a blooming anemone wrapping me within her budding, powdery petals.

"Meet me here after dinner. I have a surprise for you," she whispered, only loud enough for me to hear. After we separated, Helene grabbed my hand and pulled me toward the dining hall.

"Bi-otch, you have so much to tell me!" my bestie whisper-yelled. We left the others behind, running to the table and giggling like schoolgirls. We chatted about everything—well… almost everything. Some things—like my growing attraction to my protector—I decided to hold in until we were completely alone.

After dinner, I went to the training room alone. I promised Helene I would share all my juicy Heim gossip with her during our quasi-sleepover (she was going to room with me that night). When Heim asked if I needed anything, I told him to get some legitimate, non-wall sleep, and he rolled his eyes but agreed with a drawn-out yawn.

All the candles in the training room flickered with restrained firelight, making shadows dance on the wall. Nine young girls clothed in flowing white dresses sat in a circle with their heads bowing toward the floor. In the middle of their group sat a tall wooden stool.

Close to the wall stood three young men with buckskin hand drums. In unison, they began playing, creating an eerily slow rhythmic pattern.

"Welcome to your first soothsayer ritual, Vala. The music you will soon hear will lift the veil between the living and the dead. Soothsaying is one of the greatest gifts of the Völva.

Although it is not indefinite, you will have access to the spirit realm for a time and can visit with anyone you like."

I turned back to the door to see Figg's knowing smile. It filled me with overwhelming hope as salty tears spilled down my cheeks. She took my hand, guiding me to the stool. As soon as I was settled, she stepped out of the circle, and the young girls lifted their heads and began to sing. It was more like a chant, but it shifted to a harmonious blending of voices that enveloped all my senses.

It was beautiful.

I blinked and found myself shielded by a curtain of many colors. The scent of patchouli and praline wafted through the breeze. Instinctively, I lifted my hand to brush aside the whisper-thin material, and the veil parted to reveal my parents.

The sound of my mother's voice and my father's laughter surrounded me like a warm embrace. The dam that held my tears at bay broke open at the sight of them. I must have sniffled because, within a fraction of a second, my parents were hugging me and telling me how much they loved and missed me. I could *feel* them!

"Mom! Dad! I can't believe you are here!"

"Oh, daughter, you are so lovely and strong. We are so proud of you, Vala!" my mother whispered.

"You are everything we ever hoped for and more. Your mother and I love you so much," my father added.

"We don't have long. We must tell you something before our time runs out." Mom brushed my cheek lightly, wiping away more tears. I didn't want to think about losing them again so soon. "I need you to listen, sweet girl."

My father gripped my upper arms. "You *did not* kill us. Do you hear me, young lady?" I nodded, and he dropped his forehead to mine. "Loki whittled away at those chains for years, so we knew the time would come when he would eventually escape. That is why we were trying to leave Bend before the fire. Before Loki escaped, he sent one of his lackeys to fix a problem. Us. And you. He didn't know that you existed already, though. You see, he was a bit late."

"Wait, you know about Loki? What else do—?"

"Shh, Vala. We are running out of time," Dad interrupted, rubbing my shoulder in a comforting way. "As I was saying, Loki's henchman wasn't very intelligent and, luckily for us, didn't realize you were already born. So, you see, your poem did not cause the fire. It contained foresight, but your Skaldic magic will require more training to alter the future. Frigg will take you to Hel tomorrow to train with the best: the original poet, Kvasir."

"We are so proud of the woman you are becoming." My mother squeezed my hand. "We are so sorry that we had to leave you alone. That was never our intention. Despite our choices, you are the only hope for the nine realms and the world as you know it."

"I... uh... I will try not to disappoint you."

I was shocked. They knew. They knew everything. Was that because they were dead or because they knew all along?

"Val-ball, you could never disappoint us." Hearing my mother say my old nickname was bittersweet.

"How can I find you again? Where are you guys?"

"Hel is our home now, but you only need to come to us like this. It may not seem enough, but at least we can be together for a few moments," my father said.

"Why can't I visit you in Hel?"

"Hel does not work like that. Souls dwell in their own spaces here, and Hel's blessing is required for the living to visit."

I could feel the magic dissipating, beginning to separate the realm of spirituality from reality. The façade faded behind me. Candlelight broke through the multicolored curtain, gradually erasing parts of the spirit plane. I squeezed their hands as my tears flowed freely and whispered, "I love you, Mom. I love you, Dad. I am so sorry that I thought I hated you the day of the fire. I didn't know."

"Honey, we knew you never hated us. You were too young to understand," my parents stated in unison. "We love you, too, Vala. We love you always, and we love you more."

Just as the last bit of the spirit realm was about to disappear, I yelled into the closing void, "I *will* save you! I don't know how yet, but I *will* fulfill my promise to Hel and come for you both!"

The training room returned, and Frigg stepped into the circle to help me off the stool. Her hand squeezed mine gently. "Vala," she said with an edge of concern in her voice, "what were you talking about when you said you would save your parents? They are dead."

"Thank you, Frigg, for all of this." I had too many thoughts in my head to articulate them, so after a polite goodbye, I fled. I planned on informing the goddess about my previous chats with Hel and my dream of Jorm, but at that moment, I needed to talk to my best friend about a boy to avoid the deep ache in my chest.

CHAPTER THIRTEEN

"Wait, you did *what* with Loki?" Helene squeaked, blushing.

"I did not do *anything* with Loki!" I squealed and rolled over. The motion produced the desired effect, sending a tiny wave to bounce Helene's small frame off the side of the waterbed. She landed on the floor, giggling. I had missed my friend and having her by my side was a balm to my soul. "Hey, can I ask you a question?"

"Of course."

"You said you were the goddess of compassion. How does that work?"

"I wondered when you were going to ask about that." She moved to my side of the bed and grabbed my hand. "It's the strangest thing, but my empathy has always drawn me to you. Do you remember the day we met? That creepy clown gave you a balloon at the school carnival, and then you tripped over your clodhoppers, and it flew off into the unknown. I remember hearing you crying, so I rushed to you even though you were a stranger to me."

"Helly, who calls shoes 'clodhoppers?'" We both chuckled before she continued.

"I always needed to see you happy. If you weren't, I needed to be there for you however I could. After your parents died, I wanted to take all your grief away, and sometimes, it even felt like I could. I didn't realize then I was using the magic I was born with. Looking back now, I was able to take possession of just enough of your sadness so you could get a little sleep or eat a decent meal. Tell me, how did you feel before coming to your room tonight?"

"I was heartbroken. I saw my parents tonight, and it hurt so deeply to have them ripped away again. I felt like my heart was being gouged out until I walked into this room. I thought it was because we were reunited, but now I realize it's more. What happens to *you* when my sadness is removed?"

"Don't worry about it, Vala."

"No, you don't get to do that," I said seriously. "I need to know, please."

"Okay, but please don't pity me. You know how much I hate that." She waited for me to nod before continuing, "I… I feel it all, and it feels like a crashing wave. Every emotion you experience echoes through me, sinking into every pore. My magic allows the feelings to settle within my soul until they recycle and restructure into compassion and love to pour back into you."

Tears streaked down my cheeks as the warmth of her love ran through the contact between our hands. "Helene, I love you."

"I know, cow. Now, stop crying and tell me all about your boy toy," she ordered, waggling her eyebrows. I pulled her in for a hug, and her words came out strained due to my tight grip. "Or, at least, your version of him."

"He *is* super cute, huh?" I giggled as I pulled away. Her nose scrunched as if I were talking about her brother, which sent us into a fit of girlish giggles. We sprawled out on the bed amongst the snacks we scrounged up from the kitchen and talked about Heim until we both fell asleep from laughing too much.

Morning came, and Helene and I joined Heim and Frigg in the dining hall for breakfast. I was saddened to see no ocean rolls today… or coffee. Helene must have brought those from home, and I couldn't get used to that being a morning ritual. We feasted on the most amazing crab benedict I ever tasted, though, and the kitchen concocted a fascinating green smoothie that tasted like matcha. I sipped happily as my raging caffeine headache subsided after a few swallows of the oddly delicious beverage.

"Do you like it, Vala?" Frigg inquired.

"I do! What is it?"

"It is a mixture of green tea leaves, seaweed, and some of the fruits that grow in the nearby orchard. There is quite a lot of natural caffeine in it, which I know has been a desire since you arrived in Asgard."

My cheeks grew warm. "Thank you." I hated feeling needy.

"No need to thank me, dear. I, too, require my daily allotment of caffeine to function properly," Frigg admitted with humor. "Drink up because today we are going to Hel."

I swiped up some yolk that slipped down my chin between bites. "How will we get there?"

Heim cleared his throat before speaking. "We will use the root system. The Bifröst connects Midgard to Asgard, but the rest of the realms are connected. We can get around by foot or through the root system."

Helene must have noticed the confusion on my face because she added, "Don't worry, Vala. It's easy. Remember when we went to Portland and rode the MAX to get around town? It's like that… without the train."

"I am not afraid, just annoyingly curious." I didn't particularly enjoy feeling needy, but feeling weak was way worse.

"We know," they all stated in unison. I glanced around the table at their smiling faces, and we all laughed.

The entrance to the closest root system was not where we originally entered Asgard. Apparently, there were many entrances. We left Fensalir, hopping across the step stones that rose from the lake until we reached a giant willow on the opposite shore. Frigg placed her palm on the rough bark, and the tree shook, creating a hollowed-out archway in the trunk.

"See you two there." Frigg reached for Helene's hand, and together, they entered the tree, which promptly swallowed them whole.

"That was… interesting. How long do we wait until we can go?"

Instead of answering, Heim touched the trunk, and the process repeated. He grabbed my hand and pulled me into the tube-like center. "Hold on, Vala. The root system can sometimes be a bumpy ride." As soon as the words were out of his mouth, I was knocked into him as the hole—and the sunlight—disappeared, leaving us in the dark. My protector's solid arms were planted firmly on my waist, holding me steady. His body against mine was an anchor in the overwhelming sea of my emotions.

My stomach flipped. It did not feel like we were going up or down, left or right. No, it was like we were traveling in every direction at once. Were we teleporting? I buried my head in Heim's chest to ground myself. The chill that suddenly licked the bare skin of my arms was a welcome sensation, but the laughter I heard next was not. My cheeks burned from annoyance at the intrusive sound as I pulled away from Heim's embrace and turned to see Hel.

"Hello, Vala," said Hel nonchalantly despite her eerie laughter. She was sitting on her throne of bones, stroking Garm, who slept soundly on the ground by her side. Each breath the sleeping wolf took created a rumbling, deep snore that lightly shook the ground beneath my feet.

"Hello, Hel," I replied, searching for acknowledgment or emotion in her face and finding none. It seemed she was acting like we never met, which was odd since Frigg already knew I had met her once.

"Hel, can you kindly take us to Kvasir? Vala has a lot to learn in a short amount of time," Frigg requested politely.

"Follow me." Hel rose from the throne, her exposed bones scraping at the joints, creating a chilling clang with each step. Her movements were zombie-like, and her long silver dress stretched across her slender and emaciated body in an unearthly fashion.

Her throne room was a vast, open space of lamp-lit darkness within a rotting maze of tunnels. Roots wound along the walls and through the ground as if the entire underworld was an overgrown, noxious weed. I noted that there were no souls in sight.

After a few twists and turns through the shadowy dungeon, I *saw* words and runes. They flitted and floated around me, as tangible as the skin on my body. I reached out to touch one and jumped back slightly at the sizzle when I made contact. The bracelet on my wrist lit with every color and became akin to a homing beacon, guiding me toward an open room.

I walked ahead of the others, allowing the bracelet to magically pull my body to whatever awaited me. I stopped just before the heavy iron door and inhaled deeply, allowing the breath to soothe and calm my rattled nerves. When I turned to look at Heim, he gave a subtle nod of his chin in approval.

In the middle of the room was a giant of a man clad in white robes with long, gray hair and braids like Heim's. He was the picture of normalcy, except for his open mouth, which released flowing, tangible words. Full poems left his lips and filled the room with their existence. Each emerged from his mouth, floated around for a minute or two, and then fizzled out like a soap bubble popping.

"Greetings, Vala." The words slipped from his lips, circled me in a caress, and—upon touching them—exploded into a thousand tiny pieces. An eruption of colors.

CHAPTER FOURTEEN

When the man stepped forward, I instinctively moved back. As if he hadn't noticed my retreat, he walked closer until he loomed over me, standing at least seven feet tall.

"I see you, Vala Boddason. I know you, child, like I know myself. My blood runs through your veins. My words inhabit your soul. I have heard of your purpose and would be honored to train you in the Skaldic ways. I am Kvasir, the original poet." Each word he spoke grazed my skin and sunk deep into my being.

"Hello, Kvasir. I'm ready to learn."

He guided me to a small wooden desk with faded parchment, a pristine, white-feathered writing quill, and a small jar of jet-black ink. All the pages were blank canvases waiting to be filled. I sat down, and we began our work.

The others watched on as Kvasir spent hours with me, honing my skills with spoken and written words. He showed me how to bend each to my will. With every new success, I felt a thrill.

I can do this!

The written word was unchallenging, as it was nothing more than willing my writing into existence. Kvasir instructed me to close my eyes, imagine what I wanted from the words I wrote, and allow those desires to move through my mind and push through to the paper. Once I caught on, I watched repeatedly as the ink from my feather quill sank into the parchment, shimmered on the page, and lifted in a lyrical dance.

I practiced changing small things in the room and then wrote a brief poem about Heim.

I watched as the words lifted from the page, a whirlwind of charcoal and smokey grey. The funnel enveloped my protector and morphed into the shape of a man that pushed down on his mighty shoulders. His resistance faltered, and his knees buckled beneath the weight of the being created from my words. Once Heim collapsed, the man turned into wind again and swirled around my protector, dissipating as quickly as it came. All that was left was Heim, who got to his feet with the biggest, shit-eating grin.

Everyone laughed, everyone except Heim, who glared at me before another big smile stretched across his face.

Working with Kvasir made me feel the most alive I had ever felt, which was puzzling since we were literally in Hel. I couldn't believe I spent so long hating poetry. If I had only known why it invigorated me when I was a kid and not stopped pouring my heart onto pages.

But then I might not be here.

It wasn't until we reached the end of our time together that I could produce my first palpable word using just my voice.

"Don't forget to enunciate, Vala. Let the word take form on your lips. Think of the word becoming what it is or what you want it to become as you speak it." Kvasir's arm rested on my shoulder encouragingly.

I focused my thoughts on what I wanted to say and what I wanted to see. "Remember." The exhalation of my breath formed fluffy, clouded letters as if I were speaking outside in the dead of winter. The nearly translucent word floated before me with an aura of shimmering gold. Kvasir's gaze shone with pride, and I did a little dance in celebration that Helene copied.

As joy enveloped my being, darkness crept in and ripped it away.

"Remember." Kvasir's duplicate word slammed into me. My body crumpled to the floor, and I was overcome with emotion. I couldn't control the assault on my senses, so I sobbed while laughing with my eyes wide open in fear.

Memory after memory crashed into me, and I attempted to right myself but could not handle the onslaught of feelings that his single word, combined with my own, brought. Experiencing everything was too much. I slipped away—the light fading around the edges of my vision in a vignette effect—until only darkness remained.

I awoke to a dull throbbing in my head. As my eyes opened slowly, I silently thanked whoever thought to close the curtains in my room. *Wait, my room?* How had I gotten back? I turned my body to the side, and the waterbed rippled beneath me. Heim sat in a chair beside the bed. His eyes were closed, arms crossed over his chest, and his breathing even. He was sleeping.

"He's been sitting there since he brought you back here." Helene placed a cold cloth on my forehead, and I experienced an immediate rush of relief.

"Thank you," I sighed, the words physically escaping from my lips and dancing around my friend. "How long was I out?"

She giggled as my words gently tickled her skin. "Two days."

"*Two days?!*" The words physically projected from my mouth in a ribbon of deep, seething red and rose to settle on the ceiling before popping and raining bits of fiery-colored confetti around us. The memories that had overwhelmed me before returned at a slower, steadier pace. The initial "download" was what knocked me out. After the first wave, the new emotions were still a lot but a tad less overwhelming.

I *remembered* everything.

I remembered weekends spent with Nana Frigg at our family home.

I remembered camping with Mom and Dad. He told stories about our bloodline while she started the campfire using only logs and magical flames that had sparked from her fingertips.

I remembered visiting Fensalir. My room was the same one I used as a small child.

I remembered the day the adults decided that I needed to forget. I attempted to rise from the bed, but Helene gently tugged at my arm.

"I'm fine," I whispered, tiptoeing to the window and pushing aside the curtain. There, on the top side of the windowsill, was an engraving in the wood: *Vala was here*. I laughed softly as a tear escaped and slipped down my cheek. Helene soundlessly came up next to me and held my hand. Without looking away from the windowsill, I traced the carving. "I was here."

"Yep, you sure were."

"Vala, you are awake," Heim said behind us. His voice was thick with sleep but filled with relief. I turned around and walked into his chest, allowing his arms to wrap around me gently. His large palms spread across my lower back, and I inhaled deeply, soaking in his natural scent of freshly cut juniper trees with hints of vanilla and leather. Immediately, I felt safe.

"Thank you, Heim." I rested my ear on his chest, listening to his beating heart. My thanks waved around us in hues of blue and magenta, pulling us closer together.

His chin rested on my head. "For?"

"Carrying me back from Hel and watching over me."

"How… do you know I carried you?" There was a twinge of bewilderment in his tone.

"Well, Helly told me, but also… really? Who else could have?" I poked at him and laughed. It was comforting to hear him chuckle, too. My magic had stayed inside of me that time, but it swirled in my chest.

We separated at the sound of a light rap on the door. "May I come in?" Frigg asked gently. She pushed the door open just far enough to poke her head in. Instead of answering, I walked to the door and opened it fully to wrap my arms around her. "I am glad to see you awake, my child. It pleases me to see a smile on your face once again. You had us worried there for a time."

"I am sorry if I scared everyone." I looked around the room at each of them. They had become beyond important to me so quickly. "I don't think anyone could have prepared me for how abundantly that would hurt. I think I experienced every emotion in such a short amount of time that my body short-circuited."

"That is precisely what happened, Vala. Kvasir warned me that it could happen, but I did not want to frighten you with that news beforehand."

"For once, I am thankful not to have a heads-up." My words escaped in the form of a colorful waterfall. It looked like literal word-vomit. "Frigg, I have been here before this visit. I remember everything, all the wonderful memories. I remember everything taken from me, too."

She stepped back from our embrace and asked earnestly, "Are you okay?"

"I didn't get it then, but I understand now why they had to do it." I winced as I recalled the stolen parts of my mind.

I visited Fensalir with my parents often; we came to stay at least one weekend a month. But that last time was different.

My parents left me alone in my room to play with my toys. Dad had been teaching me how to use my words to make my toy horses trot about unassisted, so I was mesmerized watching them mosey over the wood floor, their plastic feet clip-clopping like real horses walking along cobblestone streets. A loud shout resounded from the assembly room down the hall, and I let my toys fall, curious to see what the commotion was about.

I walked as quietly as I could down the hallway and spied through the crack in the door. The room was filled with many creatures. A member from each of the nine realms convened at the table, including the ethereal winged Valkyries of Valhalla. Dark and light elves sat across the table from one another—to keep the peace, I assumed—since they had a reputation for squabbling amongst each other.

All the gods I'd met, including Helene, sat by Völva. Even the giants were present, which I—even at my young age—knew was far from normal.

"The chains are weakening. He won't remain locked up forever. We all know what the prophecy says. Moa, Leif… your two magics joined will save us all," declared a loud, booming voice. Odin. "Living in Midgard will slow things down for your family because he won't know where to look, but he will continue his search relentlessly upon his release."

"She is too young right now," pleaded my mother. An older version of Helene placed a hand on her forearm in a show of compassion.

"You both know that our hands are tied. Vala's destiny, and your own, is inevitable, set in motion long ago. You both agreed to this path, remember?" Odin countered.

One of the dark elves, a being short in stature with skin the color of onyx, muttered, "Moa, we will never forget the sacrifices you have made."

"What he means to say is that we owe you both a debt of gratitude. If that means protecting the child, then that is the least we can do," a tall light elf declared. She was the exact opposite of the dark elf: her entire being was so fair that I had to shield my eyes from her brightness. "Leaving your home in Asgard all those years ago to protect Vala has proven your dedication to the cause."

"Thank you, all, for your continued cooperation and support. My wife and I knew that this would not be easy, but we also knew that we would be leaving our daughter in capable hands," my father stated with a hint of sorrow in his voice. "Moa and I have combined our magic, uniting each within our beloved daughter. Vala has begun her training so that we can gauge her abilities. Rest easy knowing that our intentions were a success. She does not yet realize the power that she will someday harness. It is tenfold what I could even dream of, far greater than any I've ever witnessed. Written are the prophecies of Ragnarök. Some say, 'So they must be.' With proper training, Vala will harness the power to author an alternative ending for the nine realms and our world."

"As we all know, the algiz will safeguard Vala. Her protector has already been made aware and will be a guide and guard after you are gone." Frigg rubbed my mom's back lightly, attempting to comfort her. She leaned in and whispered just loud enough that I could hear, "Heimdall will keep her safe."

I hadn't realized that I was leaning against the door, straining to hear every word, and the weight of my body finally pushed the door open. I fell with a thud, making all the eyes in the room rest on me. Fear latched onto every part of my being. I opened my mouth to speak, but nothing came out.

"Vala!" Mom rushed over with tears in her eyes, and sobs racked my tiny frame as understanding hit me.

"Where are you and Daddy going?"

"Vala, how much of that did you hear?" She rubbed her hand soothingly up and down my back, and the older version of Helene placed her hand gently on my shoulder.

"All of it!" I proclaimed. "What… does… Nana Frigg mean, Mommy?"

"Darling, I need you to calm down," my dad urged. He, too, had tears in his eyes, but he remained planted like a tree by the table.

"She has heard too much," said Odin to no one in particular. "Leif, you know what you must do."

My father nodded in agreement before he knelt beside me, silently crying. My parents wrapped me in a family hug. "Vala, we love you so much. Someday, you will remember everything. When you do, you will think of this exact moment. Mommy and Daddy probably won't be with you then, but we will always be in your heart." His words sounded like a goodbye.

"When you were in my belly, Vala, we talked to you. We instilled in you all our love because you will have to shoulder a heavy burden alone. When you were born, we spoke it into and over you with each new day. As you grew, you learned all that we could teach. The rest will be up to you." They were confusing my thoughts, talking to me in enigmas my young mind couldn't understand.

"Our daughter, the time has come." Dad pulled me up from the floor as he and my mother kneeled before me. They held hands as he traced a vertical line on my forehead with his index finger, kissed my cheek, and said, "Isa. Freeze."

The sound dripped from his lips in liquid form. It congealed and grew into a puddle of goo that floated above me. As my eyes rose to look at it, it fell and covered my entire body. It drowned me. I struggled against it, reaching for my parents. But they stepped back with muffled sobs.

Helene stepped into the goo beside me and scooped me up in her arms. She held me close, hugging my frantic body tight. Her voice calmed my mind as she chanted softly into my hair, "I've got you, Vala."

"Vala, don't fight it. It won't hurt you. Let it in," my father begged. "Forget." The word stung like the spreading venom of a bee, and the goo turned to ice. And then… the world went black.

I woke from that strange dream in my childhood bed in Oregon, my mind fuzzy from obliviousness. The part of my life that meant so much was a frozen relic. Stolen from my mind. Magic was something found only in books, and life was "normal."

My consciousness returned to the present. My magic had melted the ice block my father placed on my true memories; I could finally grasp my past.

My father was right; I did not understand then. The words spoken to me that day were not for the fearful child who stood before my parents. The things they told me were for who I was to become. With the memories came the teachings, and with the teachings came understanding. I knew who I was fully. My parents took me apart that day with a promise to put me back together. I was whole again and ready.

I looked around the room, holding eye contact with Heim for a beat, then Helene, and finally letting my gaze rest on Frigg. The warmth of regained magic ignited within me. A word burned through my memory, reminding me that I could resist the darkness by stepping into the light of hope. I felt an intrinsic need to access my purpose. When I spoke, the words erupted out of my mouth intentionally, bright red with orange flames. "Naudhiz. It is time to step into my destiny."

CHAPTER FIFTEEN

Everyone stared at my little fireworks show in awe but snapped out of it as soon as I spoke again, sans flames. "We need a plan, don't we?" I asked as we walked to the dining hall. My stomach grumbled at the thought of sustenance. I couldn't even remember the last time I ate.

"I agree with Vala. We do need some sort of plan," said Heim. He stared at me continuously, waiting to see what my words would do next.

But with the return of my memories, I was instantly skilled at turning off my Skaldic magic because of the restraints my father taught me so long ago. I could speak freely without words floating about and causing a distraction.

"The first thing on the list is dealing with Skoll and Hati," Helene interjected. "Those dumb wolves have got to be the easiest thing on that list, don't you think?"

Skoll and Hati chased the Sun and the Moon, keeping the orbs rising and setting each day. Their mission was to catch their prey and devour the light, thus leading to the mighty winter—also known as Fimbulwinter. If we managed to stop them, we would prevent the first two prophecies from coming to fruition. But what could I say to rewrite the purpose of creatures that had circled the globe for generations already?

"I suppose. But how?"

"Perhaps that is a question for Mimir," Heim mused thoughtfully.

Mimir, the ancient discorporate giant. Long ago, there was a war between gods, the Aesir and the Vanir. A power struggle between the two led to excessive bloodshed. To end the war, the gods exchanged hostages as peace offerings. The Vanir received Hoenir, the god of silence, and Mimir, the god of wisdom. The Aesir received Njord, the god of the sea, and Freyr, the god of war and peace.

The Vanir, fearing deception at the hands of the Aesir, decapitated Mimir and sent his head to Odin's palace, and the Allfather instantly sought a way to save the god of knowledge and wisdom. He used herbs and primordial magic to reanimate and immortalize Mimir's head as an eternal source of wisdom. The thought of such an existence made my stomach roil.

"Do you mean the talking head?" My nose wrinkled in disgust. Helene started giggling, and Frigg smiled indulgently at me.

"I do, yes," Heim confirmed, staring me directly in the eye. "He is the wisest in all the land, despite his lack of a body." I had difficulties hiding my discomfort, but if Heim recommended him, Mimir would be a valuable option.

"Okay. Where is he?"

"For a long time, he was with Odin, but he longed to be amongst his people again," Frigg answered.

"Odin allowed him to return to Jotunheim," Heim added.

"Now, he spends his time watching over his well and searching the deep waters for Odin's eye," Helene supplied.

Newfound courage and purpose coursed through me like the blood in my veins. "Well, I guess we are going to the land of the giants."

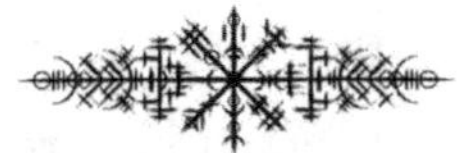

Heim loaded items into his leather bag as I said goodbye to Frigg and Helene. We all collectively decided that the trip should be only my protector and me to avoid confrontation with the giants. They were peaceful creatures if they did not feel threatened. The plan was simple enough: travel to Jotunheim—which would take about two days, attain information from Mimir, and return to meet Helene and Frigg at Valaskjalf to discuss our findings with Odin.

As we traversed the marshy canal, I asked Heim why we could not use the root system as the sole means of travel.

"The Yggdrasil is a strange being. Although everything is interconnected, the root system is unevenly dispersed. Think of tree branches: uneven and inconsistent. To travel the entirety of the tree and its subsequent realms, some foot travel is necessary."

I nodded in understanding as my mind drifted back to my high school anatomy class, where we learned that the circulatory system of the lower body resembles an upside-down tree. The human legs were like two large branches with small offshoots of blood vessels.

"Heim, can I ask you a question?" My gaze remained locked on my hand as it lazily dragged through the water, creating a trail of ripples.

"Anything."

"Why do I not remember you from when I was younger? When my memories came back, I remembered everyone except you."

"I have known I would be your protector for a long time, Vala. You have been my fate for many years. I was under strict instruction not to see you before the day we first met." He seemed uneasy as if the topic was making him uncomfortable.

"So, you had never seen me before?"

"Well, I wouldn't say *that*." His cheeks reddened beneath his beard. Was he blushing?

"What *would* you say, then?"

"Can we not, Vala?" His tone was almost pleading.

"That is not fair, Heim. You have known about me for… I don't even know how long, yet I am still getting to know you." His big arms slowly pushed and pulled the oars again and again. With rapt attention, I watched his muscles swell and move beneath his taut skin with each pass through the water. The motion was mesmerizing. *He* was mesmerizing.

His emerald eyes remained focused on the floor of the canoe as he murmured, "I can no longer count the times I watched you skipping rocks and dipping your toes into the icy river. Those were the nights you stared at the stars, talking about boys from your school with Helene. I needed to see you, to know who I was protecting, so I did." His head remained bowed. "But I knew I was breaking Odin's rule, so I always returned to my tower near the Bifröst to wait. Waiting was physically painful for me. I was flayed open. My nerve endings were sliced and torn each time I was pulled back to my dwelling. This tattoo isn't new, Vala. I've had it for many years, and with it came a certain longing. As your sworn protector, my soul demands to be near yours. I may live in Himinbjörg, but your soul is my home."

I stopped breathing altogether for several seconds. The honesty was brutal, and I knew that was not simple for Heim to admit. Anxiety set my skin on fire, layering me in my typical cloak of quiet awkwardness. My mind argued with my heart about what words—if any—I could allow myself to speak.

Why did Heim's confession affect me so? Why did his kindness and honesty feel like a thousand knives to my gut, stirring up my insides? My mind rattled with uncertain bewilderment. I was frustratingly mute while my thoughts were annoyingly loud.

You know why. It's because no one has made you feel wanted or worthy in years. This man just healed nearly eight years of loneliness with two sentences. You need him, and that's scary.

His eyes were on me, searching for something, anything. So, I decided to bring my thoughts to life. The rune that was our original connecting point slipped from my lips. As it formed, water from the canal combined with the shape, and the algiz rune soon floated between us.

"What are you doing?"

The rune grew until it filled the space between us—connecting us again. I reached through the middle of the disjointed orb of water, and Heim did the same, laying his palm flat against mine.

"Hold your breath." I inhaled a deep gulp of sweet, marshy air, interlacing our fingers. The rune orb enveloped us completely, surrounding us in its protective power as the enchanted water deepened our connection. My eyes met Heim's, and I could see in his gaze that he could feel it, too.

I moved closer, and our hair floated around us, creating a fusion of chestnut and blonde as our foreheads touched. The emerald of his eyes was intoxicating, and the thought of closing the distance between our lips flitted through my mind. But before I could act on it, the bubble burst, leaving the two of us soaking wet and laughing.

"Vala, you are extraordinary!" Heim exclaimed. There was more behind his words than what he was saying, but we needed to focus on rewriting the prophecies to stop Ragnarök. The feelings I felt for Heim were growing and becoming deeper. Were we friends? Did I want him to be more? I could not think of that without feeling selfish. I had the entire world to prioritize.

CHAPTER SIXTEEN

When we passed below the drooping willow tree and exited into the unveiled Asgard, Huginn and Muninn cawed above us in greeting.

"Vala," they said in unison. "Where have you been? Odin has been ill with unease."

"Please send word to him that all is well and that I will visit him soon with information."

"Yes, child." Together, they flew away toward Valaskjalf as Heim and I continued on foot toward a line of bushy trees dotting the horizon.

The bright blue of the sky waned, bleeding into hues of peach with variegated shades of orange. Night was falling quickly.

"It is going to get dark soon. We should make up camp and get some rest," Heim suggested as soon as we reached the forest.

He slung his leather bag onto the ground, unfastened the laces, and removed several items. A thick sheet of canvas, braided rope, and two neatly coiled bedrolls. I watched on as he wandered through the dense underbrush, collecting branches and large logs. He dropped the pile and pulled a thick iron blade from his boot to whittle and smooth the thinner branches into rods. The skill was as natural to him as breathing.

Once that task was complete, he created a shelter, using the sturdy rope to tie the connecting points of the canvas to the chiseled boughs. In record time, he was laying out our bedrolls as if it were nothing.

"I brought a few provisions, but I will have to hunt for our meal."

"Hunt… as in hunt an animal?" Wow, that was a stupid question.

"Yes, Vala. Unless you want to gnaw on some bark," Heim deadpanned. "I won't go far. Will you be okay on your own for a bit?"

I shot him a glare, and he wandered off, knife in hand. Determined to make myself useful while he pursued our meal, I piled the wood into a cone shape and stuffed smaller pieces of kindling in the holes. My lips parted, and I mouthed the word "*Fire.*" The flames harmlessly licked my lips before billowing into a pyre.

When Heim returned, the chill of the blackened sky nipped at my skin, but the blazing bonfire was a warm balm. My protector carried the lifeless body of a bristly, brown hog over his shoulder; dripping blood bloomed on his shirt in patches of deep crimson.

"Nice fire," he praised with a hint of pride.

"Nice pig," I countered, equally impressed.

Heim chuckled, "Wild boar."

We set about making dinner together but separately. Heim had offered to teach me how to scald and skin his catch, but I politely declined. *Gross*. Instead, I opted to peel, cut, and roast the carrots and potatoes in pads of butter, all sourced from our provisions. Heim's bag must've been enchanted because I found a large pot amongst the vegetables and spuds.

The finely chopped strips of boar meat were added to the pot, and the meat sizzled in buttery oils. The inescapable scent of roasting pork invaded my senses, making my stomach audibly growl with hunger. Heim chuckled as he retrieved plates and cutlery from his Mary Poppins bag. I grumbled at him for laughing at me but enjoyed the ease of being in his presence, nonetheless.

"Thank you for dinner," I murmured between chewing strips of juicy meat. Heim's gaze dropped to my lips, and his eyes lit with amusement and… an almost feral darkness. I could feel the droplets of jus dripping down my chin when his hand lifted to gently swipe the glistening liquid from my face. Keeping his eyes on mine, he languidly licked the juices off his palm.

"I… uh…"

"Delicious."

My cheeks blazed, but my gaze never wavered. "You make me nervous…" The admission was soft, barely a whisper.

"I'm… oh, Vala… I'm sorry."

"Why are you apologizing?" I asked, clearly bewildered.

"I don't want to make you uncomfortable. That was never my intention." His expression turned sullen, almost boyish.

"Heimdall, why do you do that?"

"Do… what?"

"Why do you become apprehensive when talking to me? You get all awkward and quiet."

"Isn't that the pot calling the kettle black?" he teased. Before I could retort, I noticed a change in his demeanor and let him gather his thoughts. He dropped his eyes to the fire, the flames dancing in his gaze, and released a heavy sigh. After several moments, he broke the silence. "I suppose it is because having you here still feels like a dream. I've held you on a pedestal for so long that I can't bear the idea of hurting you or scaring you away. I've been alone so long that I worry my abrasiveness isn't always kept in check. You are soft, fluid lines, while I am hard, cracked edges. I do not want to hurt you."

"Oh, please," I chided. "You have to give me more credit than that, sir."

"Why do you always call me 'Sir?'"

"Because you are *old*," I teased. "I mean, truly, how old are you?"

"I have been living for many generations. I have witnessed many eras." His voice oozed maturity. "But, when it comes to physical age, Vala, I stopped aging when I was nineteen."

I raked my gaze from his beautiful face down to his barrel chest and strong back, thick with muscles under his still-bloody shirt. I paused in my perusal, taking in the enormity of his arms and the thick biceps that lifted an entire boar as if it were a feather. My eyes dipped to his toned legs, and air escaped between my suddenly parched lips.

"So, you did," I muttered. He glanced at me with a small smile. The shadows from the blaze flickered against his skin. The sight made my blood run hot, and I hoped like Hel that Heim could not tell how much he affected me.

"Did you know that I have nine mothers?"

"What did you just say?"

"It is true. I have nine mothers," he repeated a little louder. "I have not seen them since I was very young. So many stories have existed, now lost throughout the years, buried with the bones of Skalds of old. I'm not even sure I understand how it is possible, but I do understand the inescapable doubt and insecurities they left in their wake."

"Tell me."

"Long ago, the nine mothers who birthed me also abandoned me," he said, his voice rough and thick from the pain of remembering. "I was only five years old when they left without a word."

"Do you know where they went?"

"No one does. They were there, and then… they were just… gone." His words were thick as he held back tears. "I think that is part of my callousness and… fear. I am afraid of being vulnerable because I can't stand the thought of what I care for being taken from me, or worse… leaving."

"I am so sorry, Heim. No child deserves to feel left behind."

"Do you feel left behind?"

I stilled, allowing the question to sink in, to feel every emotion it brought forth. Did I? I breathed in the smoky campfire air and relished the memory of my father telling stories of our ancestors. I watched the blaze rise higher and remembered my mom gently waving her fingers, teaching me how to play with the inferno. Then I thought of all the foster homes I'd lived in, the abuses I'd witnessed, and the cruelty I'd endured. I had known little to no love during the past several years. Well, besides Helene. For a long time I had been angry at *them* for dying and *myself* for surviving.

"No. I did for a little while. But now, I know they are still here with me. They did what they needed to do for me… for all of us."

Heim's eyes lifted to mine again, and I leaned my head against his giant shoulder. "You are quickly becoming one of my dearest friends. You are strong, brave, and softer than you know. Vulnerability is not a weakness. It is a strength that not many know how to command. What you did tonight… opening up to me… shows courage."

"Well, I don't know about all that, but—"

"Heim, I *do* know, and I am grateful you trusted me enough with your emotions." I placed my hand on his thigh. "I am not going anywhere, okay? You, *sir*, are stuck with me."

He finally allowed a smile to lift his lips, and the sight was incredible, leaving me in a daze.

This beautiful man is letting you in, allowing you to see his broken parts. Don't you dare mess this up.

An invisible wall had grown around him, built to protect his heart, yet slowly, he was allowing me access. "We should head to bed. It's getting late, and we have an early start in the morning."

I followed my protector to the tent and crawled onto the thick wool blankets spread across the bedrolls. Heim remained by the entrance with his back to me and started to remove his stained shirt. His back muscles rippled beneath his tanned flesh with every move, and I caught myself staring at the lines etched into the taut skin.

Deep black runes covered every inch I could see, some even sinking beneath the waistline of his pants. Unlike the first time I'd seen the tattoos beneath his shirt in Rowan Grove Park, I could understand what they meant. *If only I could read them all...*

I looked away quickly as he turned around and sank to his knees. He crawled into the bedroll beside mine and adjusted until he was comfortable. Heim was so close that I could almost feel his body heat.

The night air drifted into the tent from every small open crevice; it had gotten colder since dinner, making it difficult to get comfortable. I shuffled deeper into the blankets, a heat-seeking missile trying to find an ounce of warmth.

"Are you okay?"

"I am c-c... cold," I stuttered between full-body shivers.

Heim propped himself onto his elbow to look down at me. "I have a solution, but I do not want to make you uncomfortable."

"…What is your solution?"

He scooted closer, wrapping one enormous arm around my waist. Without overthinking it, I rolled to my side and cuddled in close to his chest. He gently pushed his other arm beneath my pillow, and I tucked my head in the crook of his elbow. Heim radiated warmth, and I breathed him in, allowing his aura to thaw me from the inside out. It was like having my own personal heated blanket.

"Is this okay?"

"Yes, Heim. Thank you." The words came out steady because, in seconds, my body was no longer shuddering from the cold. "How are you so warm right now?"

"I think it may have something to do with algiz." He raised his inked arm to show me the rune glowing dimly in the dark. I lifted my hand to his and gently intertwined our fingers. It was easier to be brazen when I could not see his face.

The warmth of his breath tickled my ear as he gently whispered, "Goodnight, Vala."

"Don't forget, Heim. I'm not going anywhere."

My thoughts swirled while he held me in his arms. Did he feel the same electricity that I did? Was this as intimate for him as it was for me?

I will let you in, too. But please be careful with my heart. My silly antics rattled my brain, but I allowed his rhythmic breathing to lull me to sleep. That night, I dreamt only of Heimdall.

CHAPTER SEVENTEEN

The next morning, the bedroll beside me was empty. Heim had left. With a rising sense of panic, I rose quickly, threw on a cloak, and exited the tent. Instantly, I calmed when I saw him standing by the fire, preparing something that resembled a sticky cream soup.

"Good morning, Vala. I hope you like porridge," he greeted, entirely too cheerful for the morning.

"Like Goldilocks?"

He stared at me for a moment, clearly missing the reference. "It is similar to oatmeal."

"Or mush," I muttered under my breath.

He handed me a wooden bowl full of the revolting sludge, and I begrudgingly took a small bite. *Interesting*. It wasn't that bad. It reminded me of the Cream of Wheat my mom made me when I was little. She always added a small amount of vanilla creamer for a special surprise. I tasted hints of the sweet extract and made quick work of eating the rest. "Thank you."

"You will need your strength for today." Heim let out a long, low whistle and turned to start cleaning up our campsite.

"Why did you whist—?"

Gulltoppr cantered toward us, his champagne mane billowing in the wind as his thunderous hooves rumbled the ground beneath my feet.

"We will ride for part of our trek today."

I got to work helping him pack our camp into his Mary Poppins bag. When I made the joke out loud, it went right over his head. "Tough crowd," I muttered to myself.

Heim tamped out the fire with water from his ancient bottle, and we attempted to return the land to how we found it. Gulltoppr patiently waited for us, his tail swishing and swatting at flies as he stood tall in the brightening sunlight.

After the camp was clear, Heim kneeled on one knee and hoisted me onto the horse's back like a gentleman. Of course, his mounting was a lot smoother, even without assistance, and he slid in behind me without a hitch. Wrapping an arm around my waist to keep me steady, he grasped the reins, gave a light click of his tongue, and the three of us were off.

We rode for hours through the forest and then a desert terrain similar to what I grew up with. The dry dirt kicked up beneath Gulltoppr's hooves, leaving a literal trail of dust. In the distance, we could see another horizon of trees. From what I gathered, forests bordered every part of Asgard. We dismounted when we reached the tree line, and Heim whispered something to Gulltoppr. The horse turned around and ran back in the direction we came from, dust pluming in his wake.

"Where is he going?"

"I sent him home. We will continue on foot."

Heim chose a tree near the middle of the grove, laid his palm flat on the bark, and opened the root system passage. I didn't think I would ever get used to that form of travel—not knowing which way was up or down, left or right, was too out of my control.

After a seemingly endless amount of time where my stomach, heart, and lungs seemed to rearrange themselves, an opening formed, spilling sunlight over our awkwardly entwined bodies.

I poked my head out to get a peek at Jotunheim for the first time—a flourishing countryside with rolling hills, lush green pastures lined with rustic wooden fencing, and flocks of overgrown sheep lazily munching the too-green grass. A wide cobblestone trail snaked from our tree up a nearby hill to a village of oversized huts.

Then, I saw a few giants. Heim nodded politely to them, but they completely ignored us and kept walking. They were not multiple sizes larger than me, as I foolishly anticipated. The stories I grew up with in the human world were incorrect. Kvasir was a giant, so I didn't know why I still thought they would be much bigger. I distantly wondered why everything was so immense if the giants weren't that much taller than most humans.

High above our heads was a rickety wayfinding sign with poorly written names. The plank pointing to the left read

Jotunheim, and the bottom one pointing to the right read *Mimir's Well.* It was all rather straightforward. As Heim and I followed the path to the right, we walked deeper into the dense forest, and barely any light slipped through the heavy canopy. The forest muffled all sound, leaving only silence under its leafy weight. Each step we took made a soft crunch, temporarily breaking the oppressive quiet. After several hours, we eventually came upon a sunny clearing broken only by the giant trunk of the Yggdrasil. And tucked right next to it was Mimir's well.

Giant mossy boulders piled high in neat stacks surrounded the well, and atop the largest one sat the disembodied Mimir. His piercing gray eyes unnervingly followed us as we stepped closer to him.

"Hello, Heimdall." The god's voice was hoarse and deep.

"Hello, Mimir. How are you enjoying being back home?"

"I am very much at ease now. I missed the waters of my well and the chatter of my people. But to ask such simplicities is not why you have come, is it?"

"Ah, Mimir, as usual, you are omniscient," Heim acquiesced respectfully. "We are here to ask a question that only you would know the answer to."

"Go ahead then, boy. Ask."

"Skoll and Hati are destined to catch their prey, sir," I jumped in, growing impatient with all the niceties. "Do you have any ideas on how we can change that?"

Mimir turned his eyes to me, and a half smile appeared on his lips. "Ah, Vala Boddason. Let me see you." I moved so I was in his direct line of sight, and he nodded in approval. "I will help you on one condition."

"What's that?"

"I would like you to find something for me in my well. It has been lost for some time." He peered into my soul with his steadfast, steely eyes.

I shifted under his glare. "Okay, what am I looking for?"

"Odin's eye."

My head bobbed in agreement before what he was requesting fully sank in. Finding Odin's eye couldn't be that difficult of a task, could it? Gross but doable. I climbed up on one of the sturdy rock piles, peering down into the glittering water to see if I could view the bottom. The well was deceptively deep.

"Will the water hurt me in any way?" I asked Mimir cautiously.

"It will not."

I started to undress, but Heim laid a hand on my arm. "Let me," he insisted.

"No," the god interrupted. "It must be her."

"Heim, I am fine. I am a phenomenal swimmer." I winked at him while removing my clothes, leaving only undergarments. He turned away quickly—I assumed out of respect. But Mimir kept his eyes on me the entire time.

I dipped my toe in the water and was pleasantly surprised to find it was tepid. It was an exquisite relief after all the traveling. After inhaling a deep breath, I dove down. My eyes opened underwater and saw no end in sight. Just like that, the quest quickly changed from simple to impossible as I swam around, disoriented in the liquid darkness.

I felt anger rising within, and my magic stirred. When I surfaced, the word "*Breathe*" formed on my lips, and a pocket of oxygen surrounded my head like a diver's helmet.

I dove back down, encompassed by the magical air bubble, and trustingly inhaled a deep breath. It worked! I hastily began my search because I was unsure how long the magic would last. The deeper I swam, the more my air bubble dwindled, becoming smaller around my head. I rose to the surface to refill my air supply but stayed under as long as possible. *Odin's eye must be down here somewhere.*

As I swam around fruitlessly in the inky blackness, I realized I could use my power in more ways than one. I thought of Odin's eye, reflecting on the Allfather himself, and mouthed, "*Find.*" The word itself was soundless, but I instantly felt the magnetic-like pull of something magical anyway.

Warmth surrounded my wrist, and my bracelet radiated a thread of golden light that spiraled into the abyss. I rose for a final deep gulp of air and dove back down.

The end of the thread drifted into an alcove I hadn't seen before. I reached into the hole, feeling something slippery and round.

As I held it, the eyeball turned on its own and looked directly at me. Honestly, I released an involuntary scream and almost dropped it. Swallowing down my disgust, I securely gripped the all-seeing eye and swam back toward the surface just a little too late—my air bubble diminished completely.

Being deprived of oxygen under the crushing water pressure made my head swim with dizziness, and a black border formed around the periphery of my vision, slowly blocking out my eyesight. Right before the darkness overtook me completely, I felt a tug on the golden thread that floated upward. I yanked back as hard as possible, knotting my hand around the tangible magic that had become a lifeline.

As I broke through the surface, I choked and coughed up water before sucking in deep gulps of fresh air. Heim still grasped the golden thread, even as he pulled my waterlogged body out of the well and onto the solid earth. He stroked the wet locks out of my face and held me in his arms until my breathing evened.

"You saved me."

"I will always save you, Vala." My cheeks burned beneath his intense gaze, and I became acutely aware of my lack of clothing, relishing the heat of his wandering hands as he unconsciously checked that every part of me was intact. "Always."

CHAPTER EIGHTEEN

Once I was okay, I tried to stand, and Heim helped me to my feet. I placed Odin's eye next to Mimir on the ledge where his head sat. "Here," I said gravelly, my throat sore from lack of air and choking on water.

"Good girl, I knew you could do it," he praised.

"Now, will you help me with Skoll and Hati?"

"Yes, I will. Please take Odin's eye and hold it in your hand."

"But I thought you wanted it for yourself?"

"Ah, yes. For this. This will make it easier for you to understand." I grimaced in disgust but followed Mimir's instruction and held up the slimy eyeball. "Skoll and Hati are in an inescapable loop, chasing the Sun and Moon. Their pursuit will continue until Ragnarök. As you already know, the prophecy claims their success, thus leading to the darkness covering all nine realms. How can you change their destiny?"

Annoyed at yet another riddle, I grumbled, "That is what I came to ask you."

"True. But if I tell you, you will have learned nothing."

"Wha—" I stopped mid-sentence and thought for a moment. "Fine then, let me think about it." After several moments, my deep contemplation was beginning to hurt my already rattled mind when I turned to my protector. "Heim, any bright ideas?"

"To change their destiny, we need to change something…"

"Thank you, Captain Obvious," I griped sarcastically and instantly regretted it when I saw Heim's frown. "I'm sorry. This is stressful, and I don't do so great under pressure. I need some Zen or something." I stretched my arms above my head and inhaled a deep, centering breath. Yoga always helped me think.

Mimir started to hum a low, haunting tune. The sound was nearly trancelike, and I instantly relaxed. My thoughts toiled and swirled, trying to connect the discombobulation that circulated through my mind. I looked down at Odin's eye and watched as the pupil dilated. The augmentation erased all color from the iris, leaving only the white of the eye and the blown-out center. It shrank to a tiny dot and then returned to normal size. Watching it reminded me of the balance of light and dark when it hit me.

"Oh, my gods! They are like a yin and yang, a balance of contrary forces. One is black and chases the white light of the sun. The other is white and chases the gray Moon. We need to flip them!" I blurted.

"That could work," Heim proclaimed. I looked at Mimir.

His expression was pure satisfaction, and he smiled proudly at me. "Well done, Vala."

With that solved, I needed to figure out how to switch Skoll and Hati's roles. I needed to find the perfect words to write—a reformed prophecy. The two men chatted about Jotunheim and its inhabitants as I stepped away to clear my mind.

The tall trees of Jotunheim towered above as afternoon sunlight trickled through the lush canopy surrounding the well. A dozen shades of green covered me like an awning of leaves, rich emerald, bright chartreuse, juicy honeydew. I reveled in the beauty, allowing the calm of nature to soak into me.

A breeze licked my skin. It was not cold, but it sent shivers down my spine. On the wind, I swore I heard, "*Hello.*"

A crimson leaf floated down from a branch, and I held out my hand flat to catch it. The wind caught it again, and it danced around me.

Just as simple joy filled my soul, dread quickly followed. Warm breath tickled the back of my neck before a malicious voice broke the peaceful silence.

"What do you think you are doing here, Vala?" Loki. His tone was icy and taunting. I whirled around quickly and saw nothing but a burst of dissipating red smoke. *What the Hel!*

"Show yourself, you coward!"

Again, his voice was in my ear as if he were standing right next to me. "Do you *actually* think you can change things? Don't be a fool, Lítilvölva."

"Don't underestimate me, Loki," I seethed.

He switched to my other ear. "Don't worry, *little girl*, I don't plan to." Tendrils of red smoke slithered down my arm like slow-burning incense. My body trembled in fear, but I kept it in check. I didn't want him to see me scared.

"Vala, where are you? Is everything okay?" Heim's footsteps crunched through the dirt with relentless speed.

"Ta-ta for now, Lítilvölva," whispered Loki.

"How do you keep finding me? Tell me, you monster!" I screamed at the forest.

As Heim reached me, the cloud of red smoke burst between us. I was rooted in place as the mist lingered around my body. Heim picked me up in his sturdy arms, anger and protectiveness written on his face, and carried me to the root system. We didn't even say goodbye to Mimir, but as we moved, I could have sworn I heard a small splash as if something eyeball-sized was tossed back into the water.

"I will kill him when I find him," Heim murmured into my hair as he held me tight within the trunk of the traveling tree. My body was still shaking. I hated that I couldn't control my natural response to fear. I felt like the little girl Loki called me. Within my protector's embrace, I allowed myself to fall apart with sobs of rage and terror. Heim repeated three words I allowed to be my strength: "I've got you."

Our journey back to Asgard was uneventful. I spent much of the time deep in thought, trying to figure out how to resolve the Skoll and Hati issue. It was proving to be no simple feat, and my head began to throb.

The engulfing headache that invaded my skull constricted all my attempts at concentration. A serious lack of caffeine and almost drowning were most definitely the culprits of the building pain. Being sidelined by Loki without even seeing him in person didn't help. Heim continued carrying me, even after we left the root system, and I nuzzled in the warm crook of his neck and closed my eyes.

"Vala," a woman's voice murmured.

My eyes were heavy with sleep, but the scent of patchouli and praline invaded my senses, and I sat up quickly in bed. "Mom!" I looked around, surprised. "How…? Where…? Oh gosh, never mind."

My mother's gentle laughter filled the small room. She sat beside me on the bed and stroked my hair. "My sweet girl, how I've missed you."

"I miss you so much." I wrapped my arms around her waist in a hug. "Where is Dad?"

"It is not as manageable for him to visit the dream world. This is a gift of the Völva magic, which is not as strong in him. He did, however, send a message for you." She pulled out a piece of paper from a pocket in her modest, long-sleeved slate gray gown.

I took it and read:

I read and re-read the poem. Confused, I looked at my mother for answers. "What does it mean?"

"This is the original poem about Skoll and Hati. This is what you must change, Vala." Her matter-of-fact tone was soothing to my addled mind.

"Mom, how does Loki keep finding me?"

"We are trying to figure that out, darling. I wish we had answers, but your father and I honestly do not know. Rest easy knowing that many are seeking an explanation." She kissed my forehead and disappeared as sleep quickly reclaimed me.

I awoke to a different scent, a manly scent—vanilla and leather mixed with fresh-cut juniper. It lit a fire within me instantly. When I opened my eyes, I was looking directly at Heim's ass. It was a beautiful, sculpted masterpiece of an ass, but I wouldn't dare tell him that. Had he *seriously* thrown me over his shoulder? *What a Neanderthal!*

"Put. Me. Down!" I swatted uselessly at his backside.

He laughed, the deep roughness of it enveloping me in warmth and irritation all at once. My body bounced like a ragdoll with each of his pounding steps. I bellowed several incredibly unladylike profanities, which, unfortunately, only made him howl harder.

Heim wrapped his arms around my waist and lifted me with ease, dangling my body in front of him so that we were face-to-face. "You were starting to get heavy," he explained with a devious gleam in his eye.

I glared at him as he finally set me down gently on my feet. "Well then, why didn't you just wake me?"

"You were so peaceful in my arms. And, back there at the well was... a lot. I wanted you to get your rest."

"I mean, that's sweet and all. But really? Just throw me over your shoulder like a sack of potatoes?"

"You're much lovelier than a vegetable, my little potato." I heard a flirtatious tone and blushed. Damn him, always so good at making me nervous!

"So says the eggplant." The words rushed out without thought, and I slapped my hand over my mouth, eyes wide.

"Don't mind Vala, Heimdall. She is just being a pervert. Par for the course." I hadn't realized Helene had joined us. She poked me, understanding my mortification. Perversion was not, in fact, par for the course. I had no idea where that came from.

"Hey now, Helly! Not fair. He slung me over his back like Jock McGlock used to do to the cheerleaders." I elbowed her gently, eyes wide in mock-horror. She picked up on my queue.

"Oh… Ohhhhh. Heimdall, what in the ever-loving Hel is wrong with you?" She winked at me, obviously understanding the assignment.

"She was getting heavy," my protector countered defensively, seemingly missing our teasing. I mildly pitied the poor guy as we continued to goad him.

It took a moment to gain my bearings and realize we were back in Asgard near Odin's home. Heim had carried me all that way, and there I was, being a jerk to him. When Helene started walking toward Valaskjalf, I held back and slid my hand into Heim's larger one. I interlaced our fingers and leaned on my tiptoes to whisper, "I'm sorry," in his ear. His body trembled when my breath touched his skin, and he wrapped his free arm around my waist.

The spark our bodies created kindled electricity. It was painfully obvious that our chemistry was tangible. Being close to him sent tremors down my spine, short-circuiting my nerve endings.

He had to feel this attraction… right?

A wave of satisfaction crashed over me when his breath stuttered. Knowing that he was just as affected by our connection as I was made me feel vulnerable… and powerful. I lifted my head and caught his wanton, fiery gaze. Was it from the situation we found ourselves in or his prior annoyance at my relentless teasing?

Heim bent his head and murmured, "Don't apologize for flirting with me…"

Before I even registered what he said, he placed his hands on my waist and tilted his head close to mine. Our eyes were level, lips nearly touching. I stood frozen, heart beating out of my chest, while lust built as thick as fog in the air between us. His mouth remained next to mine, and my body craved more as his breath teased my skin.

"Don't underestimate my understanding of banter. Sure, you called me a dick—because yes, I know what an eggplant stands for—but I also called you something. What did I call you, Vala?"

"You… you called me a potato. Which is actually quite rude."

"Wrong. Did you know that a single potato can generate electricity? They grow even when they are shut away in dark or tumultuous places, are one of the most widely consumed crops, and are the base of many types of alcohol. You are powerful and incredibly resilient. You survived without your parents, yet still feed hope to those you love. And you are akin to a stiff drink for me, making me vulnerable and reckless." His head twisted and before I knew it, he had gently bitten down on my earlobe before releasing and taking a step back. "Plus, you taste delicious, my little potato."

At that, he let go of me completely and walked away toward Helene, Odin, and Frigg, who were too deep in conversation to witness that little... whatever that was. The only coherent thought I could hold onto as I watched him strut away was that I liked confident Heim. I really, *really* liked him.

CHAPTER NINETEEN

"**I** saw my mother," I stated, trying my best at nonchalance after I calmed down and joined the others. I could feel more than see Heim's questioning eyes on me, but my gaze landed firmly on Odin. "Hello again, Odin."

"Hello, Vala. I trust you learned all you needed from Mimir?"

I stepped close to Heim's side despite my frazzled nerves. "*We* learned a lot."

I told the others what we gleaned from Mimir, prodding Heim to interject now and again so that it was *our* narrative instead of just mine. We were a team, and I needed his father to know that. I intended to keep the promise I made to my protector in the canoe.

We are in this together.

When I recited the poem from my father, Frigg inhaled deeply, and a look of understanding dawned on her face. "It has been so long since I have heard the lore, the prophecies of old." There was a strange longing in her voice. "Your father used to recount them each night we were together. His voice was always so melodic when he slipped into the Skaldic ways. It was truly a sound and sight to behold."

"I wish he were here now. I could use his help."

"He is here, Vala. His words are in you, and his blood runs through your veins," Heim said softly. He placed his hand gently on the small of my back and guided me inside, following Odin as he led the way into Valaskjalf.

We walked silently to the assembly hall, which was already occupied by members from each realm, along with Thor, Sif, Idun, and Bragi, who sat at the grand table.

"Long time no see, Vala. Did you miss us?" Thor greeted teasingly as I neared the table. "Or were you having too much fun with my brother?" He winked. Oh gods, had he seen what happened outside?

My cheeks burned, but a comeback came without a thought. "Oh Thor, at least your brother's bite matches his bark…" His brows shot up, and a wicked smile graced his lips. Thankfully, the joke was quiet enough to be a shared moment between only us.

"Touché," he chuckled softly.

"I have gathered you all here today because I had a vision," Odin announced. "Vala has an idea, and we are here to show her the support of the realms."

A small, espresso-colored elf stepped forward and pulled a chair from the table. "Vala," he said gruffly. Parchment, ink, and the loveliest quill sat on the table before me. I nodded at the elf, took my seat, dipped the quill in the inkwell, and wrote down the verse that kept replaying in my head since I had read the note from my father.

I allowed my magic to pour onto the page as the ink bled from the quill. Each line glowed golden and lifted off the parchment. Gasps echoed from those who hadn't witnessed my ability.

"It is true."

"She is the one."

Once I finished, the floating words enveloped me in a whirlwind. I closed my eyes, relishing the feel of them on my skin. But even behind my eyelids, I saw the words. They were what I wrote… until they weren't.

They morphed into a picture of Skoll running after the Sun and Hati, the Moon. The Moon and Sun were chariots of light manned by the twins, Sol and Mani. The image resembled a yin-yang circle.

The wolves began to move, spinning endlessly around and around as their mouths frothed from hunger and exertion. Sol and Mani continued their trek on their chariots, looking back at the beasts in fear.

I was beginning to get dizzy when the wolves suddenly stopped, frozen in place. Sol and Mani, on the other hand, were not immobile. They dragged the chariots backward until each cart was behind their respective wolves.

The siblings retrieved leather harnesses and attached them to Skoll and Hati, and the beasts enraged eyes rolled back to glare at their new masters. Sol and Mani returned to their chariots, wrapping the reins around their fists.

The cracks of whips set the wolves back into motion, their vexed bodies rearing in hopes of fighting their harnesses. Once they admitted defeat, the endless circling began anew, but this time with the twins in control. The image disappeared into a golden cloud of smoke, and I reopened my eyes slowly, sucking in a shocked breath.

Everyone was staring at me. Before I apologized for getting lost in my mind, I looked down. Written on the paper was a new poem:

"Well done, Vala," exclaimed Odin.

Had I done it? Was it *really* that easy?

What an odd feeling. I hadn't even known I was writing. The words had fully enveloped me and took over. I silently thanked my mother and father for their gifts. A sense of joy and peace seemed to blanket everyone in the room.

"We are safe from Fimbulvinter now," said the sing-song voice of a light elf.

"Of course we are," boomed Thor. He elbowed me gently with a smile. "We all knew she could do it."

"Wait," interrupted a dark elf, his voice deep and husky. "How do we know that the poem she wrote changed anything?"

"Aksel, did you not see the golden light?" Heim questioned. "Did we not just witness the same magic? Vala rewrote the prophecy of Skoll and Hati without the quill."

No wonder I didn't remember writing anything after penning the original poem. Confidence spread through me like a free-flowing river. I rewrote my first prophecy, and it was so simple. I was starting to feel like I could tackle saving the world from the Ragnarök Loki longed for.

Suddenly, darkness enveloped everything. *What the Hel?*

"Everyone outside!" boomed Odin. Heavy chairs scraped over the floor as people left their seats to leave the assembly hall.

"Do you all see why I doubted?" Aksel asked as he vacated the room.

"Shut up, elf!" Thor yelled as he directed Sif outside.

With the natural light snuffed out, everything was steeped in darkened shadows. There was no electricity in Asgard and no lit candles to light the way. A hand touched my wrist. Instinctively knowing it belonged to Heim, I allowed him to pull me toward the exit until a thought struck me.

"Wait!" I backtracked and grabbed the parchment, folding it and shoving it under my arm. "There." Outside, I stared up at the sunless sky.

The cacophony of disgruntled voices rose and peaked before Odin yelled loudly, "Stop!" The crowd fell silent and lifted their heads to the Allfather. "Come with me. We shall seek refuge in the halls of Valhalla as we formulate a plan."

Everyone followed Odin toward a grand building that shined like a beacon in the darkness. The rooftop was constructed from thousands of iron shields, and winged, ethereal females were etched upon the immense, ominous doors.

When they opened, everyone shielded their faces from a sudden burst of white light that was worse than a car's brights, and it stung my vision. Eventually, the extreme illumination dimmed to a warm yellow.

When my eyes opened, I was face-to-face with a beautiful, muscled woman. Her hair was white as snow, and it contrasted beautifully with her black iron dress-like bodysuit. The armor was obviously tailored, hugging her curves like she had been born with it.

Between her shoulder blades were giant, silver wings tipped in white. They flared out majestically behind her, and it was difficult not to stare in awe.

"Hello, Vala. I am Freya, Queen of the Valkyries. Welcome to Valhalla." She stepped to the side. *Whoa.*

Valkyries were everywhere, some in flight on their dazzling, obsidian horses. Others sat at tables. A few were even training with wooden swords and shields, sparring together with wings unfurled. Row after row of wooden tables stretched as far as the eye could see behind a heavy golden gate. Warriors dressed for battle sat amongst Valkyries, feasting and chatting. None of them looked our way as we piled into the hall.

"They can't see us," Heim explained beside me. "They cannot see anything beyond the gate."

The Hall of Valhalla was enchanted in more ways than one. When we were outside, it didn't look that large. But as I stepped past the threshold, the space seemed to expand before my eyes. I nearly forgot that Freya spoke to me when someone cleared their throat.

"Oh, hello. Freya," I greeted clumsily.

"We apologize for the imposition, Frey, but there has been a complication." I was grateful Odin was taking the lead.

"What happened?" Freya inquired, worried.

"Vala found a way to transform the Skoll and Hati prophecy, but something went awry. After we witnessed the words of the prophecy change, darkness overtook the realm."

Immediately, Freya pushed through the doors to look outside.

"What could have caused this?" questioned one of the giants.

"We saw her power work, Odin. What is going on?" asked the espresso-colored elf.

"I am not sure," he answered honestly. "We need to review the parchment for error." I glared unconsciously, hoping he wasn't referring to me messing something up. I laid the parchment flat on the closest table, ready to defend my work.

That was when I saw it—a smudge of red ink next to a poorly drawn image of a large eagle with its wings wrapped around the sun. I ran outside and screamed at the black, starless sky, "Loki! I know you are causing this! Stop being a cowardly eagle and show yourself!"

CHAPTER TWENTY

The pitch-dark sky fluttered open like a closed fist stretching its fingers wide. Through the cracks of darkness, I could see the shape of feathers. Red smoke wafted through the sky as Loki languidly beat his wings to keep the Sun contained.

"Loki, you fool! Do you not think we can make another net to capture you? Do you not think that I can wield Mjolnir and finally avenge my brother's death?" Thor yelled behind me. His voice was thunder, and his hammer pulsed bright ivory light.

Wicked, cawing laughter, followed by an ear-piercing screech, rent the air. "Thor. *You* are the fool! You all thought you trapped me, but I will be the death of you yet, nephew," Loki's voice boomed as if from the heavens. "With my children by my side, we will bring about Ragnarök. We *will* fulfill the prophecies. Wait and see."

Heim and Thor growled in anger beside me, their rage palpable as their auras gleamed brightly. An emerald glow surrounded my protector while the god of thunder emanated a piercing, white light as if he were lightning incarnate.

My golden glow combined with theirs, and our auras merged, tangling into one giant pale jade energy. I didn't even know that was possible, but I swore I could feel Heim's calmness seeping into my pores and Thor's strength filling my soul as I began to repeat the word "Teiwaz."

Frigg taught me it meant warrior and that, in times of need, I should call on the Norse runes to fill me with power.

I allowed the word to form on my lips and fall like wax melting down a candle. The symbol began to harden before me, and the arrow on the teiwaz rune became metal. I grabbed it by the shaft and threw it toward the sky with all my might, Thor's power coursing through my veins, giving me extra strength.

A silence fell over the crowd as we all awaited the result of my throw. Those few moments felt like an eternity, everyone suspended in time. When the arrow finally connected with the base of one of Loki's wings, he shrieked in pain. His giant eagle form unfurled from the sun, and its light broke through, blinding us all. As everyone shielded their eyes, a raucous, unsteady flapping ricocheted through the realm until all went silent and completely still.

When my eyes adjusted, I looked up just in time to see the arrow freefalling to the earth. Everyone in the line of fire ran and ducked for cover, and the tip pierced the ground, splattering dirt everywhere like raindrops.

Thor roared. In a blur of lightning and… feathers, he danced viciously with Loki, the eagle, creating a chaotic smear of colors when blood mixed with blinding light. Heim ran toward them, and I tried to grab his arm before he entered the fray. I missed, barely grazing his sleeve, and I felt dread at the feel of it slipping through my fingers.

The three gods twisted, knotting together like the trunk of the Yggdrasil, in a ruthless battle. The eagle cried as Heim pulled on its injured wing, and Thor jerked on the other wing until it was straight, spreading the beast like a meager set of cards. Loki flailed, attempting to gouge out their eyes with his long, thin beak, but his effort was to no avail; they held him trapped and helpless.

The men pinned him to the ground, and Heim spread his legs wide to stand firmly on each wing. As Thor lifted his hammer high above his head, he looked me straight in the eye and brought the hammer down with an audible whoosh, making dust fly when it connected with the ground.

Where was Loki?

"Damn it. Loki must have shifted, which is probably for the best because I would have killed him," Thor growled, his breath coming out in huffs. "Vala, my energy flowed into you like we were sharing it. That was one Hel of a trick. Between that new development and calling on the teiwaz, you have a lot to work with in your arsenal."

"I am not sure how I was able to do that." I glanced at Frigg. "You didn't teach me how to borrow power."

"I did not teach it because I cannot do that," she replied.

Cheers erupted from Valhalla as Valkyries ran into the now-bright sunlight, their wings glistening and gleaming. Thor slapped his hand on my back—all but knocking me over—and whooped with the rest of the men. Heim saw me falter and held onto my arm before I completely fell to the ground.

"You never cease to amaze me," he whispered into my ear as he steadied my body, acting like he felt no pain despite the fresh wounds all over his hands and arms. His words sent a shiver down my spine. I could still feel the calm of his aura filling me as I leaned on my tiptoes to wrap him in a hug.

"Ditto," I murmured. I relished the involuntary tremble I got in return. "But let's not pretend that feeling pain is weakness. Those scratches look awful."

A light elf brought us a bundle of fresh cloth, and a dark elf carried over a bucket of warm, clean water. I thanked them but ultimately went about healing Heim with my words so the elves could tend to Thor's wounds instead.

"Well, now that we have that all sorted and Loki has, yet again, cowardly scampered away, what do you suppose we should do next?" Odin's question was posed to no one in particular.

"The next part of the prophecy is that Loki will summon Jörmungandr," Frigg commented.

"Jorm and I have spoken. He does not wish to be summoned." Everyone around me stopped talking and stared.

"You met Jörmungandr?" Odin asked. "And he *spoke* to you?"

"I have. It was in what I thought was a dream, but I woke up wet, so who knows anymore? Why do you seem so shocked that he spoke to me?"

"Because no one has communicated with the ouroboros since he was banished." The Allfather eyed me quizzically.

"Tell us everything that happened, Vala," Frigg requested.

The crowd listened quietly as I relayed each facet of the short conversation between the Midgard snake and myself. At the end of my story, chatter amongst the many started.

"We cannot trust Jörmungandr!" exclaimed one of the light elves.

"He is Loki's child. A monster…" mumbled a giant.

"Silence," Odin ordered. "I trust Vala. We have learned that Jorm, as she calls him, had a change of heart during his exile in the ocean. The depths have changed him, and since he is willing, we must do what we can to forgive him for the past and allow him to change his future. If he wishes to be small again, we must help find a way to make it so."

"But how can we reverse his size?" inquired one of the dark elves. At that, Odin looked at me with a raised brow.

"What makes you think I would know the answer?" A wave of nausea hit me with immediate force. I bent over and hurled as my vision went black. The darkness was dizzying, then popped with many colors. I saw flashes of a woman's pale, sharp face with glaring yellow eyes. There was a loud cackle as her lips moved slowly, images flashing in and out of my vision. I finally made the jumble of words she spoke into a coherent sentence.

Come to Ironwood Forest.

"Where is Ironwood Forest?" I panted between ragged breaths.

"Jarnvidr, known to many as Ironwood Forest, is on Midgard." Helene stepped to my side, helping me stand upright. She tore the edge of her sleeve off and handed it to me so I could wipe my mouth. When I squeezed her hand with gratitude, she smiled in response.

"I saw a woman just now. In my mind. Her image came to me scrambled and quick, like a horrible flashing labyrinth. She told me to go to Ironwood Forest." I turned to gaze at the Allfather. "Odin, did you know that would happen?"

"I have witnessed your powers, Vala. I know that even you do not know the extent of all you can do. I trust that your gifts will know when and how to present themselves."

"You saw Angrboda. She was Loki's first wife, the mother of monsters. She dwells in the Ironwood Forest with her clan of troll wives."

"Why would she have appeared to me like that, Frigg?"

"The troll wives have many gifts. Some can see the future or shapeshift. Others are masters of incantations or are skillful at crafting magical items. Angrboda is a troll and a giantess; her shapeshifting abilities are tenfold what the other troll wives are capable of. She can become who and what she wants while also being able to briefly enter minds to send a message."

"Can she change others as well as herself?" The pieces of the puzzle began to come together. Maybe Jorm's mother could make him small again.

"There is only one way to find out," Heim commented.

"Let us sit and feast for our success today. We can make plans while we eat together," Odin suggested. He guided everyone from the messy scene outside toward the dining hall in Valaskjalf.

As food piled high on plates as far as the eye could see, we began strategizing our upcoming visit to meet Angrboda. Maps of Earth were strewn across the tables, but they were different than any I had viewed before. I saw cities I was familiar with featuring landmarks I had no recognition of. Odin placed an iron knife on a location called Senja. It was a small island toward the north tip of Norway, and just below the city, encompassed by tiny trees, were the words Ironwood Forest.

I was never the best in geography, but my father had many maps of Norway in his home office; that forest had not been marked on any of them. The map's title caught my eye: Midgard. The conversation had veered to who would accompany us and what we needed for the trip. As the others strategized, I allowed myself to draw in small amounts of power from those around me, practicing the new magic.

I secured wisdom from Odin.

I harnessed strength from Thor.
I siphoned peace from the light elves.
I drew hardiness from the dark elves.
And finally, I borrowed shapeshifting from the giants.

CHAPTER TWENTY-ONE

With full bellies, we hatched a plan. Heim and I would ride Odin's wingless, flying steed with eight legs, Sleipnir, over the Bifröst to Midgard. We would then travel over the seas to Senja.

Helene and Frigg were to join us there, riding on the backs of Huginn and Muninn, who were able to grow large for such ventures. Frigg made it clear that Angrboda would be more apt to talk to someone she knew, especially if that person were female.

Odin urged us to stay until the next morning, citing that we would need rest for the trip, and everyone helped us prepare for our travels. The light and dark elves even banded together to gather food and supplies while the giants cared for the animals.

"Are you nervous?" asked Helene as we cuddled on the big bed in the room Odin offered me my first night in Asgard.

"Should I be?"

"Angrboda is not a pure person. She is inherently evil. Some think that Loki turned from his childish pranks to what he is now because of her."

"I refuse to blame a woman for the actions of a man," I said, but I adopted a healthy fear of the woman based on my friend's words.

There was a soft rapping on the door. "Who could that be at this hour?"

"Maybe it's your *eggplant*," giggled Helene as she rolled over on the bed and burrowed under the covers.

I opened the large door, encountering a tall, bright elf. "Good evening, Vala." He bowed politely. "I am Freyr of the Vanir."

"Hello, Freyr. Can I help you?"

"I apologize for calling on you so late, but I wanted to give you something for your trip." He unclasped his leather belt with an attached pouch and handed it to me.

"What is it?"

"Open it, and I will tell you."

I untied the little pouch and found a neatly folded handkerchief nestled inside. I pulled the cloth out; embroidered on each corner was an exquisite longship connected by thin waves along the border.

"Skidbladnir," Freyr whispered.

I immediately knew what it was and what it meant for him to give it to me. Skidbladnir was the mightiest longship ever created. It was born from the magic of the dark elves and could carry all the Aesir and their supplies, including animals. When not in use, the ship folded to the size of a handkerchief for safekeeping. Shocked at his gift, I could only stare at him openmouthed.

"Don't look at me like that, child. I know what I am doing, and you will take it," he demanded quietly. I was unsure why he thought I might need it, but I was eternally grateful for the benevolent gift. "Think of it as an indefinite loan."

"Thank you."

"No need to thank me, girl. If you do your part with that ship, I will be the one thanking you when all this is finished." At that, he turned and walked silently down the hall. I held the handkerchief, rubbing my thumb over the soft material. Belatedly, I suddenly realized that Freyr forgot to tell me how to use the ship. How did the magic work? I rushed down the hall and around the corner he disappeared behind only moments before and ran squarely into Heim's stout chest.

"You have got to stop doing that to me!" I whisper-yelled.

"I was only coming to check on you and tell you good-night."

"Did you see which way Freyr went?"

"Freyr came to your rooms? Why?" Was that jealousy I sensed in his voice?

"He gave me this." I lifted the belt in one hand and the cloth in the other.

Heim's eyes widened, and a smile formed on his face. "Well, I'll be damned."

"I know, right?"

"That could come in handy where we are going. But why do you need to see Freyr again?" Envy slipped back into his tone.

"He didn't tell me how to use it."

You will know how to use it when the time comes, Vala.

Oh, ok. Thank you, Frigg. She chuckled in my head.

Heim sighed deeply, placed his hand on the small of my back, and guided me toward my room. When would I get used to the rush that his touch caused me? Probably never. The maddening man I knew for such a short time already took up so much space in my mind.

I refused to be one of those girls who would fall for a guy and completely lose themselves in him. Everything I had experienced showed how capable and independent I could be.

I was no longer an orphan, held down by my FPs, who made me feel small and alone to keep me submissive. My parents were always with me; they were the whisper in the wind. I was not weird. The kids at school could never understand my grief journey. I would always be awkward and unusual, but that was not a negative. I was free to be unapologetically me.

I was no longer alone. I was surrounded by people who loved me and fostered my growth. I had a family, *my* family. I became a powerful Skaldic Völva. I found my people and myself. I could not wait to see what was in store for us next.

I decided then and there that Heim was part of my next. I cared for him in a way I didn't know I could feel for another person. Sure, I loved Helene like family, but Heim was different. My blood ran hot when he was close by, and my nerves were always on high alert. But, unlike any crush from my past, my confidence grew in his presence instead of shrinking. Having him near allowed me the comfort to express myself and wield my magic. He protected me. He did not judge me. I reached for his hand and wove our fingers together.

"Vala." My name was like a prayer on his lips. "You cannot look at me that way anymore. I cannot bear it."

"Why?" I stepped closer, staring into his deep emerald eyes, and I swore there were lightning bolts of yellow erupting in his irises. He inhaled deeply and held his breath for several seconds before releasing it slowly.

"Because I want you, Vala. You are exquisite. I want to keep you and make you mine. To protect your heart as my own by giving you mine in return. Unnasta, ek ann per." Those last words were so deep and soft that I almost didn't hear them. Before I could ask him to repeat himself, he touched his forehead to mine. He tipped my chin up and closed his eyes. When he opened them again, the translated words I craved got lost within the swirling emerald pools.

Our faces were close, our breath hot between us. His tongue slipped out to lick his bottom lip. Then, he crossed the divide of tension we built, his mouth a fraction of an inch from mine. His soft lips awaited my approval.

I lifted myself as high as possible on my tiptoes, tangling a hand in Heim's glorious hair, and bridged the gap. The kiss began sweetly, shyly. Our lips merely touched; it was a faint, teasing connection. I pushed further into him, pulling him closer.

He was gentle, slightly opening his mouth to capture my bottom lip between his teeth. An involuntary moan escaped from my mouth, and his body reacted in kind. His arm wrapped tightly around my waist. I couldn't get enough. I couldn't get close enough. He pulled away momentarily, his heart racing beneath my palm.

He tucked a loose piece of hair that fell in my face behind my ear. "You are so beautiful." His words, combined with that charming action, sent electricity coursing through me.

I pulled him in for a deeper kiss. The dam we built with flirtation and longing glances burst open, flooding my body with tingling awareness. As if we were dancing, I jumped up and wrapped my legs around his waist. Without missing a beat, he caught me and cupped my bottom so I wouldn't fall, pushing my body against the closest wall to lift me higher so our faces were level. I reveled in the closeness, opening my mouth to explore his lips with my tongue.

He, in turn, explored mine, and our ragged breaths became in tune with the hammering beats of our hearts. Our lips broke apart, and I sucked in much-needed air.

Heim buried his nose in my hair. "You smell so good, Vala," His mouth found my nape, lightly biting and kissing the sensitive flesh. He followed the curve of my neck up to my ear and used his tongue to flick my earlobe gently between his teeth. I fell apart instantly. How did that feel so good? "And you taste even better."

I had only seen what Heim was doing to me in movies, and it felt way better than I ever imagined. I was an expanding balloon, ready to burst. It was like the feeling you get when you rub your socks on the carpet and wait for the zing of the inevitable shock. Kissing Heim was a jolt to my senses.

Everything within me simmered, waiting excitedly for a release that nature told me was coming. Heim tucked another loose hair behind my ear and stared into my eyes. When I reached for his face to pull him back in, he nudged his cheek into my palm.

"Vala, we need to stop. We must stop before I can't anymore." Even though I understood, I couldn't help but grunt in dissatisfaction. My irritation made him chuckle. "Believe me, I don't *want* to stop. But want and need are two very different things, and this is not the time or place, Unnasta."

I scrunched my nose and followed it up with a purposefully childish "Fine." We both giggled quietly as he put me back on my feet. As we walked to my room, I asked, "Heim, what does Unnasta mean?"

He smiled down at me, bent his head until our lips almost touched, and bridged the gap to kiss me so gently that everything caught fire again. My knees became weak, and I grasped his muscled arms so I wouldn't fall over. Just as I thought I might erupt from bliss, he pulled away. "It means 'Sweetheart.' Goodnight, Unnasta. Rest well."

The sound of shuffling and a giggle could be heard from behind my door, and Heim and I smiled knowingly at each other before he brought my hand to his lips, giving it a chaste kiss and heading to his room.

I inhaled a deep, centering breath, but the pleasantly provoked butterflies in my insides were completely unaffected. The door cracked open, and I squished my eyes shut but wore the biggest smile that wasn't going anywhere for the foreseeable future.

"Tell me everything!"

I awoke the next morning well-rested and completely content despite staying up too late with Helene. She had dragged me from the door to the bed, demanding details. I left out nothing, including the unusual words Heim whispered before sweeping me off my feet. When I asked her what they meant, her cheeks reddened, but she told me she could not remember. Her eyes said otherwise. I was severely curious, although I had my suspicions.

We spent the evening giggling and delighting in my first kiss. Heim gave me my first kiss. Just the thought brought back the swarm of rambunctious butterflies. Helene rolled out of bed and opened the blinds in our room. Sunlight spilled in and touched everything gold, making the room sparkle.

"Are you ready?" she asked.

"As I will ever be. You?"

"I suppose."

"But first… Idun's cider!" I followed her to the hallway and was pleasantly surprised to see Heim standing outside our door holding a tray of steaming mugs. He wore jeans and a white T-shirt, probably because we were visiting Midgard.

"Oh, thank the gods, Heim!" squealed Helene as she all but ran toward him, grabbing a mug. She started sipping it immediately and re-entered our room to get dressed for the day.

"Your father *did* say you know how to treat a lady," I joked.

"Only you. Helene got cider by default," he teased back. He handed me a mug and leaned down to kiss my cheek. "Get dressed, Unnasta. I'll be waiting."

I ventured into the room, floating on a cloud of utter happiness. I wound up in the closet, where Helene sipped her cider and stared at the empty walls.

"Why is there nothing in your closet, Vala?"

"I think Odin did that so I could begin learning my magic when I first arrived. Clever idea, I suppose."

"Yeah, sure. But what are we supposed to wear?"

"Hold, please," I said as the writing desk appeared. I jotted down a quick haiku on the creamy parchment. Then, we watched as my words did their thing.

Helene jumped as the warm wind rushed around us. Our pajamas magically removed themselves, and—thank the gods—new undergarments were the first item to clothe us. Next came new jeans. Hers were flare-legged and torn on the knees, like her favorite pair at home. Mine were bootlegs, showing off all my curves.

A black halter top appeared on Helene, followed by a denim jacket and a lilac scarf. The shirt that clothed me was my usual black crop top with a gray zip-up hoodie. To finish off the outfits, we both wore matching black Chucks.

She checked out the new getup in the mirror on the wall, visibly impressed. "Dude, you are so cool."

"I know," I joked, feeling truly awesome.

The dining hall was filled with people since Odin was still hosting the delegates from the other races. Amongst the chaos, I filled my plate high with thick strips of meaty bacon, plantain bread, and fluffy scrambled eggs. Heim sat beside me, and we stole glances throughout the meal. Helene smiled and kicked me gently under the table every time she caught us.

"I have given Sleipnir his orders. He knows only to answer to the two of you," Odin cut in, looking at Heim and me.

"Thank you."

"It is time," Frigg announced. "We have quite the trip ahead of us."

Everyone emptied the dining hall and assembled outside, where Sleipnir, Huginn, and Muninn stood, saddled and waiting. The ravens had grown significantly larger since I last saw them, standing taller than the horse beside them.

The crowd created a circle around the creatures. Many held fluttering multicolored fabric flags with the algiz rune lifted above their heads. The multichromatic view reminded me of my first time seeing the Bifröst.

Odin parted the crowd, the rainbow of flags splitting like a meticulously axed tree. Sleipnir's nostrils flared, and the creature restlessly stomped its feet. Heim gracefully pulled himself onto Sleipnir's back and patted the steed's neck, leaning down to whisper unknown words to our travel companion.

Huginn and Muninn unfurled their wide wings and bent their necks to the ground, offering Frigg and Helene easier access to their backs. Each woman mounted a raven, wrapping their arms around their black-feathered necks. They also whispered soft, calming words to the noble birds.

Odin cleared his throat and began speaking, looking at each of us in turn. "Today, we send off these four travelers. We ask that the algiz cover them in protective power. Heimdall, my son, I urge you to allow the mighty elk to guide you and protect the treasures gifted to you. Frigg, my first wife, may you carry the way of your women and use their gifts to keep yourself and the others safe."

"Helene, I give thanks for your gift of compassion and send you on this journey with the strength of your people." The Allfather knelt beside me and whispered, "Vala, I have a gift to offer you. Please take what I willingly give."

He clasped our hands, and for a second, nothing happened. When I looked at his face in confusion, the connection suddenly grew warm. The sensation spread from my fingers toward my wrists, up my arms, and throughout my body. As he rose to his full height, leaning his forehead to mine, the image of a mighty eagle filled my mind.

I peered into Odin's good eye. His iris was the golden green of the giant eagle, and I knew, at that moment, mine matched. I could feel his eagle within me becoming my own.

"Save her for when you truly need her, Vala. I am not sure how long she will last for you," Odin whispered. He blinked, and his iris was back to his own, his eagle tamped down. He knelt again to offer me a leg up, and Heim grabbed my hand to pull me from his mounted position on Sleipnir.

"Don't miss me too much," Thor yelled before belting out his rich, infectious laughter.

"I think I will miss you least of all," I replied with a wink.

The horse's eight legs started moving, and we went from a standstill to a run in less than ten seconds. The wind caught us, and Sleipnir glided into the sky, seamlessly taking flight. Cool air tousled my hair as we lifted further off the ground.

The ravens followed, soaring into the clouds gracefully. As we flew higher, the crowd below erupted into a roar of warrior cries. Leaving Asgard felt different than our prior trip. Why did it feel as if the inhabitants of the Yggdrasil were sending us off into battle? I clutched my new leather belt and the precious pouch close to my side and held onto the saddle horn as Heim guided Sleipnir toward the Bifröst.

The speed of the animals we rode was awe-inspiring. The Bifröst flew by in a vibrant vortex of color as we corkscrewed down and around the rainbow bridge. Heim pulled his map from his ever-present leather bag and opened the scroll to navigate. I couldn't believe that we were going back to Earth. Even saying it in my head felt weird and unpalatable.

"There is a grove not far off the coast of Norway where we can land and make camp."

"Will we be flying all the way there from Oregon?" I asked. We veered to the left and crossed through an invisible threshold as if in answer to my question. Above me, the sky was a bright, cobalt blue with tufts of cotton candy clouds. Below, the endless sea was a churning, toiling navy blue. "Whoa." I held on tighter to the saddle horn, and Heim wrapped his arm around my waist.

"You are okay, Unnasta. I've got you," he whispered into my ear.

There was a large landmass in the distance. The coastline was dominated by towering, jagged mountains lined with forest green trees. The furious waves of the Norwegian Sea seemed tamed by the land, slowing to a lull as they reached the shore. There were tiny creatures on the beaches scurrying about, and it took me a second to realize they were humans doing human things, ignorant and oblivious.

Was I jealous?

No. I had a purpose.

We flew further inland, over the craggy cliffs. We passed an enormous peak that looked as if it could pierce the sky. When we began our descent, it started slow and progressively got faster. The tips of tree limbs lightly scraped my skin as we sunk deeper into the forest, but it was nothing more than a harmless brush of leaves. Our creatures were skilled at narrowly missing branches and safely guided us to the ground.

Once we landed, Heim tied Sleipnir to a thin tree trunk, and we relieved the animals of all they carried and set up camp. We had traveled for most of the day. It all happened so fast, but the sun was already setting in the sky, and the light peeking between the trees was growing darker quickly.

"I missed this place," Helene stated as she hung thick canvas from branch to branch, creating an enclosure.

"You have been here?"

"Well, I haven't been to Norway since I met you, but yes." It was difficult to grasp that Helene had a long past before me. Instant guilt struck my consciousness; her life changed so she could babysit me.

"Vala, stop it. I can see that look on your face, and I don't like it. You are my best friend, and I love the fact that I know you better than anyone. You, cow, are a blessing."

"Helly, I am just sorry that I sometimes forget you led a whole life before we met."

"Shut up and help me with the bedrolls," she ordered as she bumped her butt against mine.

"Yes, ma'am."

Helene looked utterly disgusted. "Um, no! You do not get to call me that!"

"But you *are* old, like, *really* old," I teased, trying not to laugh.

"Girls, I am glad you are having a good time, but it would be wonderful if you could hurry up and help me with the fire. We need to make some food," interrupted Frigg. Helene and I both laughed and rushed to finish our project.

Later in the evening, we all sat around the fire that I set with my words. Heim had hunted for our dinner and field dressed the catch before placing it over the blaze, and I became lost in the flames licking the meat. Tiny sizzling sounds mixed with the aroma of our upcoming meal; the charred brown of freshly cooked deer was tantalizing. It smelled so good, and I was starving.

The meal was paired with the same starchy side dish as last time—fire-roasted carrots and potatoes. Venison was unlike anything I tasted before. The texture was like steak, but the flavor was wholly unique. It tasted wild, earthen, and rich.

As we devoured our dinner, we talked about the lore of troll wives. They were a spirited group of women. They enjoyed using their magic to trick others and could be dangerous crea-tures. Frigg explained that they were taller than the giants, and she warned me not to hold eye contact for too long with any one of them.

"Why?"

"The longer they look into your eyes, the easier it is for them to take your form fully. Most shapeshifters can make themselves look like someone else but never fully encapsulate them. You can tell by their eyes. But the troll wives can replicate everything if you let them gaze into the windows of your soul."

I shuddered at the thought of being able to see and touch a mirror image of myself.

"Ladies, we should get to sleep. We have an early morning," Heim suggested.

"Okay, Dad," Helene muttered under her breath.

"Does that make me Mom?" I whispered to her, giggling.

"Okay, you two," he interrupted. My friend and I nudged each other, still laughing, but followed Frigg and Heim into the tent.

The bedrolls were laid side by side in a line. Frigg snuggled into the blankets of the farthest one, Helene followed suit next to her, and Heim crawled into the one closest to the makeshift door. That left me a spot between him and Helene.

I climbed in and grabbed Helene's hand like we used to do when we were younger. Heim rested flat on his back, staring at the patch of canvas above, and I reached out my other hand and intertwined our fingers. Their breathing deepened; I knew sleep was taking over their bodies. Before they succumbed to slumber, I whispered my father's nighttime ritual to them:

"I love you more than all the Aesir in Asgard. More than all the light elves in Alfheim and the dark elves in Svartalfheim. More than all the humans in Midgard. More than all the giants in Jotunheim. More than all the fire and ice in Muspelheim and Niflheim. More than all the darkness in Helheim and more than all the Vanir in Vanaheim. That means I love you more than all the inhabitants of the Yggdrasil, and that, my dears, is an awful lot!"

Heim's hand gently squeezed mine, and I turned my head to see his face. His lips moved ever so slightly. The words were so quiet there was almost no sound. "Ek ann per, Vala."

My insides became molten magma; I was almost sure I knew what those words meant. I allowed the warmth teeming within me to pull me under, descending into a dark balm of sweet dreams.

CHAPTER TWENTY-THREE

I stirred awake. The glistening dew on the leaves dripped onto my face and ran down my skin like rhapsodic tears. Light spilled through the branches, and beautiful orange-chested birds flitted about. Warblers sang their morning song, and the wind floated through the trees, gently tickling the skin on my arms.

I sat up slowly and looked around. Frigg, Helene, and Heim weren't there with me. Neither were the animals. The sudden crunch of dirt and dry branches startled me, and I swiveled my head to see what made the noise.

I stilled. A majestic, gray reindeer with soft, fuzzy white antlers stood in the middle of an opening in the trees not far behind me. The creature was grazing, head down, and nibbling on the green grass growing in the meadow.

My hand moved a fraction of an inch, and the earth beneath my palm shifted. The reindeer's head shot up, and its glowing yellow eyes met mine. I held my breath, not knowing if the stag was gentle or dangerous. It held my gaze and lifted a giant leg, scraping its hoof on the ground as it rose. As my mouth opened to scream, the beast charged.

All I could do was lift my hands in front of my face. I thought about using my magic, but before the creature reached me, it evaporated into a thousand specks of shimmering dust that seemed to fly through my body. What the Hel? The bits of dust rained on my skin, leaving a layer of caribou ash.

There was a loud cackle, and I whirled around to find myself face-to-face with… myself. This was a trick. I knew it wasn't real. But she looked exactly like me. I was frozen in place.

"I knew you were coming," said my copy.

"Who are you?"

"Don't be stupid, girl. I know you came to see me."

"Angrboda?" She cackled again and then changed into the form of a snow-white fox. The creature circled me slowly, never taking its yellow eyes off me. "Where are the others?"

I didn't expect it to talk until a shrill voice came from its mouth.

"They are gone, Vala. And soon, you will be gone, too." The small fox pounced and sank its teeth into the flesh of my arm. Blood, thick and sticky, spilled from the wound, and I screamed involuntarily.

"Vala. VALA!" Heim was shaking me. My eyes flew open, and I realized it was just a dream—well, more of a nightmare. "What the Hel happened, Vala?"

"I… I'm… I'm fine…" I stuttered, almost soundlessly, between ragged breaths. I had been dreaming. It was just a dream. But then, why was…?

The pain kicked in. A pulsing, stabbing sort of pain. Wincing, I lifted my arm and saw blood trickling down from a deep bite mark. Helene rushed around the tent, looking for the first aid kit the elves packed for our trip.

"Oh gods, I can't find it. Where is that damned thing?" Items flew from her bag as she threw them carelessly during her search.

"Calm down, Helene." Frigg wiped the sleep from her eyes. "Vala, you can heal that. Remember your training."

Oh… yeah. I whispered the healing spell and watched as the flesh began to mend itself. The ripped muscle reattached as the skin grew back together. Helene poured fresh water from a canteen into a bowl, wet a clean rag, and cleaned the blood from my arm. All that remained beneath was a pink scar.

"Thank you," I whispered, my voice hoarse from screaming.

"I got you, boo." My friend's tone was more serious than I expected. "Sorry for my momentary freak-out, but your screams scared me."

"It's alright. I would have done the same thing if the roles were reversed."

"Vala, I need to know what happened. What did you see in your dream?" Heim asked.

"I woke up, and I couldn't find you guys. I was alone in the forest, and there was a reindeer. But it turned into… well, me… and then I… she… turned into a fox, and the damned thing bit me."

"You met Angrboda," Frigg stated matter-of-factly.

"I suspected," Heim agreed.

"I figured that out during the dream, but how? Is it like when she sent me the message? This was so much more *real* than that."

"The troll wives are known for entering our dreams and turning them into nightmares. It is just another of their tricks," Frigg explained. "Did you look the reindeer in the eyes?"

"Yes," I admitted sheepishly. "I figured when you told me about eye contact, you meant specifically with people. I won't make that mistake again."

"I apologize, child. I should have put a protective spell over all of us last night, but in my weariness, I completely forgot."

"No one is to blame, and Vala is okay," Heim said. "Let's discuss a plan so the troll wives don't catch us off guard again."

We ate a meager breakfast of eggs and toast—items packed by the elves—as Heim pulled out the map of Midgard. We studied it, finding a route to take. When I looked at the map with Odin, I thought the entire patch of trees was the Ironwood Forest, but it actually only covered a much smaller portion of the area we were currently in.

We set off north. I was not the best at navigation, and I didn't know how long we needed to walk, so I just enjoyed the beauty of nature along the way. There was plenty of wildlife and a sprawling lake with water so clear that I could see to the bottom; the smooth stones beneath the surface glittered in the sun.

The deeper we walked into the forest, the more I could sense Midgardian magic. The trees surrounding us radiated auras like a dense, enchanted blanket. I was peering up at the limbs above when Heim's strong hand grasped my wrist and gently tugged me toward him.

"Shh," he whispered into my ear. Helene and Frigg had stopped, too, frozen in place. Ahead of us was a cloaked figure. It was hobbling silently, its giant body swaying back and forth. In its arms was a basket filled with mushrooms and twigs.

"What is that?"

"That is a troll," Helene answered softly.

Despite the softness of our voices, the troll stilled and turned around. Beneath the cloak, her eyes gleamed like two silver dollars, and her long, bulbous nose sniffed the air. "Come now, darlings. I could smell you from a mile away." The female's voice was a menacing croak. She started walking again. "Let's go."

I looked over at Frigg, awaiting her approval. She jutted her chin slightly in the direction of the troll, and we all slowly trailed the path. The troll's dark cloak swayed with each step, and she grunted as each limb lumbered forward.

An iron fence materialized. Fox and wolf skulls decorated the tops of each spike, and spider webs spread out between the posts, shiny with dew drops in the sunlight slipping through the trees. We passed into a crude village with scattered huts, fires with red logs that heated cauldrons filled with steaming concoctions, and troll wives going about what I could only assume was their normal business.

"I've been expecting you," a soft and feminine voice said. Given what I had gleaned of trolls, it was completely unexpected. A towering woman stepped out of the hut closest to us. Her hair was black as the night, and her skin was porcelain smooth. She wore a cloak made of fox furs and boots that resembled the color of the reindeer from my dream. "Hello, Vala. I am Angrboda."

I lifted my head to her but did not look her in the eyes. My breath caught in my throat, but I would not allow myself to show any fear. Frigg stepped forward and placed her hand on my shoulder. She must have sensed my apprehension. "Hello, old friend. We bear no ill will. We only came to—"

"I know why you are here," interrupted Angrboda, looking directly at Frigg. I took the chance to glance at her eyes, seeing that they were the same eerie yellow as the fox and reindeer from my dream. "I saw you coming."

"If we can just speak with you and get the answers we seek, then we can leave you and your clan in peace," I spoke confidently, despite my internal fear.

"Follow me." We entered the hut. It was more spacious and nicer than it seemed from the outside. There were rugs made of animal hides on the floor, wooden stools set up in a circle, and in the corner was a large bed with a plush fur blanket that stretched out on all sides.

Angrboda sat on one of the stools and waved her arm, a silent order for the rest of us to sit. We obliged. The troll we followed through the forest entered the hut with a tray of steaming wooden mugs, handing one to each of us. I was wary of the drink, but it smelled amazing. Cinnamon and cloves mixed with a hint of something different but alluring.

"Please, try the mushroom tea. Astrid brews it herself, and it is quite delicious." Angrboda lifted a cup to her lips, and she drank deeply. I glanced at Frigg; she gave a slight wink and took a small sip. Everyone followed suit. It was delicious. Savory, yet sweet and soothing. "Alright, now what is it you would like to know?"

I started telling Angrboda everything that happened to that point. I told her about my visit with her daughter, Hel, and my dream of Jorm. I started telling her about the prophecies when she interrupted me.

"Vala, do not be insolent, child. I know that my children have sought freedom. I have also known of your destiny far longer than you. You require information that will return

Jörmungandr to his original size. You think that because I am his mother, I would know."

I kept my eyes on the floor as I responded, "Well, yes. That is what we were hoping."

"And what makes you think I would kn—"

"Excuse me, but *you* are the one that interrupted my thoughts in Asgard. You are the one who told me to come to the Ironwood Forest!" Each time I spoke the word "you," the word rushed out of my mouth in a stream of fire, popping and sizzling in the air before extinguishing. I was over her rudeness and interruption.

One of Angrboda's brows lifted, and her mouth tilted in a sinful smile. "There you go, Vala. I wanted to see that fire, little girl."

"Do not call me a 'little girl,'" I countered, biting back my anger.

"Oh, but I do love a feisty one!"

"Enough, Angrboda!" Heim yelled.

"Come now, precious. Call off your guard dog. I was only trying to have a little fun."

Enough was enough.

"Bind." The word, formed from my anger, became a solid ribbon and tied itself around the terrible woman's head, covering her mouth. She stared at me wide-eyed, and I glared back at her. "That will stay on there unless you are ready to cooperate. If you so much as make a sound that I don't like, it will shut you up again. Do I make myself clear?"

Angrboda nodded, and I let the tie slip enough for her to talk. "Good show, Vala. I have what you seek. It is in the form of an elixir. One that you must somehow allow my son to ingest."

"It will make him small again?" I asked. I thought about the woman's reputation for trickery and added, "And it will have no ill effects?"

"Vala, I hope you would know that I would not harm my own child."

"Fine. Let's have it."

Angrboda rose cautiously, went to her simple wooden nightstand, and pulled out a small vial filled with a galactic, cloudy liquid.

"As I said, you must pour this down Jörmungandr's throat and allow his body to ingest it. The spell will act quickly. All of my clan put pieces of themselves into the spell itself after I witnessed your plan in a vision. I may not be a good person, but I would do anything to free my children."

"Prove it."

"Excuse me? How would you like me to do that?"

"Drink some," I instruct flatly, ready to free my words on her again if she didn't comply.

Her eyes widened as she saw my mouth begin to open. "Okay, okay!" Angrboda popped the cork from the bottle and lifted the potion to her lips. She allowed a tiny drop to fall on her tongue and quickly replaced the cork. A few seconds passed, and my anger boiled until her body began to writhe.

The troll, who was once at least three times my size, started to shrink. When the potion's magic came to an end, Angrboda stood no more than four feet tall, glaring up at me.

"Thank you."

I reached down to grab the small bottle, and as my fingers wrapped around it, Angrboda snaked her slender fingers around my wrist. She pulled me toward her, and she shapeshifted. Her wicked smile was the last thing I saw on her face before she completely transformed in a cyclone. The wind lifted us both, spinning us in its wild whirlpool, and then set us down on the other side of the room. When everything settled, the figure that held my wrist was my worst nightmare.

My ice-blue eyes stared back at me.

She was me.

"Vala!" Heim stepped toward me and my mirror image.

"Heim, stop!" commanded Frigg. "We do not know who the real Vala is. Look at their eyes. They are the same."

"Shit, I failed. I knew I wasn't supposed to look her in the eyes," said the carbon copy next to me. Angrboda had even taken on my voice.

Heim stepped toward her, eyeing both of us warily, while Helene and Frigg looked from her to me. My protector stood still in front of the imposter, staring deep into her eyes. She looked back at him, and I wondered if that was how I stared at him. Her eyes were filled with respect, trust, and something else. Was that lust? Heim leaned toward her and whispered something in her ear. Her body stiffened, and her even, exhaled breath released slowly. He straightened and inhaled deeply.

He glanced at me, then stepped directly into my line of sight. I dropped my eyes to the ground. What if Heim didn't recognize me? He gently lifted my chin and gazed deep into my eyes, penetrating my soul and seeking the heart I'd willingly given him.

"Heim, I'm right here." I nuzzled my cheek into his palm.

"Prove it, Vala," Helene demanded, making me roll my eyes.

Heim kept his gaze on mine until he leaned forward to tuck a loose strand of hair behind my ear. He inhaled and released a whisper so feather soft that I doubted anyone could have overheard, "I told you before, Unnasta, your soul is my home. I know when I am home. That woman could never trick me, even if she possessed your eyes."

Heim's hot breath near my ear sent a shiver of joy through me, but I contained it. He may know me, but I couldn't blame Helene and Frigg for not trusting either version of myself. Heim stood tall again, and we looked at one another, not moving. I saw his eye twitch, almost as if he was giving me one of his stupid winks, and I tightened my lips to hide my smile.

"This is ridiculous," I said, letting the last word hiss off my teeth. The breath between the spaces in my mouth sizzled the word into existence. It was filled with air, blowing up like sticky, chewed-up bubblegum that flew in front of Angrboda's face. It popped, covering her features in the sticky substance.

She let out an exasperated huff. "Stupid child! I was only trying to have a bit of fun in return for that stunt you pulled earlier." In another cyclone of power, Angrboda returned to herself, but she was still shorter than before.

"Well played, Angrboda. That *was* fun."

"Leave this place now before I make you regret asking for my help."

"Happily," I huffed. Despite my annoyance with her childish games, I promptly added, "Thank you again."

We exited the tent, and as we headed out of Ironwood Forest, I could hear her evil laughter following us on the wind.

CHAPTER TWENTY-FOUR

"What did you whisper to Angrboda when she looked like me?"

"Maybe I will tell you that when you tell me what happened with Loki in your bedroom that first night," Heim teased. Oh wow, I hadn't thought that subject would ever resurface.

"Well, with all we have been through, I am not opposed to telling you what happened now."

"Oh?"

"Loki tricked me into thinking it was you in my bed instead of him," I admitted. "I woke to your voice, thinking it was you with me. You… I mean, he… asked if I wanted a kiss."

His next question came out unsure and lacked his usual confidence. "Did you want me… him… to kiss you then?"

"Heim, don't make me answer that," I pleaded. My cheeks burned. "I had only just met you then. Even now, I don't understand all I feel for you. Everything has happened so fast."

"I do realize it is unfair of me." He laced his fingers in mine and continued, "I have known about you for a long time. I see you, Vala. I know what you stand for. I see your hopes and dreams. Your strength and vulnerability. I spent so much time observing you before we met in person. I knew my feelings for you before I heard your alluring voice say my name. Before I touched your soft skin. My heart has always known, and I wouldn't have it any other way."

I was stunned into silence, and a tear slipped down my cheek. His exposed emotions seeped into my pores, filling every empty place with his adoration. We stopped walking. Helene and Frigg continued on, allowing us a moment. Heim lifted his hands to my face but did not touch, looking to me for acceptance. I turned slightly to nuzzle his palm. It was all the invitation he needed.

My protector held my head between his strong palms, gently swiping away my hot tears. I closed my eyes, relishing the feel of his hands on my skin. His body shifted forward, and the gentlest of kisses peppered my flesh. In the lightest caress, his lips brushed against my eyelids. As his thumb ran softly over my bottom lip, my eyes opened again, and our gazes met. "Will you be mine, Vala? Because I have long been yours," he whispered.

"Yes." The statement was a mere breath before he tenderly took it away. He kissed me softly, repeating a single word each time his lips left my mouth.

"Mine."

"Okay, you two, enough of the grossness," Helene yelled, cutting into the sweet moment. "Don't forget about cooties, Vala!"

Heim and I laughed. After intertwining our hands, we ran to catch up.

"Cooties… are… not…. real," I gasped.

"Duh," she giggled.

We were almost out of the forest; beyond the tree line were the jutting cliffs we saw when we flew in. The charcoal rocks were in stark contrast to the icy blue of the ocean beyond.

Frigg snuck beside me. "Can I speak with you for a moment?" Heim nodded respectfully and veered toward Helene, the two falling into comfortable chatter.

"Of course. What's up?"

"Much has occurred over the past several days, and I realized that I never got the chance to ask you what you meant the night of the soothsayer ritual. You told your parents you would save them?"

"I meant to talk with you about that." Her eyes were kind but questioning. "I made a bargain with Hel."

"I figured. Did you not think you could tell me?"

"I wanted to see if I could trust Hel on my terms. I hold onto hope that I can save them, but I'm still not sure I can trust her. Do you think the bargain was a mistake?" I asked, vulnerability lacing my voice.

"I think the person making the choice is the only one who can decide whether that choice is a mistake."

"Uh… thank you for being cryptic." I stared at the ground, shuffling and dragging my feet. I wasn't frustrated at Frigg;

I was annoyed at the decisions that I needed to make and the answers I did not yet have.

"Vala, you know what is best for you. I trust that Hel wants what is best for her and her siblings. She has been tortured long enough, and if you choose to help her, I commend you. I do not worry about the choices you make. I trust that you know what you are doing."

"Thank you, Frigg. I appreciate your confidence in me."

"You are stronger than you know, my darling." She reached over and squeezed my hand. My thoughts were bombarded with an overwhelming sense of peace. There I was, walking with the most important people in my life. Helene—the truest friend I ever knew. Frigg—the maternal force that took me in and loved me like her own. Heim—the protector I needed, the confidante I didn't know I wanted, my first kiss, and possibly my first love.

I missed my mom and dad every moment of every day, but I realized that I found a family. My heart was full, overflowing with strength. I had spent so long feeling alone and never wanted to let the feeling of togetherness go. I thanked the trees, the earth, and the sky for my luck in finding this group of people who fully accepted and loved me.

We were crossing the rocky terrain of a cliff when a bellowing siren attacked our aural senses. The sound was a blaring noise that left pervasive ringing in my ears each time it stopped. One drawn-out, high-pitched wail followed promptly by an equally long, low, warbling moan persisted at full volume.

"What is that?!"

"I don't know," replied Heim, stepping to my side defensively.

The ocean became angry. The once-calm lapping waves were violent, crashing into the shore with fierce intensity. Whitecaps rose higher and higher, slamming into the innocent beach below. The town in the distance was a bustling horde of tiny people shuttering windows and tethering outdoor furniture.

It finally clicked. That sound was a tsunami alarm.

The wind kicked up and blew the salty scent of the sea in our direction. I peered into the void of the ocean, attempting to view the horizon. There was nothing but massive waves. I clutched my belt, held Heim's hand, and closed my eyes, remembering my training with Frigg from the not-so-distant past. I was a seeress and needed to *see* if this was a storm or something more sinister.

I allowed my body to relax—despite the chaos—and let my mind open. Every sound disappeared, and my mind vacated my body where I stood. I could see myself and those I loved as my spirit rose, flying past the cliff, out over the water to the middle of the ocean. I scanned the endless waters, and my gaze landed on a dark, daunting shadow below the surface. Fear gripped my spirit when I realized that the shape was eerily snakelike.

I was not afraid of Jorm, but I feared what Loki could make him do. I knew what the prophecy stated. What was coming.

"Vala, the time is near. I have come to warn you. Loki is readying his ship, and he controls me. I am unable to disobey him."

"Jorm! I know how to help you. Come to the surface, and I can fix you!"

"I am powerless against this measure. I cannot fully rise until the time comes. Save me, Vala. I must go; he cannot know I warned you."

Suddenly, the ocean grew still as the shadow sank back into the darkness. I turned back toward the shore to return to the body I'd left behind and to tell the others of my findings. As I soared through the open air, a gull rose and leveled out in flight beside me. The white bird stroked its wings, the left side slightly catching with each lift.

The barely noticeable impediment caught my attention, and I scanned the bird to see if there was anything else off about its presence. Then I noticed the red rings surrounding each beady eye.

"Hello, Lítilvölva." The voice emanating from the gull was smoothness laced with a belittling edge. Loki. My anger writhed, creating a bursting gold glow tinged with fiery orange. "Don't get yourself in a tizzy, little girl."

"Do not call me a little girl, Loki!"

"Ah, but Lítilvölva, you *are* still a child. Not yet eighteen. You have no idea who you are. You do not even have access to all your power yet." His words bit at me, further unleashing my rage. "My son thinks I did not see him rise to warn you. He must think I don't know that you can hear him speaking. Foolish snake. I see and know all."

"Why are you doing this, Loki? Why do you want Ragnarök to happen, anyway? Isn't it written that you will die?"

"Of course it is. This immortality, this life, is unacceptable. No man should live forever," he spewed angrily. "I have accepted my fate, dear girl. It is the others who cannot agree to their deaths. I long for the darkness of eternal rest, the end of all things for my kind. I crave the chaos that will overtake the world, allowing the Yggdrasil to rot and wither, thus creating a new world—a fresh slate. I also crave vengeance, for them to feel pain the likes of which they burdened upon me all these years."

I pondered his words. My mind momentarily rested on the idea that a fresh slate wasn't so bad. The world was a dark place, a dying planet full of selfish people. Loki's negativity seeped into my being, the darkness clawing through me with slices of all the great and terrible things. Murder, homelessness, greed, and many more sinister images flashed through my mind.

Suddenly, an immediate relief washed over me, a blanket of hope wrapping me in comfort.

"I got you, boo."

I hadn't realized how close to the shore we were, and I could see a soft lavender light gleaming like a beacon on the cliff. Helene rested her hands on my shoulders, whispering into my ear. Her warmth enveloped me, followed by flashes of the good in the world. The things worth saving.

Loki could feel his talons tearing from my psyche as his gull writhed. Fresh blood spilled from the wound I inflicted as Helene's aura poured into me, mingling with my gold. I neared my body, screaming on the inside. I could feel the trickster god splitting from me, attempting to rip through my soul as we pulled further apart.

"You cannot break me, Loki!" I screamed into the void.

"I can certainly keep trying, though," he viciously laughed once we completely separated. He soared above us, allowing his uninjured wing to carry him high on the wind. "I cannot wait to spill the blood of the ones you love, Vala. I'm most looking forward to gutting that pretty man by your side just to see you shatter."

With that, he flew off into the now-bright sky.

"What is he talking about?" I asked, grabbing the hand still on my shoulder and gazing into Helene's eyes. Heim moved closer to me, his strong arm wrapping around my waist in a protective stance.

"The prophecy says Loki will kill me."

CHAPTER TWENTY-FIVE

Memories of the prophecies of Ragnarök invaded my mind. Somewhere, deep down, I knew Loki intended to kill Heimdall. I knew the stories, knew the fates of all the gods and the Yggdrasil. Why was knowing Odin and Thor were doomed unless I could reverse the prophecies not hitting as hard as realizing Heim—my Heim—would be savagely murdered by Loki?

My confidence wavered. Loki was right; I was still technically a child.

"What happens when I turn eighteen?"

"We aren't completely sure." Frigg rested her hand on my upper arm in a maternal, comforting way. "But we know that a Völva comes fully into their power at age eighteen. That means the magic you have exhibited thus far is only a fraction of what you will be capable of in a few short weeks."

A whirring of magic zipped through my body, starting in my toes and tingling its way up to my head. My golden aura erupted at the thought of even more abilities, of more ways to disrupt the words of the Skalds of old. Heim bent and softly kissed my cheek, sensing the anxiety that matched my excitement.

"Don't worry, Unnasta. We've got you."

"I know. Thank you."

The relentless sun's rays beat down on us, burning the pale skin on my cheeks. The warmth bit like pinpricks, turning into a sting with the salty air of the coastline. If we didn't move to the shadows, we would all surely burn up.

Once we were all under the shade of the trees, I reached for Heim's pack and pulled out his water flask. I drank deeply, my mouth stale from the oceanic air.

"I wish that Loki wasn't such a douche," Helene commented, making me spit out the sip of water I took in a very unladylike fashion.

"Helene," Frigg scolded. Heim's shoulders dipped in silent laughter.

"When you're right, you're right. I'm sick and freaking tired of him calling me 'little girl.'"

"Don't worry, Unnasta. You may be young, but you are chosen. Little does Loki know that age does not equal power. That lies within the person. We see you, chosen one." Heim wrapped his arm around my waist, placing a light peck on my forehead. "To us, you are as old and wise as dirt."

I shoved him away while Helene and I laughed. "You're a shit, you know that Heim?"

"Yup." He wink-blinked, and his smile devastated me, the deep dimples drawing me in. I could stare at him all day.

Frigg began walking into the forest, and the three of us followed behind her, tittering like schoolchildren. We walked for miles, the smell of salt evaporating into the musky scent of the dense forest. The glaring sun sliced through the trees, creating an eerie glow between the limbs. Dust particles floated in the beams of light like glitter. The deeper we ventured, the quieter we became.

My mind raced with the happenings of the past few hours, and Angrboda's potion jostled in my pouch as I thought of what Jorm told me.

Loki is readying his ship.

We neared the campsite, welcomed by the animals we left behind. Huginn and Muninn cooed a synchronous "Hello" while Sleipnir whinnied and brayed. Heim tended to the creatures, feeding them items from his pack and sneaking the horse some sugar cubes from a small pouch he pulled from his pocket.

"Jorm said something about Loki getting his ship ready," I mentioned as we sat for a much-needed break.

Friggs's voice was like ice. "Naglfar."

"The ship of the dead," Heim added.

Naglfar was a mighty warship. It was crafted entirely of the toenails and fingernails of dead giants. The idea was repulsive, and my mind conjured images of a yellowed, fungus-rotted vessel floating on a churning, foaming sea.

"Yeah, it's disgusting." Helene scrunched her face in a look of utter distaste.

"No kidding." I patted the pouch at my waist. "At least we have Freyr's ship."

"We may have the ship, but we need more than that," Heim said. "I think it may be time for us to visit Vanaheim."

"Yes, Heimdall. I think you are correct. We need to see Njord." Frigg's gentle countenance was becoming more and more rigid, her maternal nature morphing from nurturer to protector and creating an ache for my mother. The wind picked up, swirling the sweet scent of patchouli and praline through the air. My mother's love surrounded me. She was always with me. I took solace in knowing that I had Frigg in physical form and my mother in spirit.

"Why do we need to see Njord? And… when did he go back to Vanaheim?"

"He is the god of the sea," Frigg explained. "We will need his blessing to grant us safe passage if we are to bring a fight to Loki by boat. He returned home many centuries ago, long after the Vanir–Aesir war ended.

"Vanaheim is both near and far." Her words were cryptic, but I didn't mention that, lest I annoy her. "The isle is not on Midgard because it is not of this world. There is a spot in the middle of the sea that will allow us entry. Let's go. Quickly."

The urgency in her voice pressed everyone into action, and just like that, our short reprieve was over. Heim helped me mount Sleipnir while Helene and Frigg hopped on the giant ravens. We rose from the ground, the beasts twisting and turning through the trees gracefully until we flew high above the blanketed forest. We flew west, directly toward the ocean that lapped lazily toward the shore.

The salty air overtook my senses again, the scent filling my nose with its brine. When the animals dipped toward the water, I suddenly understood Frigg's near and far statement. We were flying directly toward the water at a pace that seemed far too fast. I opened my mouth to scream as Heim's grip on my waist tightened.

Frigg lifted a fist, and her voice boomed, "Skor!" Just before we hit the surface, she released something from her open palm.

The water beneath us suddenly split. Waves tore from each other and reformed above our heads, creating a tunnel along the seafloor. The deeper we went, the darker it got. In the murky wall of water beside me glided a giant blue whale. It hummed a deep, melancholic, and chilling tune. It was yet another surreal sight, but Sleipnir and Heim's steady arms grounded me.

Spray from the ice-cold water sprinkled over my face, and my body involuntarily shuddered. The ocean was endless. The darkness chilled me to my core. And a sense of dread caused a chill to skate down my spine, stealing the breath from my lungs. I tried and failed to draw in air, choking. Heim attempted to soothe me, rubbing a hand over my back in light strokes, but it was useless. I was afraid of the dark. My body betrayed me, allowing fear to invade my consciousness.

Everything went numb as the panic rose. I was going to pass out. I could feel the lack of air taking its toll.

A word flitted through my mind, and I opened my mouth, allowing it to form before I could faint. "Sigel." The word came out soundless, but my magic allowed the rune to take shape in the silence. White light, like Thor's aura, bloomed in the abyss. My body relaxed, and I could see the others ahead of us flying through the murky tunnel.

A new fear quickly replaced the prior ease of my anxiety. I could see… everything—creatures that no human should have ever been able to witness. Prehistoric beasts larger than a whale roved the deep waters, their eyes cloudy white. They resembled sharks but with limbs that protruded from beneath them like amphibians. Their long tails swished from side to side, propelling them forward, and rows of teeth the size of school buses hung from their jaws.

The giant sharks surrounded us, their cloudy eyes drawn to the light of my magic on all sides. One got so close that its giant tooth slipped into the tunnel, and Sleipnir twisted, narrowly avoiding collision. My panic set in again, fear of the unknown overtaking me. The sharks picked up speed, swimming around in a frenzy. What had gotten into them?

Heim physically winced, and I turned my head to see what caused his pain. His shoulder bore a jagged, bloody tear. The razor-sharp tooth had grazed him. Oh, my gods, the blood! The creatures must have smelled it because they were feral. Hungry.

One of the giant sharks' eyes was trained on Heim. It saw prey, and it was on the hunt. The predator swam fast, gaining on us. Heim wrapped me in a protective hug, and I screamed. Just as the creature was about to break through the tunnel and devour us whole, I closed my eyes tightly, wishing we were anywhere but about to meet our death. Water splashed my face, and I prayed to drown before feeling the pain of those teeth biting into my skin.

Frigg's strong voice yelled, "Skor!"

"Vala, open your eyes," Heim coaxed gently. There was no pain, and I said a silent thanks to whoever allowed me to succumb to death so quickly.

"Heim, I am so glad you passed with me."

His arms were still wrapped around me, but his grasp loosened. "We are not dead, Unnasta."

"Wait, what?" I opened my eyes. We were on a shoreline, and the ocean spanned miles behind us. A deserted island. Beyond white sandy beaches was a lush rainforest that covered a tall peak and went on as far as the eye could see.

An elderly man, sculpted with muscles that were impossible for someone his age and a long white beard, walked toward us. He carried a trident in one hand and a conch shell in the other. He brought it to his lips and blew, creating a bellowing call. "Hello, Vala. Welcome to Vanaheim."

CHAPTER TWENTY-SIX

Njord, the god of the sea, had piercing blue eyes, and in his gaze, I saw kindness and quiet strength.

"Hello, Njord." Frigg bowed her head slightly, and he returned the gesture.

"You look well. My wife will be pleased to see you."

"Ah, Skadi. How I have missed her all these years."

The two gods turned and began walking through the white sand, their footprints leaving a path. They spoke only to each other, but Frigg lifted a hand and beckoned for us to follow.

"What the Hel just happened?"

"Well, Heim got a boo-boo and almost got eaten by a shark, but we made it just in the nick of time," Helene mused. "See what I did there? Because you got *nicked*?"

"Helly, stop it! I literally thought we were dead!"

"Well, you *literally* aren't…" She bumped her hip against mine and winked.

"Helene…" My friend side-eyed Heim but continued walking, giving us a moment. "Vala, I am okay. It was just a scratch. I dislike that path to Vanaheim, but desperate times called for desperate measures."

I raised my hand to his shoulder, using my magic to heal the wound. "What is skor?"

"Skor is the sea," he said between gritted teeth. Once the injury was fully closed, he breathed a sigh of relief and inter-laced his hand in mine. "I am sure you heard Njord mention his wife, Skadi, to Frigg. They have been friends for centuries. Vanaheim is the most difficult realm to travel to, so long ago, Skadi gifted Frigg a sea stone. It grants the owner safe passage." Heim waved his arm to encompass the stunning island.

We followed Frigg and Njord's footsteps as they traveled further up the beach. As we approached the forest, their sandy prints morphed into dense depressions in the moist soil. I looked around, taking in the towering palms and lush undergrowth. In the wind, birds sang joyously, harmonizing with the deep chirrups of rainforest frogs. The hot sun was a blanket of warmth, filling the air with sticky humidity.

Along the damp path were bright red hibiscus flowers sprouting yellow stamens. Technicolor dragonflies flitted about, emitting a happy buzzing sound. I was too invested in my surroundings to think of silence. Not being lost in my head for once was a welcome reprieve.

The gods stopped to let us catch up.

"Njord has offered to take us to Skadi's home so that we may rest. We will discuss the business of our visit soon, but first, we must recharge." Frigg continued walking. "It is a bit of a hike to the top."

"I thought we were going to recharge," I muttered quietly, intentionally speaking my thoughts out loud, but Frigg did not answer.

The path to the peak was steep and lined with large, slippery stones. I tripped many times, and Heim held onto my hand to keep me from falling entirely, lifting me with each misstep. Helene chuckled, and I tossed her a glare over my shoulder, just to almost trip again.

"The rocks are deterrents." Heim's voice was even, setting my anxiety on edge. He didn't seem phased by the treacherous hill, and I became self-conscious when I realized I was the only one struggling.

"Deterrents…from…what?" I gasped.

"From enemies."

"I must be… the worst… kind of enemy." I sucked in a gulp of humid air and ran a hand through my sweat-soaked hair. "I'm… deterred." Heim chuckled, never fully releasing my arm. I wasn't mad about it.

We finally made it to the summit, and the view was almost worth the grueling workout. Before us was a panorama of island perfection; the trees faded from hunter-green to lime, and the beach surrounding the island glittered in the sun, contrasting greatly with the cerulean-blue sea. Behind us was a cliff that rose to an angular jutted point.

A weather-worn house sat nestled into the cliffside, almost like it had merged with the rock. The thatched roof was yellowed with age, and the outer walls were constructed of the same smooth stones I struggled to hike on.

"Beautiful," I whispered, taking in the three-hundred-and-sixty-degree view.

"Yes," Heim replied, gently tucking a fluttering piece of hair behind my ear. "You are."

A blush stained my cheeks instantly.

"Heimdall is correct; you are lovely, Vala," stated a tall, fit, androgynous woman I hadn't noticed. Her smile reached her warm brown eyes, softening her features and allowing me a glimpse of the femininity hiding behind her mask of neutrality. "I am Skadi. Come in, come in, and make yourselves at home."

Skadi paused by Njord's side. They were the same height, gazing into each other's eyes with flirtatious affection. She kissed his cheek and whispered something in his ear. The couple laughed about their shared secret, teasing each other as they entered the home. They were adorable. Heim looked at me and attempted his odd wink, and I swear, had I not already been falling for him, I would have tumbled into the deep well of emotion at that moment.

Skadi's hands waved enthusiastically as she guided us through the house. She showed us all her guest rooms, assigning one to each of us as we passed. They had comfy-looking beds that boasted fluffy down comforters and plush pillows. The comfortable living area had a worn leather wrap-around couch that just begged to be sprawled upon, and the dining room was stocked with exotic fruits in decorative bowls atop a large, hand-carved table.

The last room she took us to was at the end of the house, where the main structure joined with the towering cliff. Two heavy, insulated doors opened to a cavern lined with smooth rock, slick with dripping water and moist moss. Billowing steam from a natural waterfall sprinkled us in a feather-light mist, and the scent of fresh falling rain melded with damp earth reminded me of a summer rainstorm in Central Oregon.

"This is where we bathe. It is my favorite room."

"Mine, too," said Njord teasingly. Skadi looked shocked for a second, gently elbowing her husband in the ribs. Those two were clearly in love, and it was all I could do to tame my blush as Heim's hand snaked around my waist.

"You, sir, need a shower," I joked, looking up at him.

"I think we all do," he said, obviously missing my flirting. I was second-guessing my attempt when he yawned, making me realize belatedly how tired we all were.

"I would like everyone to make themselves at home. Shower, have dinner, and rest. We will discuss the reason for your visit in the morning," Skadi instructed.

I could not argue despite my need to resolve everything at once. My body betrayed me, sagging with sleepiness and the need to be clean. Everyone headed to their respective rooms; mine was painted in shades of teal and tan. It reminded me of when my parents took me to the Oregon Coast and how the colors seemed to blend with the sea beyond.

A giant bay window offered me an uninterrupted view of the island. I curled on the bench, watching the orange sun sink into the horizon. Its aura seeped into the sky, surrounding it and melting into fuchsias and Tyrian purples. I heard footsteps behind me but kept my gaze locked on the enchanting scene. Arms wrapped around me as I was pulled against a large, warm body.

"I know the last few days have been hard," Heim whispered into my hair. "I am impressed with your ability to adapt to our world, Vala."

"Well, I don't have much choice, do I?" The words came out bitter; the acidity tasted wrong on my tongue. "I'm sorry. I'm just exhausted, filthy, and incredibly overwhelmed. I am trying, though."

"We see you, Unnasta. You will succeed. I have no doubt."

"Thank you, Heim," I whispered as a hot tear slipped down my cheek. With our hands entwined, he gently pulled me up, fully enveloping me in a hug I hadn't realized I desperately needed.

"Come with me."

"Where are we going?"

"I would like to wash your hair… if you would let me," he answered timidly, pulling back from our embrace. The look in his eyes was uncertain and shy. Was he asking me to shower with him? Would that mean we would be naked? Together?! Just the idea of it invigorated my exhausted body with a plethora of nerves.

Fear clashed with desire as I yearned to feel his hands tangle in my hair, massaging and cleansing me.

His eyes met mine, and I knew he sensed my internal battle. He started to step away, cautious and… hurt. I grabbed his wrists, pulling him closer to me.

"I would… like that very much," I stuttered nervously. "But… I don't want you to see me… naked."

He grinned from ear to ear and reached into a pocket, withdrawing a long piece of black cloth. "I suppose I should have started with this…" His words eased my coiled nerves until we reached the shower room. A new wave of anxiety crashed into me, building with each step toward the waterfall.

I was about to shower… with a man.

CHAPTER TWENTY-SEVEN

Water spilled from the rocky cliff and bounced off the floor, soaking our legs. Heim reached for the hem of his shirt but stopped short to stare at me with a question in his eyes. I nodded, and he peeled the dirty garment from his body in one graceful move, revealing his incredibly defined abs and muscled back—tattoos and all.

His hands slowly went to the button on his pants, but he stopped again, awaiting my response. My breath caught in my lungs.

"Are you okay?" His voice was rough and deep.

"Ye-Yes. Are you wearing anything under those jeans?" The question brought heat to my cheeks, a brutal reminder of my naivety.

He gave a gentle laugh. "I am. And I plan to keep them on… if that's your concern."

"Okay!" I didn't mean to sound so relieved, but damn he was making me nervous. He took my breath as an allowance and pulled the jeans off, freeing his strong legs. Seeing him so… naked broke some rational part of me. He was beautiful, like a Greek god.

Oh, wait, what was I thinking? He was like a Norse god. He *was* a Norse god.

I closed my eyes tight, shaking the silly thoughts from my mind. When I opened them again, I was met with a view of his back glistening with water droplets. Heim held a hand up, clutching that piece of cloth from his pocket.

"I need your help."

I stumbled closer, realizing yet again how tall he was. If I were to lean in and wrap my arms around him, my head would rest between his shoulder blades. I wanted to do that. Instead, I grabbed the cloth and leaned on tiptoe to wrap the blindfold gently around his eyes. My body pressed against his back as I tied the loose ends, knotting them, and he let out a soft groan.

"Too tight?"

"No," he said, a little too quickly. "Not at all. It's just that your body is so warm and very close."

That broke my fragile restraint, and I did what I wanted. I leaned into him, wrapping my arms around his waist, closing every gap between us. His skin radiated soft heat, and I melted into him, allowing my head to rest between his shoulder blades. We fit perfectly. A small moan of contentment left my lips, the hum sending a tremble through Heim's body.

"Take off your clothes, Unnasta." Heim's voice was raspy and thick. At my sudden intake of breath, he reassured, "I can't see anything, and I promise I won't look."

I nervously followed his instructions, letting my zip-up sweatshirt slip from my shoulders and fall to the floor. I peeled off my sweat-stained shirt and unbuttoned my jeans. Heim hissed a ragged breath through his teeth. He couldn't see me, but the sound of me undressing made us both start to unravel. After I dropped the pants onto the pile of grimy clothes, I stood there, self-conscious, in just my bra and panties.

An internal battle to remove the remaining articles of clothing was waged within my mind. Ultimately, I chose to keep them on. I could not be stark naked in front of Heim. Not only would that be mortifying, but also not something I trusted myself with. I adored him, and whenever we were alone, my body craved him. My human nature longed to take over, but I couldn't allow that. I was not that kind of girl, and despite not knowing his past, I knew he was different with me.

"I'm… er… I'm ready," the words stuttered from my mouth, tripping on the way out. I gripped his hand to pull him toward the water and was pleasantly surprised the downpour was warm, and the pressure was like a gentle stream raining down on us. We breathed a sigh of comfort, and I opened my eyes to see his giant form slick with water. His linen shorts clung to his body, and it took considerable effort not to stare at his visible bulge; my curiosity tried to get the better of me, but that wouldn't have been fair unless I were willing to reciprocate.

I lifted my palm to his chest, resting it above his hammering heart. He covered my hand with his, turning my body so that he was behind me. We just stood there for several moments, allowing the water to wash away the past few days.

"On the ledge is a bar of soap. Can you hand it to me?"

I turned to look at Heim, assuring myself the blindfold was still in place. It was, so I reached for the soap and placed it in his hand. My body went rigid as he began rubbing it between his hands, building a lather.

"I can feel you looking at me," he teased gently. "Turn around so I can wash your hair."

"Yes, sir," I laughed. My humor was quickly waylaid by his hand snaking around my waist. He pulled me back, still far enough that our bodies did not touch but close enough. He reached for my hair, and goosebumps immediately rose on every inch of my body.

He ran his hands gently through my long hair, using his fingers like a comb. Once he lathered every strand, he massaged the bubbles into my scalp. Holy Hel! Every atom of my body awoke. It was the most delicious feeling I ever felt, and my eyes involuntarily closed. A moan escaped my lips unintentionally, and his hands tangled in my hair, pulling me a little bit closer.

The water grazed my back as he pet my head with delicate strokes. I never knew having someone wash my hair could be sensual and intimate. He gently pulled me back under the spray, pushing the soap from the top of my scalp down. The frothy mixture tickled my body as the bubbles fizzled, some popping and causing an overload of sensation as they slid along my skin. My breath halted as his touch traveled to my shoulders.

"Is this okay?" He gently stroked down my arms and back up.

"Yes." I reveled in the feel of his hands exploring. All too soon, they left my body, and a lonely chill swept over me. A fire that spread from my very core quickly replaced that feeling when Heim put his hands high on my waist, right below my bra. His large fingers sprawled across my ribcage, pausing their movement completely.

"How about this?"

"Y-yup." He roved my midsection, grazing my belly button but never going any lower. The soap made his palms slick, allowing them to glide seamlessly over my skin. Every cell in my body was on high alert. His breath came out in ragged pants, and it was gratifying knowing I wasn't the only one affected. He turned me around again and leaned in to kiss my forehead before dropping to his knees. He caressed my waist, paused at my hips, and then continued exploring my legs.

"And this?" His warm breath tickled the flesh of my abdomen, sending shivers up my spine. I nodded, forgetting that he couldn't see me. "Answer me, Unnasta."

"Oh, gods, yes." He let out a sultry laugh and kissed my stomach. My abs tensed beneath his lips, and he trailed the path of my tightened muscles with his mouth. Meanwhile, his hands ran up and down my legs, washing the stress away with each passing touch. I tangled my hands in his wet hair, attempting to leave the blindfold in place.

When the sensations became too much, I sank to my knees, yanking the soap from his hands. I lathered it between my palms and flattened both on his chest. It rose and fell in deep breaths, and his heart pounded beneath my touch. I moved to his hair, slowly hooking my fingers beneath the blindfold. His hands flew to my wrists as I started to pull on the material.

"Vala," he choked.

"Shhh," I breathed into his ear, lifting the fabric completely. I pulled back and looked into his emerald eyes. He stared directly into mine, unwilling to break his resolve. I lifted his hand to my neck, placing it beneath my collarbone. "Look… please."

His eyes pleaded with me, but his gaze finally dropped to where his palm rested, and his pulse quickened even faster. His gaze toured my body, and I watched intently for his reaction to each new landmark.

"Beautiful," he murmured.

I finally left his hand resting on my hip, returning the favor by washing the parts of him I could see. I lathered his stomach, arms, legs, and hair. As the last bubbles of soap rinsed down his body, I placed my hands on his face.

"I trust you," I stated with a newfound confidence. I leaned in and kissed him, abandoning all modesty as I tipped my head to deepen the connection. His mouth met my fervor, tasting my need and tracing light circles around my back. The slight touches sent shocks of energy through me.

Suddenly, the doorknob jiggled. I pulled back from Heim, sucking in the humid air. His eyes were feral, darkened with lust.

"Vala, hurry up and get out of there! It is my turn to shower!" Helene's voice boomed through the closed door.

"Oh, my gods." I jumped back from Heim, immediately rushing for one of the plush towels hanging on the nearby wall. I wrapped it tightly around myself and yelled, "Be right out, Helly!"

Heim just stared at me, water cascading down his beautiful body, and it was all I could do to not jump back into his arms.

"Heim, I need you to be very quiet," I whispered, unable to break the gaze that held my own.

"I can do that, but I need you to turn around." His hands crossed over his lap below his hips. Heat blossomed under my skin as I put two and two together and instantly spun around to face the wall. His footsteps sounded behind me, and I saw his large arm reach over my head to grab another towel.

"How are we going to get out of here?"

"Come on, you two! Get the Hel out of there… now!"

Heim's laughter enveloped me as he leaned in and said, "I think, Unnasta, that we can just walk out."

CHAPTER TWENTY-EIGHT

Heim stood behind me as I flung the doors open. Helene jumped back in shock with an astonished laugh. My protector chuckled, and I slammed my elbow into his stomach, causing a satisfying whoosh of breath to leave his mouth. I grimaced at my friend.

"Stop it with that face, Vala. You look like Lucius Malfoy!" Helene barked. I gasped exaggeratedly, bringing my hand to my open mouth. She gave me a once-over, pausing at the bra straps visible above the towel, and then glanced at Heim. "I expect you to tell me everything."

"What happens in the waterfall room stays in the waterfall room."

"Young adults, it is nearly time for dinner," yelled Skadi from the other room. "Hurry up and get dressed.

Heim walked away with an obvious swagger toward his room. When he reached the door, he looked at me and half-winked, making Helene and I break into a fit of giggles.

Lying on the bed in my room was a simple, flowy linen pink dress. Pink was never my favorite color, but the pastel hue reminded me of the sunset. I slipped on the garment, admiring how the fabric felt on my skin. It was soft and smooth, cool to the touch where I'd been so hot only moments before.

As I relished the feeling, I thought of Heim and how he felt on my skin. Being near him—with him—was a rush. I read books and watched movies about people falling in love, but I never understood why they called it *falling*.

I was buried alive before I met him. All my grief, awkwardness, and jokes made at my expense were handfuls of soil people kept throwing on my grave. Then, he found me. He reached his hand in and broke through my figurative coffin, letting the light and air seep into my being. The emotions he stirred in me lifted me out of death and into life. I yearned to live. With him, I finally could.

A knock at the door interrupted my chaotic thoughts. When I glided over and opened the door, I was instantly face-to-face with a clothed Heim. I took his hand, and we walked to the dining room together. It was certainly a plus that I was a self-proclaimed foodie because each new table I encountered in the realms produced offerings that instantly made my mouth water.

Skadi and Njord's table had goblets of ice-cold water, condensation dripping from each glass, and a large wooden bowl with rising steam sat on a woven trivet in the middle. The smell of the broth combined with sprigs of fresh basil and scattered bean sprouts reminded me of my favorite Vietnamese restaurant back home. I also saw chunks of tropical fruit and slices of warm bread with coarse pink sea salt freckling the browned crust.

We joined Frigg and Skadi, who were already busy eating and gabbing between sips of soup. The way they acted together reminded me of Helene and me. I glanced around for Njord, but before I could ask where he was, Helene walked in. Her hair was wet, and her dress—a pastel purple version of mine—clung to her body.

"Why are you still all wet?" I asked, feigning innocence.

"Because someone… or should I say *someone's* decided to use all the allotted shower time for themselves."

"Believe me, Vala. I know how easy it is to lose track of time in that shower," Skadi commented nonchalantly. She made an *oof* sound, and Frigg glared at her. She must have kicked her under the table. I turned several shades of red. On top of getting caught, Skadi had just admitted to using the shower for the same—if not worse—purposes. Gross.

I glanced at Heim, who was also, thankfully, a deep shade of red beneath his beard. I was glad we were in this state of embarrassment together. Attempting to change the subject, I tried to grasp the question I sought pre-mortification. "Where is Njord?"

"He doesn't live here," Skadi stated as if it were the most natural thing to say. "His home is down the hill, next to the bay."

"But why?" I hoped my question didn't come off as rude. I was just incredibly curious.

"Well, when you have been together as long as we have, sometimes space is necessary."

"Oh, yeah. I suppose that makes sense."

Skadi looked at Heim and then at me. She appeared wise beyond her physical years, and her next words proved that. "If I could give you any advice, my dear, it would be to keep things fresh. When things become too normal, relationships tend to go awry. We are curious, creative, and caring and must foster those traits. We can also become callous, cold, and comfortable. We must strive to avoid those. I call it the rule of Cs."

I nodded. It was sound advice. It made me realize I was not *falling*. To fall is to move downward. With Heim, I only went up. He fostered my curiosity by allowing me a glimpse into himself, leaving plenty more to find out. He gave me a safe space to practice my magic, allowing my creativity to grow. He was there for me anytime I needed him, caring in a way I didn't know I was missing. I could jive with Skadi's rules of Cs.

We ate and chatted until Helene's mouth dropped open in a large yawn, and the older women urged us to head to bed. None of us argued. We dragged our feet, zombie-walking our way to our rooms. Between the travel and the food, we were exhausted.

When I got to my door, Heim kissed me goodnight, and I stepped into my room. The curtains rustled in the sweet, salty breeze drifting through the cracked window. I curled onto the big bed, closed my eyes, and fell asleep immediately.

I awoke in the morning before the sunrise to the sound of talking. I could pick out Njord and Skadi but didn't recognize the others.

"Why are they here, Njord?" questioned a deep, masculine voice.

"I told you, she hasn't asked yet, but I would venture to guess that it has something to do with Loki."

"We need to get rid of them fast," another interjected. "The sea is swaying. This hasn't happened in centuries."

"I know, my friends. I will not let their presence here cause any harm to come to any of you."

They continued to discuss our visit, some arguing with Njord about getting rid of us. Others—including Skadi—tried to reason with the group. I rose begrudgingly from the comfortable bed, dressed quickly, and snuck down the stairs just as the original man started to argue with Njord about helping us.

"I'm sorry, but we just need Njord to grant us a blessing of safe passage for our impending battle with Loki." My words were direct but polite, making all the eyes in the room turn toward me.

"Vala, I apologize that we woke you," Skadi said. The gods' people stood all around the room, adorned in lightweight linen attire with thick braids plaited down their backs in dense ponytails. Each of them wore a necklace made of white shells. The adornments reminded me of my dad and his puka-shell days. My mom told me he wore them back in his popped-collar-going-to-marry-Kelly-Clarkson era—aka the early two-thousands.

"I am not sorry," the man stated stubbornly. "Our ocean connects to yours, and it is angry. We have lived here in Vanaheim, untouched by the outside world, and as soon as you and the others stepped on our shores, the seas became enraged."

The supporting presence of my friends appearing behind me gave me courage, so I spoke again, "We intend no ill will to come upon you or your families. Njord, as the god of the sea, we need your assistance. Freyr gave me his ship. A fellow Vanir entrusted me with his gift. Can you please help us?"

"You have Skidbladnir?" Njord's gaze dropped to the pouch on my belt.

"I do."

He turned toward his people and spoke with authority. "Vala is destined to rewrite our history. Her gift will allow us to continue in the peace we have created." His arms spread wide, as he turned to me. "I shall command the wind and the seas to bend to you and yours. In exchange, you must proceed with your task and save this realm."

"I promise I will do everything I can to save Vanaheim." I nodded my thanks to him and the others. Skadi smiled at me, but there was worry clear in her gaze. I turned and saw a similar concern in Frigg's eyes. Heim and Helene, on the other hand, were proud. The next words that left my lips sounded far more ominous than I intended, "I suppose it is time to prepare for Jorm and Loki."

CHAPTER TWENTY-NINE

A few hours later, we stood on the sandy beach near Njord's home, the ocean rolling wildly behind us. Vanir came down from the foothills of the rainforest. They snuck out between the trees carrying loads in their arms or on their backs. Some brought us food, others brought weapons and armor. With each new gift, we said our thanks. The Vanir were decent people, but they were scared. I could not fault them for that.

The pouch at my waist felt heavier each time I thought about our quest. It was nearly time to use Freyr's gift, but I still wasn't sure how to. I opened the pouch and pulled out the cloth to admire the craftsmanship.

The ocean reacted; tendrils of waves snuck up the shore like liquid limbs reaching toward my ankles, making me startle. The shock changed quickly to delight when the salty spray tickled my skin. The water turned to mist, sending flurries of droplets raining down on me. Some splashed onto the handkerchief, soaking into the material.

The wind caught the damp cloth, whipping it around in the breeze until it stilled, suspended in the air before me. The moistened spots burst with amber light, sending beams of color across the beach and making the white sand sparkle. Suddenly, I knew what I must do.

I snatched it from the air and ran toward the sea. Heim hollered my name, but I was too excited to pay attention. As I approached, the waves pulled me closer like outstretched arms preparing for an embrace. When I stepped into the low tide, the bottom of my water-logged jeans became heavy. If this worked, it would be worth the uncomfortable, sticky feeling of sopping denim. I bent over, fully submerging the handkerchief.

Amber light exploded from the tide as a loud, cracking sound rent the air. I stepped back to watch the fabric transform into curved planks of oak timber, each panel creating a new overlapped layer of a massive hull. Unearthly snapping and clicking sounds drowned out the waves as iron rivets were magically drilled in neat vertical rows to hold the wood in place. The keel followed, creating an ornately chiseled spine-like bond down the hull's center, and the stern sprouted a devilish wooden tail with meticulously carved prongs.

On the bow, an elaborate dragon's head took shape. Its brow was sharp, its nostrils flared, and its open mouth bared long, pointed teeth—a perfect image of rage. At least a hundred long oars dropped from each side of the ship, and above each rested an iron shield painted a different color. The longship was ready for battle.

A towering mast grew, adorned by a burgundy and white striped sail that billowed in the wind like Steve's beer belly after a night of heavy drinking. Tight, thick ropes angled down from the mast, tying off at various sections of the hull.

There she was—Skidbladnir—in all her glory.

"Isn't she spectacular?" Njord's voice was filled with awe as he stood by my side in the water. I hadn't heard him approach.

"Yes." The tumultuous waves smacked against the starboard side, which towered at least twelve feet tall. The rhythm sent the boat rocking back and forth. "Hey, Njord. This might be a stupid question, but I'm curious. How are we supposed to get on board?"

He smiled at me and snapped his fingers. In less time than it would take to blink, I found my feet planted on the flat bottom of Skidbladnir as she swayed. Beside me were Heim, Frigg, and Helene, along with our animals. Stacks of supplies were nestled between each or lining the starboard and port sides of the ship.

The sea god remained in the same spot; his trident raised high. "Vala, I give you and yours my blessing of the sea. May the wind carry you safely and swiftly. May the waters be calm and the waves be your guide. May the beasts of the depths become friend and not foe. In this time of need, I send my power from high above and the deep below."

After his blessing, Njord dipped the tips of his trident into the sea. Threads of rich cobalt surged from the tines into the ocean, heading straight for us. The tendrils of his magic climbed the ship walls, steadily wrapping the deck and everyone on board in a glittering royal blue hue. Something tickled my nose, and when I reached up to scratch the itch, I noticed my hand was sticky with paint.

I gazed in awe at my companions; each bore a unique painting on their faces. Frigg's art was all thin lines, an elaborate interlacing of runes stretching from one ear to the other. Helene's paint was a deep indigo mask that covered her eyes, making her hazel irises pop. On her forehead was a single rune. She held two fingers in a peace sign, placed them at the top of the mask above each eye, and dragged them down to smudge the color onto her cheeks. The result was vaguely intimidating yet alluring.

I turned to Heim and watched as fingerless magic painted a labyrinth of runes that stretched diagonally across the right side of his face. Thick, swooping circles wove around feather-light runes, capturing their safety within. The image was stunning. One rune was a common theme amongst all of their markings—the laguz.

"I know how curious you are, Unnasta. I can see in your eyes that it's killing you to view us but not know what covers your beautiful face. Let me show you."

Heim pulled a mirror from his bag. Yup, I knew it was definitely enchanted. I mean, who carries around a mirror the size of a box of cereal on everyday excursions?

When I glanced at my reflection, I nearly dropped it in shock. I wore a mask, but unlike Helene's, mine was shaped like an eagle. Its body and head, which were filled in with white laguz and algiz runes, rested along the bridge of my nose and forehead. Thousands of wisp-thin runes created the outline of every intricate feather, and from the tips of each spread wing, paint dripped down my face.

"Wow," was all I could mutter.

"Njord's blessing. He sends us with the protection of the laguz," Frigg stated. "Now, hold on."

The sea rose, lifting the longship from the shore. We all stumbled back as Njord blew wind directly at the boat, pushing it toward the open ocean. The water began to circle like a slow-draining bathtub and gradually gained speed and intensity, becoming a whirlpool.

As we sailed toward it, I latched onto Heim, suddenly terrified of the unknown. Njord would not cause us harm, would he? It seemed unlikely after all the trouble he went through allowing us in his realm. I glanced back at the shore to see Skadi and the Vanir waving at us; their words carried on the wind. "Goodbye, Vala."

As the bow tipped forward and fell into the spiraling water, we all collectively shouted our goodbyes—mine was probably a little hysterical, and the longship dropped into the deep.

What happened next was unexplainable. It was as if we were simultaneously falling and motionless. The sensation was like traveling through the root system but not as chaotic. The whirlpool swallowed us whole. We were upright, then nowhere, and finally upright again.

On the other side, the boat swayed in the same, gentle way, but the ocean was different. Angry. The island was gone, and the sea stretched for miles. The water was darker, a menacing shade of midnight blue, and there was turmoil in the sky.

Grey clouds pulsed, sending down streaks of white lightning. Thunder rolled so loud that I could feel it throughout my body. The storm made an ominous feeling settle in my gut.

"Do you feel that?" asked Frigg, her voice carrying despite the noise. We all nodded. A sudden chill hit the air, and goosebumps rose on my arms immediately. Rain poured out of the darkened clouds, violently slamming into the ocean, but nothing touched us. The showers slid in angry rivulets down a protective ward around the boat and into the waves below.

"What is happening?"

"Naglfar is rising." Cold dread washed over us all at Heim's menacing deduction. We knew it was coming. It was why we were there. But the knowing didn't remove the foreboding of what was to come.

"Njord's blessing is protecting us…" Frigg pointed at the invisible bubble that enclosed us, her gaze locked on the horizon. "…for now."

"As it was written in the Völuspá—the final prophecy—so it is supposed to happen," whispered Helene. She looked at me with confidence that I longed to soak in myself. Warmth spread across my body as our invisible bond poured her as-surance into me.

"I need to see it."

Frigg pulled a rolled-up scroll from one of the crates, and we kneeled on the deck as she flattened the worn parchment. Sprawled across the page were the words of the prophecy, the truth I was so desperately trying to bend to my will.

I waved my hand above the parchment and watched the ink glitter and float upward. The words swirled in the air, a literary ballet. I guided them toward me, using my hands to usher them closer. I opened my mouth as if it were second nature and devoured the words that tasted like magic, sizzling and sweet. They sank into my being and became part of me. I closed my eyes, and the prophecy began to play out in my mind like a feature film.

Heimdall blew on an S-shaped horn that resembled a curled antler as we stood at the base of the Bifröst. The trumpet was so loud that the earth shook beneath my feet, making the Yggdrasil tremble. From my vantage point, I could see each of the nine realms as if the veil that hid them from Midgard lifted.

Giants left the forests of Jotunheim to wander the realms. The light elves scurried about in panic while the dark elves chaotically organized their forces. The Aesir sat atop the Yggdrasil, looking down upon the mayhem while murder-ous fire giants rose from the fiery pit of Muspelheim. They stumbled across the earth, dripping magma with each step.

Each footfall left a singed impression along the previously undisturbed ground.

Beyond the land, the ocean churned. Violent waves crashed against the shore, growing larger with each crest. The seas parted on the horizon, and from the depths emerged a massive ship, faded and worn to a grayish yellow with ridges, like a mycotic nail. Its tattered black sail swelled in the wind despite its many punctures. A giant man stood at the bow with a large shield, his roars echoing throughout the realms.

My vision flickered, fading in and out like a bleary-eyed dream. I saw flashes of the scene.

A shadow under the sea slithered to the surface.

Darkness.

The water surged upwards as Jörmungandr burst from the depths.

Darkness.

Evil laughter erupted as Jörmungandr's eyes clouded over, turning milky white.

Darkness.

Red smoke rose. Red hair floated in the wind. Red eyes gleamed in the darkness. Red blood spilled, filling the sea.

CHAPTER THIRTY

I opened my eyes. The vision was gone. In its place was the storm, pounding on the protective shield with a newfound might. Skidbladnir had sailed a great distance in the time my eyes were closed. We were now in a wide channel where towering cliffs stood proud on either side despite the relentless waves crashing against the rocks.

Beyond the bow, the clouds bunched into a giant mass that acted like a vacuum, sucking the rain and ocean water upward. From the abyss rose blood-red smoke, creating an eerie fog.

From the mist burst forth longships manned by crews of putrid, discolored giants. The sheer numbers of the fleet that sailed toward us filled me with terror. There were so many of them.

A massive, ornately carved dragon head made from rotting ivory rose behind the fleet of cadaverous giants as another ship surfaced from the depths. The giant I saw in the vision stood at the helm, his shield rusted and covered in barnacles.

"Who is that?" I asked loudly, trying to hear myself over my pounding heart and the terrified animals onboard; Huginn and Muninn took to the sky, circling the air above us.

"Hrym." Heim placed a gentle hand on Sleipnir, calming the horse. "He is the leader of the fire giants cursed to Muspelheim, those who were murderers and wrongdoers. The lost souls were banned from Valhalla and shunned from Hel, sent to burn for eternity in the realm of fire until Hrym called them to action."

"If he is the leader of the fire giants, then what are those dead-looking creatures in all the longships that seem to be pointed directly toward us?"

"That is Loki's undead army, sent from the depths of Hel."

Why did Hel allow them freedom? It was a valid question, but there was no time to ponder it, so I set it aside. "I don't think we can do this alone. There are so many of them." Heim lightly kissed my lips before pulling away to march toward the stern. He pulled out a long, curved horn from his bag, just like the one in my vision.

"Cover your ears, Vala," yelled Helene. I followed her instructions, but nothing could have prepared me for the piercing sound that resonated from the horn. It was a wailing, melancholic moan that reverberated through my entire being.

The sky parted, and from the clear, blue patch of sky flew a winged horse carrying Thor clad in Viking warrior attire. His hands, covered in heavy iron gloves, were wrapped steadily around Mjolnir, and a thick leather belt was buckled around his bare waist. Odin's ravens soared around him, cawing their greetings. The god's white aura bathed the eerie fleet of undead giants in light.

"Finally! I thought you would never call," Thor thundered. He dropped from his horse onto the deck, clearing the shield with no issue and rocking the boat with his weight. Huginn and Muninn dropped down to rest on his giant shoulders.

"Where is Father?" Heim inquired.

"He is rallying the troops, awaiting a further call of distress." The brothers nodded at each other in silent communication. "What are we dealing with?"

"Naglfar," I stated, watching the main enemy ship slowly rise from the belly of the sea. It was so large that only half of the keel had breached the surface. Everything seemed to be happening in slow motion. Even the ships carrying the undead halted in the water as if they were magnetically pulled by Naglfar.

After several minutes, the Naglfar finally surfaced fully. The exterior was exactly as I had envisioned, a truly disgusting abomination that was made all the more revolting because of the tendrils of red smoke seeping like blood across the deck, through the oar holes, and down the wooden sides.

Loki's vibrant red hair floated wildly in the wind despite the torrential downpour that wreaked havoc across the sea, and his evil smile was wide and maniacal.

"Hello, Vala. How I have missed you, Lítilvölva," his voice whispered right next to me. I whirled around to punch the vapor that wafted in the air and was only rewarded with an echoing evil laughter that mocked my efforts. The trickster god's next words sounded far away but were still crystal clear: "Are you ready for this, little girl?"

"By the blood of the Boddason name, I have never been more ready, *old man*!" I shot back with a seething growl of rage. Loki reappeared on Naglfar, right where he'd been before. A conniving smile was plastered to his face as he stared straight at me. Despite the distance that separated us, I could see the wild glee in his red-rimmed eyes.

His arms lifted to the sky in supplication. "Rise, my son!" Loki's voice carried across the channel, slamming into me like a battering ram. The sea knocked us from side to side; Sleipnir's hooves scratched across the deck as the beast tried hard to remain upright. I risked a peek over the ship's rail, gazing into the inkiness of the deep as the long, dark shadow of Jorm surged upward.

The force of his assent set more waves in motion. Tsunami-sized swells crashed into the cliffs, the force splitting the rocks bit by bit. Large boulders broke off and fell into the sea below, sending opposing waves back into the channel. Skidbladnir quaked; our protective shield was the only thing keeping the ship upright.

Jorm's giant head broke through the surface near Naglfar, his yellow eyes filled with pained remorse.

"Vala, I'm sorry..."

He continued skyward, slithering around his father's ship. Loki reached out to touch his son's scales, and red smoke twisted around the giant snake's body—a corruption. Jorm's eyes blinked slowly. When they opened again, a milky white film stained his retina.

The snake's mouth opened wide, revealing long, sharp fangs that dripped with pus-like venom and a tongue that flicked in and out as he hissed. The sound vibrated throughout the realm, instilling a sense of fear in me that the Jorm I knew was gone. The creature that caused such chaos was just Loki's monster. I clutched my belt, ensuring Angrboda's potion was still safely tucked within the pouch.

Skidbladnir and Naglfar lurched in the storm—a standoff of sorts, and Huginn and Muninn returned to the sky. Loki was staring at me again, peering into my soul. Hrym remained still and silent. Thor and Heim glared at them, their natural fierceness creating a palpable force that Helene, Frigg, and I stood behind, ready for whatever was to come.

"Ganga," Loki's voice rang out. "Go!" Jorm disappeared.

The mindless snake appeared above us in the blink of an eye, slamming his protruding fangs down into the force field. The shield held strong until a trail of venom seeped from Jorm's fangs, splintering whisper-thin cracks across the surface. I barely held back a scream as the protective barrier broke like glass.

"Vala, get back," Heim ordered. He barreled into me, and the clink of the potion bottle escaping my pouch sent a shock of instant panic down my spine. It rolled across the deck, my arms grappling to reach for it to no avail, as Jorm's head dropped to where I had been standing. His fangs punctured the deck, leaving two large, splintered holes in the wood when he pulled back.

The reality of Jorm's possession hit me. The Jorm I knew would never hurt me, but he wasn't here anymore. In his place was Loki's monster, the child of a trickster god who was treated as no more than a tool to do his bidding. I needed to get to the bottle.

A bright light burst before my eyes, and Jorm released a pained hiss as blood poured from a fresh wound on his side.

"No!" Thor began to harness another lightning bolt. "Don't hurt him!"

"Vala, he tried to kill you!"

"I don't care. It's not him. I made him a promise, and I won't break it." The ship tossed back and forth again, sending the bottle careening across the deck. How could I keep Jorm at bay without hurting him and buy myself time to retrieve the potion? Before I could concoct a decent plan, the longships started advancing toward us... quickly.

"Oh, my gods, there are so many of them!" Helene cried.

Jorm writhed in the water, his jerky movements stirring the waves. Despite the never-ending displacement of the ship, Heim managed to stand and raise a newly acquired bow with a nocked arrow, aiming right for Jorm's eye while the ravens circled the other, talons and beaks at the ready.

Power pulsed within my chest, fueled by overwhelming fear for my friend. Golden light radiated from my body as I lay slumped on the deck after losing my footing for the millionth time. As if he had read my mind, Heim lowered his weapon right before I recalled the word I needed to utter to quell the beast, if only for a short while.

"Isa!" I cried the same word my father used to freeze me all those years ago and understood at that moment the pain it must have caused him. Hot tears spilled down my cheeks as Jorm's body grew cold, ice spreading along his scaly back and across the bleeding wound like stitches, staunching the spilling ichor. He became rigid as a statue as the hoarfrost spread like wintry branches of the Yggdrasil.

There was no way to tell if his entire form was frozen under the sea, but I had served my purpose. The venom that dripped from his fangs froze into long, spiny icicles. He was safe—for the moment. The ship steadied a bit, and I scrambled toward the potion bottle, scooping it up before a wave could knock me to the side again. I slid it back into the pouch, tightening the leather straps down before glancing up in time to see an oncoming troop of giants.

The longship closed in, releasing arrows to anchor onto Skidbladnir. Thor jumped back as one hit the deck. It narrow-ly missed his calf, and he cursed as another nicked his bicep.

The ropes attached to the arrow shafts became taut. The giants were climbing onboard.

Thor swung Mjolnir at a giant as its hands grasped the edge of the deck on the port side. Its head was swept clean off, landing with a dull thud beside me—a torrent of inky blood sprayed from the gapping neck cavity like a gruesome water fountain.

Heim ripped the arms off another giant with his bare hands, tossing the limbs behind him carelessly. His opponent roared in pain and fury as his lifeblood seeped from the ragged stumps of his shoulders. Sleipnir used his eight legs to buck and kick, leaving clear hoof impressions on those who got too close. The giants' blood mixed with the rain and painted everyone and everything in violent crimson streams.

Njord's words—and those terrifying ancient sharks—flooded my mind. *May the beasts of the depths become friend and not foe. In this time of need, I send my power from above and deep below.*

As the men continued their brutal assault on the giants that attempted to board our ship, I ran to Frigg's side. Hot, sticky blood covered us from head to toe that even the rain couldn't completely wash away. The ichor ran in rivulets, painting the deck burgundy beneath our feet.

"We need to summon the sharks."

A look of confusion quickly followed by understanding crossed Frigg's face. "Oh, blood. We need more blood!"

"Helly, help us!" Frigg and I hurried around the deck, tossing all the dismembered body parts over the side. We fell to our knees and used our hands to push as much of the dark red sludge overboard as we could, turning the water around Skidbladnir a sickly blackish red.

"Vala, I know this might seem like a stupid question, but how do we know the sharks won't attack us as well as the giants?" Helene's question was—for once—asked without any edge of sarcasm.

"We don't. But I feel like Njord's blessing will protect us. At least, I hope it will."

Scattered limbs littered the bloody ocean around us like chum. Long moments stretched with no change, but just as I thought the plan wouldn't work, I made out a ragged dorsal fin in the distance. Another grazed the surface, heading straight for one of the longships. It popped out of the water, devouring the entire boat in one large bite. Whatever remained sunk to the abyss. Screams filled the air, a chorus of woes, a serenade of sorrow as the shark attacks became frenzied.

The surviving giants became fiercer in their assault, angry at the loss of their ranks. Hrym roared a deep bellow that shook the crumbling cliffs, but Loki was visibly filled with sinister jubilation; even across the channel, it was obvious by his crooked smile. The cliff faces quaked and split. A jagged chasm, gleaming with a fiery orange glow, formed on either side of the channel.

Red lava spilled from the rock like the very earth was bleeding. Everyone froze, including our foes, as the rubble shifted. A hulking, fiery head seemed to coalesce from the magma: eyes, ears, a nose… and a long, jagged crack opened wide with a vicious roar.

CHAPTER THIRTY-ONE

Glowing eyes. The giant was made of molten magma. Its body was humanoid like the other giants in Jotunheim, but it was more like what my mind originally thought of when I conjured images of "giants." Huge. Fully formed, the fire giant lumbered from the chasm and climbed the rocky wall to the ridge above.

More fire giants emerged from the lava, forming a unified inferno on either side of the channel. Hrym hummed a pleased sound that carried on the wind. His army stood ready and waiting for their leader's command. Even the sea stilled.

I stood frozen, afraid to make any sudden movements. Despite our daunting adversaries, Helene's gaze was steady and unwavering, and Frigg's rose-pink aura encompassed them both in a cloud of protective power. Thor's face was a mask of pure hatred, and his furious stare was directed entirely at Loki. Our creatures were restless with rage. My gaze drifted to Heim last, and his eyes were glued to mine.

"Vala! Get out of the way!"

I barely registered his mouth moving before the wind was violently knocked out of me. I stumbled, and the backs of my legs caught on the side of the boat, my momentum throwing me overboard. I threw my hand out, clawing at the wood paneling for purchase. Blood dripped from torn nail beds as I held tightly to a loose rivet that jutted from the overlapping hull. The rusty metal bit into the skin on my palm, but I refused to succumb to the pain.

The ocean beneath me churned into a boiling roil. I fought the urge to look down, knowing that my steadily dripping blood was undoubtedly attracting the same sharks that had helped us only moments before. Helene may have been right about the sharks not understanding whom they were fighting against. A small whimper escaped from my lips when water splashed on my dangling legs as a massive shark jumped from the sea, jaws wide and ready.

A hand reached overboard, wrapping tightly around my wrist. I grasped the forearm firmly and felt a strong tug lift my body, narrowly missing the sharp teeth and an impromptu leg amputation. The beast splashed back to the ocean below as I flew onto the deck, falling onto a raggedly breathing Helene. I grabbed my best friend in an awkward embrace, still holding her arm in a death grip as silent sobs racked my body.

"I've got you, Vala." Her token phrase wrapped around my heart like a bandage, compassion magic seeping into me and filling my soul with calm ferocity.

I rose, pulling her up and into a quick hug. "Thank you, Helly." When we broke apart, I found the cause of my stumble. A smoldering hole in the deck close to where I had previously stood. A large, round hunk of steaming coal rested on the level below.

A rosy glow encompassed the entire ship, rebounding incoming huge spheres of fire into the sea with ear-popping sizzles. Frigg stood on the bow, hands outstretched to maintain the force field, but her body quivered, and a light trickle of blood dripped from her nostril. Her power was taking its toll.

I closed my eyes and lifted my arms, drawing from Heim's protective power and allowing my magic to join Frigg's. Helene stood behind us, placing a hand on each of our backs to reinforce our efforts. Our auras combined into a shimmering rose gold, casting a stronger shield of protection and alleviating some of Frigg's strain.

"Thor, we must call reinforcements!" Heim's voice boomed. "The ladies can't keep this up. It will deplete them."

"Already done, little brother." Thor smiled wryly, still focused on Loki in the distance. He held a small rolled-up parchment toward the sky, rubbing the material raw between his finger and thumb.

Huginn and Muninn have sent me your message. Help is coming.

My eyes darted to the sky; the ravens were nowhere to be seen. Thor must have sent them to Odin when I fell overboard. *Thank the gods.*

Loki's eyes were heavy with rage. As if he knew what was coming, the trickster god looked at the sky. Thunder rumbled, and lightning cracked. From the gray clouds rained a barrage of flying horses carrying winged women. The Valkyries had arrived.

They flew in a linear V formation, guided by Freya herself. The fire giants let loose their cannons, aiming at the ethereal warriors. I watched in horror as one of the women toward the back of the ranks was knocked from her horse after a fireball went straight through her abdomen. She fell from the sky and into the dark sea. Dorsal fins quickly surrounded the fallen warrior, tearing her lifeless body limb from limb.

The army of winged women drew their glinting weapons and charged toward the fire giants. Upon impact, Freya swiped her gleaming sword through one of their necks. Magma spewed from the end of her blade as its head rolled down the cliff and into the sea. Another woman leaped from her horse, wings unfurled to catch the air current as she ran her spear through a torso.

As the Giants and Valkyries fought, I reached for Frigg, pleading with my eyes for her to release her magic as I dropped my own. She hesitantly obliged, lifting her sleeve to her nose to wipe away a steady stream of blood. The sound of battle was overwhelming, but the giants were no longer focused on us.

I needed to get the potion to Jorm, and it seemed as good a time as any. I turned to check that Loki remained on Naglfar, but he had once again disappeared. Oh, my gods, where was he? A trickle of foreboding ran down my spine. I ran to Heim. I would not let Loki kill him.

My protector reached for my hand, twining our fingers together and setting off his tattoo and emerald aura. Knowing that he and I were protected, provided we were together, filled me with confidence as I drew in borrowed magic, seeking guidance and power from my people to avoid Loki's wrath.

When I opened my eyes, I viewed the world through Odin's sight. Instilled with his wisdom, I could see differently. Movement was tracked in light, and a red glowing thread weaved around Heim's body, trailing toward the stern and a sardonically smiling Loki.

"Did you think it was going to be that easy?" His voice was like sharp metal, intended to slice me to my core. His next words dripped like poison, meant to sting and burn. "This is far from over, *Lítilvölva*."

Loki wrapped his legs around the tail of the wooden dragon and threw his body over the side. With an agonized scream, flesh and muscle tore apart as his body elongated. Under his smooth skin erupted rough, red patches and scales. His arms and legs twisted into thick, cracking stumps with sharp talons. A long scaly tail with a spiky knob on the end, like a flail, grew from his spine. His face, which was once hauntingly beautiful, morphed into something truly monstrous with a long snout, red reptilian eyes, and a wide mouth full of razor-sharp fangs. His long back cracked and split as spiked, translucent crimson wings unfurled.

Loki the dragon soared into the air, his screams of agony turning into a primal shriek of rage. He nosedived, spewing flames from his mouth that danced above the water and melted the hoarfrost imprisoning Jorm. The ice cracked and broke off in chunks as the snake started to move. The chaos between the giants and Valkyries still raged, and with Jorm's awakening, the situation didn't bode well for us.

I glanced at Thor, who looked frightened. *The prophecy.* If I didn't figure something out, the snake was destined to kill the god of thunder. His body alone could sink our ship.

An idea dawned on me, and I clumsily stumbled toward Heim. My face slammed into his chest as I tripped on a piece of splintered deck. "Heim, I will do anything to keep you—everyone—safe."

"Vala." He said my name like a plea. A prayer. Worry filled his eyes, but his hand sprawled on my back, pulling me closer.

"Just so you know," I whispered into his ear. "Ek ann per… too." My words took on life, tying us together in a hot pink embrace. His hold tightened around me as he released a breath like he'd been holding it for generations.

I leaned up to kiss his lips softly before stepping away from the man that I was, without a doubt, in love with. Thank the gods that it was raining because I didn't want him to see me crying. I quickly removed my belt and pouch and handed them to him. His eyes flashed with frustration and understanding, but he finally tucked them into a pocket in his pants.

"Thor, I have an idea, but I need you to promise to steer clear of Jorm, okay?" I yelled over the crashing waves.

"I planned on it!"

"What is *your* plan?" asked Heim.

"I need to get the potion to Jorm, but I don't think I can get around Loki as a dragon in my human form due to these damn waves. I could use some help."

Our little group moved closer together, forming a small circle as everyone laid a hand on me, allowing their magic to spill into my body through their touch. Thor's strength, Heim's protection, Helene's compassion, and Frigg's guidance coiled with my magic. In my mind's eye, I drew from Odin's eagle.

I looked around the circle, and each of them stared at me with awe and wonder.

"Vala, your eyes," Helene whispered.

"What is wrong with my eyes?" I briefly allowed my insecurities in, even though I knew what they saw when they looked at me. I could feel the mighty bird unfurling within and knew my eyes resembled Odin's eagle eye when he bestowed his gift upon me.

"There is nothing wrong with you, Unnasta." Heim cupped my cheek. "You are perfect. You are ready."

I let his words of love and support build my confidence. I channeled all the emotions that swirled within and sacrificed myself to them. Urgency struck my chest as Loki's pointed tail whipped against the ship with a resounding crack.

"I have never felt strong. I've never felt like I could help anyone in need. I was a broken, lost soul with only one friend in the whole world." A tear escaped as my truth spilled out. "But then you all found me. You spoke life into me with your words. If there's any way for me to help right now, it can only be done on the wings of a word because yours are what saved me. Let me use mine to save you."

My aura exploded, covering the people I loved in a blanket of golden illumination. I strode confidently to Sleipnir and easily pulled myself onto his back. I bent down and whispered into his ear, letting him know my plans, and he whinnied in response. Glancing one final time at my friends and family, I declared, "I love you."

We took to the sky high above Skidbladnir. The sea spanned beyond us, and the war lit the channel in a macabre glow. Sleipnir steadied himself midair, and I carefully stood on his back. I brought my hands together, palms touching as if in prayer as words fell from my lips in a succession of hope. "Arnar. I'm ready for you, eagle."

Like a glittering amber ribbon, they shrouded me in a golden cocoon of power.

Then, I dove.

CHAPTER THIRTY-TWO

Sensation coursed through my body as I plummeted from the sky. Fear, hope, need, and love enveloped me. I closed my eyes, confident that my power would transform me. Without sight, the sting of my insides rearranging tore through me with unrelenting agony. The unnatural cracking of bones snarled within. A metallic, bloody flavor filled my mouth, and the salt of the ocean stung my nostrils as I got closer and closer to the roiling waves.

I opened my eyes, and everything was sharper. The view of the world around me was crisp and new. I saw wings where once there were arms. I spread them wide, extending each plume; the soft brown feathers were flecked in gold and layered like downy armor. The wind caught me before I hit the water, and I flapped my new appendages, gracefully soaring upward.

I almost allowed myself to forget the destruction around us as I reveled in the freedom of flight. I was never before so alive, so powerful. No wonder Odin chose an eagle for his other form.

My eagle was much smaller than Loki's dragon, and if a dragon could sneer, I swore he did. He flew quickly toward me with a wildness in his gaze. I drew my wings inward, gracefully diving away from Sleipnir, and the dragon followed. When Loki bobbed, I weaved.

Heim stood on the deck with his hand lifted high, and something flashed in the darkness. The potion bottle. I swooped low, flying as fast as possible so that Loki wouldn't get too close. I grabbed the glass bottle in my beak, my wings softly grazing Heim's face as I drifted upward, heading away from the ship. The dragon closed in behind me, his pointed wings loudly dragging along the side of Skidbladnir as he changed course.

As Loki neared, he released a stream of flames. I dodged, barely avoiding a burn to my tailfeathers in the nick of time. Below us, the waves tossed so hard that the ship tipped from port to starboard, water cascading onto the deck with each tilt. Jorm's large body was fully free of ice. He could squeeze his body like a constrictor and smash Skidbladnir to bits if he chose to.

I circled with Loki on my tail and watched the scene unfold below. Heim pulled a stubborn Thor behind him as Jorm tangled around the ship. Frigg and Helene stood behind the two men, guarding Thor's back with their combined magic. Across the channel, giants and Valkyries spilled blood and lava with metal and flames. It was chaos, death, and destruction all rolled up into one bloody battle. A distraction. Thank the gods that we were in a remote area of the world. No harm would come to humans, nor would they witness the brutal violence.

Loki was gaining on me. Flames licked along my feet and legs, and my beak opened with a pained shriek. The bottle slipped out and plummeted toward the ocean. My heart stuttered in my chest, and I dove down, catching the bottle in my talons as misty saltwater tickled my feathers. I flew upward.

A pang of fear sent a shockwave through my body. Jorm's head was above the water, his cloudy eyes darting between Heim and Thor like a predator stalking his prey. In my distraction, Loki's talons tore into my wing, throwing off my flight pattern. I rolled helplessly through the air as the snake struck out at Skidbladnir. Loki then used his enormous tail to whip me sideways, sending me into an awkward corkscrew tailspin.

My head screamed at me as Jorm lunged again. His teeth left splintered holes across the deck. I *needed* to get close. I pulled my wings in, diving toward the serpent as his wide maw opened, preparing to strike again. His head dropped, his sharp teeth nearly grazing Thor's body when I flew directly into his large mouth.

I squeezed the bottle between my claws until it shattered. Shards of glass sliced into my legs as the magical liquid seeped between my claws and onto his tongue. Human hands wrapped around my feathered body and yanked me out before Jorm could close his mouth.

He pulled his head back, retreating from… what? The magic? Jorm's body quivered, the milky color of his eyes bleeding out like ghostly tears. Bursts of silver light popped around him like fireworks as his body moved away from the ship, involuntarily creating waves that rolled toward the rocky cliffs. I perched on an oar to watch as Jorm's body slowly shrunk.

His eyes, which had returned to their serpentine hue, stared into mine. The ocean convulsed as he seemed to wither away, becoming smaller and smaller. Loki flew above us, his dragon raging. Fire burned in waves as he flew around the ship, spewing more flames with each pass.

As Jorm's body dwindled, I lost sight of him within the haze despite my sharpened eyesight. *"Vala, help me, please."*

I took flight again and spotted Jorm entwined around one of the abandoned ropes that infiltrated our ship earlier. The waves crashed around him, causing him to slip toward the sea. I dove, barreling toward my falling friend.

My bones began to crack midair. What was once a graceful glide turned into chaotic convulsing as my human body warred within the eagle, demanding freedom. The transformation finished just in time for me to scoop up Jorm, flinging him upward toward Heim's outstretched arm before heaving in a deep breath and crashing into the misty red sea.

The water was icy and hot, stilling my body completely while incinerating it from the inside. My mouth opened to scream, and air bubbles vacated my lungs, stealing the little oxygen left. My legs were useless, dangling below me like solid blocks of concrete. I felt like an anchor sinking into the deep, unknown abyss. My eyes squeezed shut as the light dwindled.

"Vala, open your eyes," my mother whispered in my mind.

My eyes stung from the salt water. I was surrounded by darkness, but my wrist was warm. The bracelet dimly glowed, illuminating my surroundings and leading me toward a pocket of brighter light just ahead. Despite the pain, I kept my eyes open as I used my arms to propel myself forward. My body hurt all over as I exerted energy with no air, slogging through the heavy liquid toward what I hoped was my salvation.

I was nearly there when a bony hand extended from the light, reaching out for me like death calling me home. I could feel my body failing me, and I accepted my fate. At least one of the prophecies was stopped before my life was snuffed out. My eyes closed again, and as the light faded behind my lids, a strong tug on my arm pulled at me.

"It's alright, Val-Ball." My dad's gentle timbre filled my mind with peace. *"You must open your eyes."*

"Quit being melodramatic, Vala," reprimanded a familiar female voice. "Now, open your eyes."

I slowly lifted my lids, one at a time. Air rushed into my open mouth, filling my hungry lungs as I took in the sight before me. I was standing in Hel.

"What! How?"

"My father truly outdid himself this time." Hel untethered Garm's leash, and the giant wolf stalked toward me. I shrank back, afraid of his intentions. "Do not fear Garm, Vala. You have reversed the second prophecy. For that, he would like to bestow upon you a gift."

Wait, did I? Jorm was free from Loki's control?

The massive wolf stepped closer to me and abruptly stopped. He stretched his front legs out, chest low, and leaned down on his elbows. Garm was bowing to me. I gave a curt nod, and he rose. His large head nudged my hand, and I ran it between his ears and down his neck as he nuzzled his face into my ribs.

Garm rose to his full height. The creature was significantly taller than me, but I was suddenly no longer afraid. When the wolf lifted a paw, I stared incredulously at it.

"He wants your arm," Hel stated as if I were insolent for not understanding what the wolf wanted. I reached my hand out, and he gracefully used a single claw to slice an odd-looking Z into the skin of my forearm.

"Ouch!" I winced and pulled back. Tiny droplets of blood rose from the thin laceration; it stung more like a papercut than a jagged tear of a wolf's claw.

Hel gently grasped my arm, slowly grazing her bony hand over the wound. The flesh wove together beneath her touch, leaving behind a pink, puckered scar. "Eihwaz."

"Eh, what?"

Hel smiled at my question. "Eihwaz. It is the rune for immortality. Repeat after me, Vala: Eihwaz."

"Eihwaz." The word burst out of my mouth like lightning, striking the scar and infusing it with a glowing opalescence. Invigoration flooded me. I was strong, healthy, and so alive. Garm gazed into my eyes and bent his head, giving the shining scar a single lick. My nose squished, and a giggle bubbled up in my throat. "Thank you, Garm."

"Garm has bestowed the gift of immortality upon you for your willingness to save us all." Hel cupped my cheek, pulling my head up to look into my eyes. "You need his gift for what my father has planned next. You must remain calm, Vala, and take a deep breath."

"Wha—?"

"Now. Breathe, Vala!"

I sucked in as much air as my pained lungs could hold, then the world went dark.

CHAPTER THIRTY-THREE

My eyes opened to the same watery darkness Hel pulled me from. I was flat on my back, floating just below the waves. Red mist filled the air my lungs craved for just above the surface. I could hear the muffled sound of Helene's voice screaming my name at the sea. Bubbles floated nearby, and I turned my head to see Heim swiftly swimming toward me. He wrapped one large arm around my waist and proceeded to drag my limp body to the surface.

We broke through, coughing up water and dragging in deep gulps of air. Heim's arm never loosened around me as he used his strong legs to swim toward Skidbladnir. Loki's dragon still soared above, circling and spewing flames.

"Where. Is. Jorm?" The question came out fragmented between coughs.

"He is safe. Duck!"

Heim pushed my head underwater, using his body to weigh me down as Loki let loose a stream of flames where we bobbed like buoys. We resurfaced and swam to the ship as a rope was thrown overboard; Heim's arm remained fastened around my middle as he grasped it tightly. Frigg and Helene hefted the rope hand over hand, pulling us to the safety of the deck.

I was livid. Loki had caused nothing but destruction, and the giants had taken the lives of so many Valkyries—although the winged women had nearly won the battle. I unleashed my anger, allowing it to come to life with a single word. "Algiz!"

The word gushed from my mouth in a furious rush of power. Rivulets of golden magic rose around us, covering the entirety of the ship in a solid encasement of protection. Tendrils of energy continued upward, lighting up like fireworks splashing across the sky above the raucous North Sea.

Orbs of gold surrounded each warrior on our side, encasing them in an impenetrable covering as the battle continued. One by one, the fire giants fell, slashed down by the swords and spears of the Valkyries. My power rose fresh and alive. Words stirred under my skin, longing to be spoken or written.

Numerous people I came to know as friends and family told me I was Völva. But only in the middle of war did I truly grasp the magnitude of the Seiðr magic coursing through my veins.

Above us, Loki rammed repeatedly into the protective shield. His wings flapped violently, smacking against the glass-like structure I had created with a single word.

"Is everyone okay?"

My gaze shot to Frigg, whose expression was a mask of profound sadness I had only witnessed when she spoke of Baldr.

Helene, who knelt beside her, carried a beautiful brown and gold snake with yellow eyes coiled around her wrist—Jorm, and her left hand held onto something under a bundle of blankets.

I scanned the deck, searching. *No. No, no, no.*

"Where is Thor?" I asked, fearing the answer. No one spoke, but Heim interlaced his fingers in mine, and Helene whispered something unintelligible to the bundle before her. I ran toward my friend and dropped to my knees. She was holding a large, calloused hand. I gently pushed back the pile of blankets and gasped.

Thor's skin was white as snow, with black veins, like tributaries, covering the expanse of his body. His breathing was labored, coming out in short, sputtering bursts. Poison. How had it happened? Hadn't we fought so hard to stop this result from coming to fruition?

"Val… a. I see… you…finally found… yourself," he choked out, his carefree personality attempting to lighten the mood with a forced smile.

"What happened?" Helene continued to hold his hand, obviously siphoning his pain using her gift of compassion. Her stamina was weakening, though; the color was visibly waning from her cheeks. Knowing my best friend, her strength was less important to her than his comfort.

"Just before you flew into Jorm's mouth, one of his fangs grazed Thor's shoulder," Frigg explained somberly. "It was not a bite, but because of the wound that was already there, venom found a way in. He fell right after you did."

Jorm untangled from Helene, slithering around my arm. His head rested on my bicep, and I swore I saw a droplet form and slip from his reptilian eye.

"*I am sorry*," he hissed sorrowfully. He had shrunk to about three feet long and was as wide as a broom handle. I lifted my arm to gaze into his sad yellow eyes. He was bewitchingly beautiful.

"It is not your fault, Jorm. You had no control." Resentment boiled up as I bit out, "Loki did this."

The dragon pestered us relentlessly, setting my nerves on edge. I looked at the sky and glared in his direction. There was a twinkle in his eye. Thor's injury *pleased* him. He flew down, directly across from where I knelt and snorted gleefully. Thor grunted in pain as the poison tore through his veins, traveling toward his weakened heart.

"There must be something we can do!" I placed my hands on Thor's shoulder and said every word I could think of to heal his body. Cobalt-tinted tears slid down my cheeks as his breathing grew shallow. Heim knelt beside me, wrapping his arms around my shoulders. "Uruz. Heal. Uruz! Heal!"

"Vala, even you cannot change this. There are certain parts of the prophecies that, once they begin, cannot be stopped." Heim's voice was gentle and soothing, but it infuriated me that he was ready to give up on his brother. Anger and agony coursed through me as I shoved him away and bent my head to rest on Thor's big chest. His heartbeat was faint beneath my ear. Bile rose in my throat.

"There are some things that words cannot take back or give us." Frigg's voice rang in my mind. The truth of her words gutted me. Fresh tears of understanding and acceptance sprang from my eyes as I lifted my head and grabbed Thor's other hand, holding it gently.

Damn it, Frigg. I don't need your wisdom *right now.*

"Can you… tell Sif… I love her?"

"Of course." I tucked his matted hair gently behind his ear. "You became my brother, Thor. Thank you for reminding me to embrace the radiance of life." I pulled back and softly kissed his icy cheek, smiling in response to the ever-cheerful grin he wore like a badge of honor.

"Frigg. Will… will you sing my favorite song?" Thor pleaded; defeat glazed his gaze as his smile faded into a thin line.

Heim retrieved his bag and pulled out a lyre. He began to pluck a tune, a hauntingly lovely riff. Frigg gently touched Thor's cheek and began to sing along. Helene joined in, harmonizing perfectly.

"Drømde mik en drøm I nat um silki ok aerlik pael." The translation weaved its way around us, her voice like a salve. "I dreamt a dream last night of silk and fancy fur."

Thor stared at the sky while Frigg's melodic voice drifted through the air. His breathing slowed, and his eyes lost their light. Suddenly, yet peacefully, his chest stopped. Frigg moved her hand from Thor's cheek to gently close his eyes for the final time. Thor was dead.

CHAPTER THIRTY-FOUR

Thor was wrapped in the blankets Helene used to keep him comfortable in his final moments. We worked silently, pulling his lifeless body to the bow of the ship.

"We will take him home to Asgard," said Heim. "He will be prepared for a proper burial."

I owed my protector an apology for shoving him away. He had not looked me in the eye since then, and I worried I hurt him more in his time of need. Thor was his brother. No matter how much my own heart ached, his pain must have completely ravaged him. Helene must have felt my emotions and deduced what I needed because she held her arm out for Jorm, allowing the snake to carefully spiral around her wrist.

I cautiously stepped in front of Heim, wrapping my arms around his waist and resting my head against his powerful chest. I hadn't realized how much I needed him to be safe and okay until then. I reveled in the strong beat of his heart against my ear, delighting in the movements of his chest as he breathed in and out.

"You saved me from the ocean, and then… I…" When he started to speak, I interrupted before he could get a word out.

"I'm sorry, Heim. I'm so sorry." I didn't even say what I was apologizing for, but his hands wrapped around me, pulling me closer to rest his chin on my head.

"You have nothing to be sorry for, Unnasta," he murmured.

"No, but he does," Helene commented, staring at the dragon.

I looked beyond the trickster god toward the cliffs. All that remained of the fire giants were chunks of charred earth. The Valkyrian army hovered mid-air in a line atop their steeds, the rise and fall of their wings undulating in perfect unison. Sleipnir was positioned proudly beside Freya, awaiting a call to action.

"Why are they not protecting us from Loki?" I asked, dumbstruck. An entire army could surely take down a single dragon.

"They can't," Frigg stated.

"Why?" The repetitive smacking of Loki's claws against the shield grated at my nerves. I was tired of hearing him and didn't want him to overhear our conversation. "Silence!" Thank the gods, the clattering stopped.

"That was not part of their objective." Helene's face was still too pale, and her movements were sluggish. A renewed sadness washed over me as I realized I could no longer draw strength from Thor. I would have given anything to pour his resiliency into my best friend the way she selflessly took our pain from us.

"This is not the war, Vala. This was merely a battle to be fought," Frigg explained. "There are still prophecies to be undone, and the Valkyrie warriors know that."

I stewed over that, my mind racing with thoughts and ideas. Even if we won this battle, Loki did all he could to break through our barrier. He was out for blood, and I was safely assuming he craved mine the most.

"It is unlikely that he will shapeshift any time soon. He knows he has the advantage of being larger than any of us," I deduced. I considered calling Odin's eagle but remembered his warning that it was not something that would last long. Even so, my eagle was too small to cause any real damage to Loki's dragon. Suddenly, a thought occurred, and the name flew out of my mouth. "Nidhogg!"

"Badass," marveled Helene; a smirk played on her lips. Nidhogg was the most legendary reptile in Norse mythology. He fed on the corpses of criminals and the roots of the Yggdrasil. He was an enigma because he displayed the head and body of a dragon, but his tail was long and thin with a rattle at the tip. When his mouth opened, his forked tongue could stab a man clean through, and then Nidhogg would incinerate them with his flames.

"Nidhogg is unpredictable," warned Heim.

"That may be true, but I think Vala may be onto something," Frigg mused. She looked at Helene, staring at the serpent she wore like armor, and a genuine smile spread across her face. "Jörmungandr, you can speak into Vala's mind, correct?"

"*Yes.*" I nodded, a physical show of his internal response.

"Can you speak into the mind of a fellow reptile?"

"*Yes. I will do whatever I can to avenge Thor.*" I repeated his words to the others.

"I think we may have a fighting chance of escaping a watery grave."

Jorm would call Nidhogg using his telepathy, and Heim gave an unknown signal to the Valkyrian army that dismissed them to Asgard. We did not want them harmed during what would surely be a precarious fight. Loki had no clue what was coming for him thanks to my silencing spell, although the dragon demonstrated the good sense to seem alarmed when the winged army retreated, leaving only him, Hrym (who did nothing without his army, who were all dead), and us.

The rain stopped, and the ocean settled back to the normal to-and-fro of open-water waves. Loki hovered above us, methodically swishing his wings with a look in his eye that made me think he was considering a plan to break through our defenses.

"*He's coming.*"

As soon as Jorm spoke the words in my mind, a shadow passed over Skidbladnir. My chin tipped up toward the sky as a large creature flew above. Gleaming silver scales armored the extensive beast, and each sterling wing was as long and wide as our warship. The head of the dragon was much like

Loki's, except Nidhogg had long tufts of silken, white fur from the top of his head to his back, which swept behind him like a snowy mane.

His large legs tucked in close to his body as he flew, and the tip of his rattler tail dragged across our shield. I thanked the gods again for the silence because I knew that would have been ear-splitting. Loki's dragon eyes were wide with fear. He froze mid-air and glared at me. I raised an eyebrow, smirked, and pointed sassily at Nidhogg.

"Remind me to ask about that new scar when this is over," Heim murmured quietly beside me. I had nearly forgotten about Garm's gift.

"Jorm, did you communicate with Nidhogg about his role?"

"Yes, Vala. He knows only to aim for the red one."

Nidhogg leveled out, and his black eyes caught sight of his target. He was as intimidating as Hel, and he knew it.

"Remember, we are going to set sail when Loki is distracted!" Frigg yelled. "Everyone to their places!"

We scattered; the women went to the oars, and Heim handled the sail and the rudders. Skidbladnir could steer itself, but we weren't willing to take any chances. We needed to return the ship and Thor's body to Asgard safely. We stood at our stations, watching Nidhogg finally propel straight toward Loki. The red dragon swooped out of the way, but his smaller wings could not cover as much ground as Nidhogg's.

The sky became a blur of red and silver. Loki's only defense was size, and he used it to duck and weave through Nidhogg's attacks. As the dragons fought, we lifted the heavy oars and moved away from the raucous battle. My sights stayed set behind us, waiting for Skidbladnir to rise from the ocean and take us home. I glanced before me just in time to see Nidhogg's sharp claw rake down Loki's face. It slit from the crown of his head to below his jaw.

I uncloaked sound, craving the auditory satisfaction of his agonized cry. It was the least he owed us for ripping Thor from this realm. Every noise returned, and our ears were filled with shrieking roars and guttural grunts. Skidbladnir lifted into the sky, freed from the water. As the ship gained speed, Nidhogg opened his gaping mouth to suck Loki in and snapped his jaw shut. Had he just killed Loki?

Tufts of red smoke billowed out of Nidhogg's massive nostrils. He shook his head and released a fiery sneeze that sent streams of flame over the waters we hastily abandoned. High above the silver dragon flew a blood-stained white gull. It was so minuscule in comparison that it was no surprise Nidhogg either chose to ignore it or didn't even notice it. I knew it was Loki, but that didn't matter. I possessed one more plan of attack that was sure to be a blow to the trickster god's ego.

"Jorm, come here."

"Yes, Vala?"

I whispered to him and smiled as we watched Nidhogg change course and soar toward Naglfar, his long tail dragging through the ocean and making giant waves. The dragon opened his mouth and sprayed flames until the enemy ship—including Hrym—was a disintegrated cloud of ash sinking into the open waters of the North Sea. The last noise radiating through the realm before Skidbladnir picked up speed was the piercing cry of a wailing white gull.

CHAPTER THIRTY-FIVE

Skidbladnir passed over the sea, heading straight toward the Yggdrasil, and Nidhogg followed above us, his long tail weaving in the wind. Once we reached the world tree, the silver dragon dove toward the roots and disappeared into the underworld. The Bifröst spanned beneath us as we traveled the path toward Asgard. In the distance, I could see the people—my people—we left behind. In the center of the masses stood Odin with Huginn and Muninn perched proudly on his shoulders.

Everyone standing at the realm's edge parted ways as the giant ship crossed the threshold into Asgard. As the keel dug into the earth, we braced ourselves, slowing the boat as soil spilled in waves on either side of the bow. Clouds of dust plumed in the air, cloaking the world around us in a blanket of fine dust. As it all lightly began to drift toward the ground, we could make out the figures running toward us.

Odin materialized on the ship, transporting his large body from the ground to the deck in the blink of an eye. He took inventory of everything; his gaze wandered over each of us, ensuring we were unharmed. I saw the sadness strike as he stared at the wrapped blanket.

"Thor." The Allfather's voice was rough and dark with dismay.

The mournful wailing of a woman pierced the air. Sif. Sobs racked her body as she fell to the ground, screaming. Helene leaped from the ship, landing gracefully beside her. She wrapped her arms around the grieving wife, allowing her power to ease some of the pain. My stomach heaved at the sound of her pure sorrow.

Odin's gaze fell back on me, and the snake wrapped around my neck. Jorm watched him with caution, slightly retreating into my hair. I understood his reservations. After all, the Allfather was the one who originally banished the ouroboros to the depths of the sea. I touched his scales lightly as a sign of assurance. Odin's eye widened briefly, taking in my new scar, and he tilted his head to me in a nod of unspoken thanks.

"It was not his fault," I stated quickly, keeping a steadying hand on the snake.

"I know. I do not blame you, Jorm. Thor's death rests on Loki's soul. Not yours."

Jorm loosened around me, his tension unwinding. "*Thank you, Allfather,*" he hissed gently. Odin nodded. Of course, he could hear the snake.

"The loss of my son…" Odin glanced down at where Thor lay before looking at Heim. "…was a risk we understood.

To reverse the prophecy—which looks to have been success-ful—Thor died an honorable death. The death of a warrior."

Odin lifted Thor's bundled body as if it was as light as a feather. A tear fell from his eye as he disappeared from the deck and appeared on the ground below. Sif rose from the ground and touched the cloth. Silent tears spilled from her eyes as they both began to walk toward Odin's home.

"Where are they going?"

"They are going to prepare his body, Unnasta." Heim wrapped his arms around me from behind and placed a kiss on the top of my head.

"Vala, it is, unfortunately, time for another funeral," Frigg said solemnly. "But we do things differently than where you are from. Here in Asgard, the mourning and funeral process occurs for more than one day."

"What does that even mean?"

"It means that now is the time to get some rest." Her voice took on her maternal nature, slightly bossy but still caring. "Head to your rooms. Take a bath. Get some sleep. You will need your strength for the coming days."

Heim helped Frigg and me off the ship, his strong hands grasping ours and lowering us gently to the ground. Then he jumped down and knelt beside Helene. She looked exhausted; the color had drained from her face, and she was weak from offering too much of herself. He scooped her up in his arms, and I held her frail hand as he led us toward Valaskjalf.

Behind us, all the creatures of the realms that gathered to welcome us began to hum lightly. The tune was dreary and depressing but hauntingly beautiful. They were mourning the loss of Thor. The success of Jorm's freedom could not overshadow the monumental loss of Asgard's greatest warrior. Slick tears covered the soil in Asgard, leaving a soggy stratum of mud beneath the feet of the motionless mourners.

We entered the doors of Valaskjalf, where we were met by a group of women clad in flowing white dresses. Heim gently lowered Helene into the waiting arms of one of the women. The others circled them and began walking away, down the halls toward one of the guest rooms.

"Where are they taking her?"

"Those are the Völva healers," Heim murmured reassuringly. "They are taking Helene to her room to rejuvenate her body and soul."

"But I could have healed her. I could have…" My voice trailed off on a drawn-out yawn.

"Come, Unnasta," Heim laced his fingers with mine and pulled me toward my room.

I silently followed, exhaustion feeling like weights on my limbs. He pushed my door open and guided me inside.

"Sit." I obeyed, flopping down on the creamy chaise lounge and curling my feet underneath me. "I will be back in a few minutes."

I spread out on the couch, pulling a luxuriously soft fur blanket over myself. My eyes were heavy with sleep. I fought to keep them open, but I was overcome with the burden of their weight. I watched the light in the room fade as my eyes involuntarily closed. I hadn't realized how exhausted I was.

Sleep took me under, and dreams rose from the abyss of my mind. There was a nudge on my hand. I was suddenly standing by Garm. His wet nose nuzzled my hand, and I petted his large head.

"Thank you, Vala," said Hel. Of course, I would dream of her now. "For saving my brother." Jorm's body uncoiled from around my neck and wound into a ball at my feet. When I looked down, he was nowhere to be seen. I felt like I was in two places at once, curled up on the chaise with a sleepy snake coiled between my legs and also in Helheim, listening to Hel and cuddling Garm.

"He's my friend, Hel. And I think you are, too?" That last bit came out as more of a question than a statement. I was not afraid of her anymore.

"You have proven yourself worthy of our trust." She stroked her bony hand down Garm's back. He grunted gently at her touch and scooted into her legs, craving the attention of his master. The motion jostled the skeletal side of her body; she chuckled softly while stabilizing herself. "You are my friend."

"Why did Garm grant me immortality? And how does it work?"

"As long as the rune remains on your skin, Vala, you are safe from mortal death. I know my father. He dislikes feeling bested. He will be fuming from his loss."

"Yeah, I kind of figured that."

"I do not know how he will come for you, but rest assured that he will. He will not let this go easily."

"Thank you for the warning, Hel."

"Take care, Vala. Please give my regards to Odin for his loss." Her voice grew gentle, almost warm. Her last words were so low they were nearly discernible: "Do what you must to survive when he comes."

That shook me to my core, filling me with icy dread.

I was transported as a gentle swaying motion pulled me from my dream. The smell of juniper and leather embraced me. I lay swaddled in the safety of Heim's arms, my head tucked into his shoulder as he carried me. My eyes fluttered open, and his breath tickled the loose hairs across my face.

"Where are we going?"

"I ran you a bath, my love." My cheeks flushed. We entered the large bathroom, and a harmony of scents invaded my senses. Lavender, eucalyptus, and mint swirled in the air. The golden clawfoot tub was filled to the brim with gleaming bubbles and water that sent tendrils of steam to the heavens.

"Heim… I—"

"I have set out some fresh clothes, and one of the healers is ready at the door once you are undressed and submerged." He placed the softest kiss on my forehead. I loved that he knew

I wasn't ready to go too fast, too soon. I loved his respect for me. I loved him. He gently set me down before the tub and bent down to whisper in my ear, "Ek ann per, Unnasta. I love you."

I pulled my head back to look into his gorgeous emerald eyes. He towered above me, but it didn't stop me from standing on my tiptoes and burying my hands in his hair. I pulled him forward until our lips met. The kiss was soft at first but filled with need. His mouth on mine melted away every sour memory of the past few days. I finally understood what it was to need someone.

When his tongue slid over my bottom lip, I understood how two people could become intertwined. When his hands tightened around my waist, I grasped what it meant by being half of a whole. His gentle moan against my lips taught me why I never felt as alive as I did at that moment. Heim was my person. I always thought that was the lamest thing I had ever heard, but I finally understood. I didn't need him because I couldn't do things alone. I needed him because he complemented my power, allowing me the space to be myself while igniting a fire within me to be better.

"Heimdall." I gently bit his lower lip. "I love you, too."

CHAPTER THIRTY-SIX

Heim left me alone in the bathroom. I undressed and stepped into the warm bath. The steaming water and essential oils immediately relieved the tension in my aching muscles. After a few minutes, there was a soft knock on the door.

"Come in." Frigg entered the bathroom, looking freshly bathed herself. Her long, dark hair hung loose. I had never seen it down and was mesmerized by how soft it looked.

"Hello, my dear."

"Hi, Nana Frigg."

She stepped toward the bath and began washing my hair with a salve that smelled of tea tree oil and spearmint. The mixture made my scalp tingle as her pastel-pink aura surrounded me. Her voice spoke soft, nonsensical words. It was like a chant, and I attempted for a second to make out what she was saying.

My veins glowed with a faint pink shimmer as her magic worked through me. By the time she finished washing my hair, I was a new person—energized and ready to take on any challenge.

"Thank you," I whispered, impressed by her power.

"You are very welcome, Vala. Get a good night's rest as the funeral procession begins tomorrow."

Frigg left the room, and I climbed out of the bathtub. Although my body felt incredible, I could still feel the heavy weight of tiredness pulling me down. I dressed quickly in the clothes Heim chose—a set of golden, creamy silk pajamas. It seemed he thought of everything. I dried my hair as best I could before giving up and letting it fall damply across my shoulders.

Heim lay sprawled across the chaise lounge but stood abruptly at the sound of the bathroom door opening. His long hair was also damp, and he wore nothing but low-slung black linen pants. I stared at his shirtless torso, enamored with the perfection that was his tattooed body. He was a work of art. My very own Adonis. I walked toward him and lightly ran my palm along his perfection, tracing his indented abs. He shivered.

"You, sir, are perfect."

"Perfectly tired, Unnasta. Any chance I could talk you into letting me sleep in your bed tonight? I don't want to be anywhere you aren't."

"Oh, I suppose you may be able to," I joked. He raised a brow. "I think I'd like that very much."

We walked into the bedroom and climbed into the large bed. Heim didn't try anything with me. Obviously, he re-membered my wariness from Loki's trickery that happened in that very room. Instead, he held me in his strong arms and told me stories of old as I drifted into the world of sleep, lulled by the deep timbre of his masculine voice.

I woke up the next morning, hearing voices in the hallway. Heim stirred behind me, and his hand left my hip to rub small circles on my upper arm.

"It is time, Unnasta. Today is a day of mourning followed by a feast in Thor's honor this evening."

I turned to look into his eyes, and he leaned in for a kiss. I placed my fingers on his lips. "No, sir. Morning breath." He chuckled lightly and reached into the pocket of his bag that sat on the bedside table.

He procured the tiny orbs of minty magic we used daily. There may not be toothpaste or toothbrushes in the realms, but those small chewable tablets were akin to the best dental cleaning I'd ever experienced. I popped one in my mouth, reveling in the freshness, and leaned in to kiss him after he chewed his.

After we dressed, we left my room and joined the many in the assembly hall. Everyone was dressed in shades of black. Heads were bowed, and silent tears fell. I approached Helene, who stood by Sif, and slipped my hand into hers. I rested my other hand on Sif's shoulder, and she turned to look at me with eyes filled with pain.

Helene's hand squeezed mine, and I noticed that she looked much better. The color had returned to her face.

Odin stepped to the front of the room and began to speak. "Today, we honor my son, Thor. His sacrifice is one we will never forget, for it allowed Vala, the chosen one, to fulfill part of her purpose. We shall appropriately mourn the loss of a warrior who fought valiantly for generations for all realms. We will feast in his honor this evening. Until then, I release you to mourn as your realm sees fit."

The crowd parted silently, filing out of the room one group at a time. Those from Asgard remained where they stood in the hall. I hadn't noticed the large stone slab on which Thor's body was laid to rest until the room cleared. He appeared so peaceful, as if he were only sleeping. His hands—covered by his iron gloves—lay crossed over his body, and the handle of Mjolnir rested between them. He wore the finest leather trousers, a cream linen shirt, a jacket lined with soft salt and pepper fur, and leather boots strapped up to his calves.

Sif neared his body, placing her hand on his neatly brushed and braided hair, and bent to kiss his cheek as a tear spilled from her eye. She tucked an ornately carved wooden brush into his jacket pocket and whispered something into his ear. Odin pulled the massive belt Thor had worn during the battle from behind the slab and rested it on his son's midsection, adjusting Mjolnir so that the hammer rested on the leather.

"That is Megingjord, the belt that doubles Thor's strength. The gloves allowed him to use Mjolnir," Heim explained to me. "Part of our mourning involves providing the fallen with their prized earthly possessions so they can take them to the afterlife."

Dozens of Asgardians filtered through the viewing hall, placing items on and around Thor's body. I wished I could give something, anything, to the man who became like a brother to me in such a short amount of time. A memory flitted through my mind, and I dropped Helene's hand and ran toward the dining hall.

I stood next to the large table and thought back to the first night I'd met Thor. When I opened my eyes, I found the goblet Thor stole from my hands. I clutched it to my chest, relishing the memory of Thor's goofy teasing. He always made me feel comfortable, and I missed him terribly.

I returned to the assembly hall and walked to the stone. There was hardly any room around Thor's body, but I found the perfect place to set the chalice. I tucked it between his left bicep and chest to get it as close to his heart as possible.

"Thank you, brother," I whispered as I bent to kiss his cheek. My words came out of my mouth and formed ribbons of translucent gold. They braided together and covered Thor's body and belongings in a beautifully woven blanket.

The rest of the day was a blur of tears and grief. Night fell, and everyone migrated toward the dining hall. What once was a single, long table had become many tables decorated with large, lit pillar candles, bathing the room in a warm glow, stunning black stone dinnerware, and mounds of deliciously roasted foods. All of Thor's favorites were included in the evening's feast.

Everyone sat down to enjoy their meal, the chatter amongst the tables quiet and solemn. Odin stood from his table and clinked a stone knife against his goblet. A resounding chime echoed through the dining hall, and all the talking stopped, all eyes glued to the Allfather.

"Thank you for joining us this evening in remembrance of Thor," he bellowed. "The deep sadness we feel cannot be in vain, for Loki did not win. Thor would not want us to be forlorn at his loss but use it instead as a fire to ignite us to fight harder against the god of trickery. We cannot allow my brother to win or take away our peace when Freya comes to guide Thor's soul to Valhalla. Thor may be gone, but his strength lies in each of you. Let us combine our forces and fight in honor of my son!"

Cheers erupted, joyous and inspiring. Glasses clinked, and people drank to the dawn of a newfound union of forces. I became hopeful that, with the help of the nine realms, we could take down Loki and stop Ragnarök and the death of all gods.

The rest of the evening was full of endless food and stories of Thor's adventures. One at a time, they rose and shared a tale from their memory. Some were silly, and some were brave. Others still were terrifying or gory. Thor was a god of many facets. Some found him insufferable; others found him entertaining. The consensus was that he was loved for the warrior he was and the safety he provided the realms.

I went to bed that night with Heim by my side, surrounded by the memory of Thor. Tears turned to laughter in that hall, and love abounded, creating unexpected peace.

"Is that why the funeral process lasts so long here?"

"Hmm?" Heim questioned, half asleep.

"I was just wondering if this peaceful, full feeling I have is normal?"

"Mmm, yes, Unnasta. We allow our grief to be seen and heard. Then, we allow the memories to bring the person closer to us before we send their body off. They may be gone physically, but our process allows part of them to remain. They become ingrained within us, part of our heart and soul."

I snuggled into Heim's chest as he traced the rune on my arm. We had yet to broach the topic, but he was patient due to the circumstances. His heart beating gently against my back was the lullaby of serenity, sending me off to a dreamless sleep.

CHAPTER THIRTY-SEVEN

The next day was full of funeral preparations. Giants from Jotunheim carried massive tree trunks and set them on the ground as the dark elves used iron tools to remove the excess branches. Light elves sported large, sharpened axes to split the wood, turning the rounded tree trunks into perfectly squared-off beams. Asgardians transported the beams toward a growing stack in an open area. And Heim stepped in to help a group of men build something.

Helene and I sat on a rock, the sun kissing our skin, as we watched the men working. Little by little, I recognized what was taking shape—a boat very similar to Skidbladnir but on a much smaller scale.

Beckett, a snarky dark elf, sat beside us, humming a tune and whittling away at a hunk of tree trunk. He was forming the dragon's head that would decorate the bow. Another elf sat across from us, working on the dragon's tail for the stern. The focus with which everyone worked was impressive.

Helene and I rose a few times to get refreshments for the men. Each time we did, we spoke little, content with only being in each other's company. Asgard was bustling with organized chaos, everyone darting back and forth to prepare for the funeral.

On one of our walks indoors, I finally asked a question that burned within, "Helene, why are they building a boat?"

"It's a funeral pyre."

A vague memory of my father telling stories of our people's burial resurfaced, but I was so young when he told me that the exact recalling was hazy.

"The men will build the boat and place Thor's body and belongings on the deck. We will then each add kindling and straw, tucking it around him. Sif will add the garlands of flowers she has been painstakingly weaving together all day, and Idun will scatter some of her golden apples for their aroma."

"Then, we will push the boat into the lake just outside of town, and the warriors will send burning arrows toward it from the shore," I finished for her.

"Yes, exactly."

Once the boat was finished, it looked like a miniature of Skidbladnir, which made sense since that was where Thor passed on.

"It's beautiful."

"*You* are beautiful," Heim whispered. "But you owe me a story about that scar on your arm."

All that remained of the nearly faded mark were lightly raised edges that shimmered in the sun when I twisted my arm. "It is the eihwhaz rune."

"I know what rune it is, Vala." Heim used my name instead of his endearment for me. He was serious. "How did you get it?"

"Garm."

"What?!" he barked, anger temporarily overtaking his features. "That damn dog scratched you?"

"Heim, I am fine. It was a gift."

"But why?"

"I'm not sure, but Hel said I might need it."

"Do you know what this means, Unnasta?" His tone was more sincere and calmer than before.

"It means I am immortal, as long as the rune stays on my skin."

"It means you can be mine… forever." My breath caught. Heim tangled his hand in my hair and pulled my face to his. He gave me the softest peck on my mouth and then peppered sweet kisses across my face. "Forever with my love."

"Does this mean that Idun's apples will keep me young?"

"Yes, Unnasta," he said with a smile.

"Oh great, just in time for my upcoming birthday," I laughed.

Evening fell over Asgard, the clear night sky a shade of cobalt, broken only by a scattering of diamond-bright stars. Odin and Heim stood on either side of the boat loaded with Thor and his belongings. The two men, accompanied by six others on either side, lifted it and slowly marched toward the lake. A procession of realm inhabitants followed close behind.

The boat was set on the shore. One by one, people approached and added small pieces of wood or straw. Sif weaved her flower garlands between the ornately carved handrails. Pops of red, pink, and yellow adorned her husband's final resting place in a vivid way that represented his outgoing nature. Heim and I added bits of straw to the mouth of the dragon on the bow and stepped away.

Odin pulled on a rope attached to the mast, making the sail unfurl and billow in the evening wind. It was adorned with a bright yellow lightning bolt.

"For you, son." Odin waded ankle-deep into the water, pushing the boat toward the middle of the lake. It glided steadily, leaving gentle ripples in its wake. A long row of warriors lined up with their fiery arrows, nocked and ready.

"Rest in peace, Thor. May Freya guard your soul in Valhalla until the end of time," bellowed Odin. He lifted a hand and threw it down, commanding the warriors to fire.

Hundreds of arrows soared through the air, their tips like shooting stars in the dark sky. Each hit its destination, setting the boat instantly ablaze, and the smell of fresh-baked apples filled the air.

A bright light erupted high above us. Hundreds of Valkyries decorated the heavens, their white wings glowing around them. Freya descended, dipping down toward the inferno.

"Oh, my gods! She's going to—" Heim cut me off, gently pulling me into him and covering my mouth with his hand.

"Shh," he whispered into my ear.

Freya sunk into the fire. I stopped breathing, but after a moment, I saw her wings lift her above the flames. Holding onto her hand was a ghostly version of Thor. His shape and features were the same, but the night sky glittered through his glowing outline. His feet kicked below him, clearly uncomfortable with dangling from the earth.

"Will you stop acting like a cantankerous child?" Freya yelled at Thor's ghost.

He looked up at her, waggled both eyebrows, and then blew a kiss directly at Sif. Freya heaved his body upward and flung him behind her on her winged horse. I couldn't help but smile at his antics.

Silence overtook the realm as the reality that Thor was gone enveloped us. The once-bright burning ship became a small pile of embers burnt out by the lazily drifting water. Melancholy threatened to take over again until Sif stepped toward the shore, her bright eyes staring into the night sky.

"Oh, gods! Poor Freya." Her tone lacked any emotion. We all stood completely still until she turned to us and spoke again. "Now she has to put up with him."

Everyone broke into fits of laughter.

"Thank you, all, for joining us in honoring the life of Thor." Odin stepped toward me and continued, "The time has come for us to honor another. Vala, the chosen one, your sacrifice of leaving everything you knew and reintroducing yourself to the realms has not gone unnoticed. Please, everyone, join us for dinner. Tonight, we celebrate Vala's victory in this fight by welcoming her home."

Home. I finally felt at home. Did you hear that, Mom and Dad? I'm not alone anymore.

Odin's announcement left everyone cheering and dispersing toward Valaskjalf and the promise of Asgard's delicious delicacies. Heim turned to follow, his hand resting on the small of my back. I grabbed his hand and gave it a light squeeze.

"I will be right behind you."

"Is everything okay?"

"Yes." I stretched to kiss his cheek. "There is something I need to do first."

"Okay." He joined Helene, and they walked inside together.

"Tell them I said hello and that I miss them. I know how proud you have made them, Vala."

"Thank you, Odin," I whispered, holding back tears. The Allfather walked toward his home, leaving me standing on the shore of the lake alone.

I looked at the water and then upward toward the dazzling sky and stars. Witnessing the death and funeral of my beloved friend brought up past emotions. I fell to my knees on the earth, allowing pent-up tears to flow. I wished I could have honored my mom and dad in the way we honored Thor. I wished I knew about my past—my roots—when they died so they could have undergone the proper send-off. I allowed my power to stir within me, grasping my bracelet in my hand.

"I am so sorry. I always wanted my home to be with you guys." I projected my sorrow toward the rippling water.

"*Vala, you have no reason to be sorry,*" my father whispered through the wind. The air swirled and wrapped around me in a hug.

My mom joined the sighing wind. "*Hel found us in the darkness, sweetie. She guided us to a new home, but we will be together again someday.*"

I reveled in the closeness of their voices, allowing their presence to soothe my pain. "I love you both."

"*We love you, too. But that is not the only reason we came, darling.*"

"What do you mean?"

"*We have something to tell you; something we only just learned ourselves.*"

"What is it?"

"*It is about how Loki keeps finding you.*" Trepidation laced their voices. "*You must know. We had no idea.*"

"You guys are scaring me."

"*It's just that Þorbjörg Lítilvölva, a Völva of old, is our ancestor, Vala. We had no clue that Loki—*"

"Did you just say lítilvölva?"

"*Ye—*"

A sudden movement beside me abruptly cut my mother's words off, and my head spun as a burst of red smoke appeared.

"Vala, watch out!" Worry laced their voices as my parents' words reverberated through the empty air.

Before I could open my mouth to speak or scream, smoke entered through my nostrils. It traveled to my brain and through my veins, incapacitating every cell in my body until I was nothing more than a statue. The mist left my body and materialized into Loki, as dangerously beautiful as ever, with a handful of iron chains in his grasp.

"You, lítilvölva, have been a naughty girl," he seethed. He grabbed my arm and spat on my rune scar. "For that, it is time for your punishment."

He wrapped the chains around me, coiling them from my ankles to my neck. He snapped his fingers, and magical locks appeared on the connecting links, binding my body in the glowing red manacles.

"VALA!" Heim screamed, his body a shadow moving at lightning speed toward us.

"She is mine now." Loki laughed maniacally, heaving my body into his arms. He pulled my face to his and forced our foreheads to touch. My mind rebelled but my body was useless against his violation.

"No! Unnasta!" Heim was so close to us; I knew he would get to us before—

We disappeared in the blink of an eye, nothing more than a cloud of red smoke on a dark, starry night.

Acknowledgements

You guys… I wrote a book! I am still in shock, and there are so many people I need to thank. I want to start off by thanking my family. Anthony for supporting me through this crazy process, Briar for allowing me to constantly ask, "Would you or your friends say this?", August for his constant belief that I can do anything, and Raven and Poe for being the best emotional support animals a frazzled writer could ask for. I love you guys more than all the stars in the sky!

To Dad, thank you for trusting me. I've been a tough cookie sometimes, but I am definitely your daughter. To Sharon, thank you for being just as excited as I have been throughout this journey! I am beyond grateful for your input, advice, and countless conversations about "what's next?" Thank you both for financially backing this project.

To Mom, thank you for always being excited for me and helping make this book a reality! I feel the prayers you send up for us. Logan, thank you for an INCREDIBLE map and the many hours on the phone as I wrote, edited, and brainstormed (oh, and for fixing the sizing on my cover and interior art).

Having a "seestor" that is also a book bestie is one of the greatest gifts God gave me!

A huge thank you to my editor, Samantha Swart. Girl, you are freaking magic, and I'm so grateful to you for shaping On the Wings of a Word into a diamond (because she was rough before you)! Huge shoutout to C.A. Greico as well, for offering an indie scholarship and the chance to work with Sam. The indie author community on TikTok is a very special place.

Thank you to my alpha readers: Maria, Sareya, Kate, Brandi, and Shelley. Every bit of advice helped, and I appreciate each of you! Thank you to each of my beta readers: Anna, Jinna, Liz, and Samantha. The tough love, incredible feedback, and stellar editing helped form this book into what it is now. I've learned so much throughout this process, and I appreciate the kind and useful lessons!

Don't worry, Angela (alpha reader) and Jimmy (beta reader), I didn't forget about you! I can't say enough how blessed I feel to have gotten to know you (Ange) through the alpha reading process. Between that, traveling book club, your hubs beta reading (and correcting all my pop culture reference errors) for me, and the financial assistance you guys provided, I don't think I would be sane right now. I adore you guys, and I am blessed to know you! Thank you for believing in me.

To Jennifer, thank you for reading early excerpts and believing in me enough to urge me to start my GiveSendGo campaign. I appreciate the donation made by you and your family, which allowed me to publish! Thank you for the stunning raven bookmarks and your amazing friendship. I know God set our paths to cross, and I'm so grateful for that!

Thank you to every person who donated to my GiveSend-Go campaign. This book wouldn't be here without you, and I will never forget your kindness!

Thank you to my outstanding cover artist, Saira. I will be back with books two and three!

To all my book besties and fellow indie authors on Book-Tok, I am forever grateful for each of you who stuck with me during this journey, cheered me on, and poured out kind words for a stranger on the internet. A big shoutout to M.A. Ramsay-Scales for helping me through formatting and curbing some potential author freak-outs, and to Geri Banuelos for being a wonderful friend from the start!

To my dear friend Katie, thank you for always listening to me talk about my book and this process. I love you! To my friend Jenn, thanks for being a cheerleader and being excited for something I know isn't a primary interest. It means a lot to me! To my friends Brad and Alyssa P. Kelso, who read the first draft of chapter one and urged me to keep going, thank you! To Kathy, who told me my writing was beautiful, awakening the words that dwelled in my soul, allowing an outpouring to occur: I wouldn't have restarted this project without you. Thank you!

I will forever be grateful to my ARC readers for the last-minute "oops" fixes and the hilarious Discord chats. Thank you for reading and hyping up my book before release!

To you, the reader, thank you for reading this book! Thank you for allowing my dreams to come true. I also need to shout out Dr. Jackson Crawford. Without finding your YouTube channel, I would be lost in attempting to pronounce anything in my book. I hope I honored Norse culture with this story.

Last but most importantly, thank you, God, for reigniting my passion for writing, pouring these words into my mind, and allowing me to heal through the writing process. I owe you my life, my sobriety, and everything. For such a time as this, Lord. May I do your will always.

If I forgot anyone, I'm so sorry. There are many people I could thank. Please know that if you are not listed here, you are still appreciated!

Follow me on TikTok and Instagram for updates on the Loki's Monsters Trilogy.

Username: authorcmsinner

Love you, bye!

ABOUT THE AUTHOR

C.M. Sinner is a nerdy, mythology-loving writer who lives in the PNW. She spends most of her time with her family and their two dogs, Raven and Poe.

Along with writing, she enjoys listening to true-crime podcasts, exploring the PNW, watching movies with her kids, and going on dates with her husband. Two of her favorite authors are Kerri Maniscalco and Ruta Sepetys. Even though she writes fantasy, you can find her reading pretty much any and all genres.

Writing has always been a way to release emotions for C.M. Sinner. She wrote poetry throughout high school and early adulthood which helped spark the storyline for On the Wings of a Word. As someone who always saw the magic in words, she was pleased to bring that to life in this book.